THE EIGHTH DETECTIVE

THE EIGHTH DETECTIVE

A NOVEL

ALEX PAVESI

HENRY HOLT AND COMPANY
NEW YORK

Henry Holt and Company
Publishers since 1866
120 Broadway
New York, New York 10271
www.henryholt.com

Henry Holt® and ᴴ® are registered trademarks of Macmillan Publishing
Group, LLC.

Library of Congress Cataloging-in-Publication Data

Names: Pavesi, Alex, author.
Title: The eighth detective : a novel / Alex Pavesi.
Other titles: 8th detective
Description: First edition. | New York : Henry Holt and Company, 2020.
Identifiers: LCCN 2019057808 (print) | LCCN 2019057809 (ebook) | ISBN
9781250755933 (hardcover) | ISBN 9781250755926 (ebook)
Subjects: GSAFD: Suspense fiction.
Classification: LCC PR6116.A94 E54 2020 (print) | LCC PR6116.A94 (ebook) |
DDC 823/.92—dc23
LC record available at https://lccn.loc.gov/2019057808
LC ebook record available at https://lccn.loc.gov/2019057809
Our books may be purchased in bulk for promotional, educational, or business
use. Please contact your local bookseller or the Macmillan Corporate and
Premium Sales Department at (800) 221-7945, extension 5442, or by e-mail at
MacmillanSpecialMarkets@macmillan.com.

First Edition 2020

Designed by Meryl Sussman Levavi

Printed in the United States of America

1 3 5 7 9 10 8 6 4 2

THE EIGHTH
DETECTIVE

I

SPAIN, 1930

The two suspects sat on mismatched furniture in the white and almost featureless lounge, waiting for something to happen. Between them an archway led to a slim, windowless staircase: a dim recess that seemed to dominate the room, like a fireplace grown to unreasonable proportions. The staircase changed direction at its midpoint, hiding the upper floor from view and giving the impression that it led up to darkness and nothing else.

"It's hell, just waiting here." Megan was sitting to the right of the archway. "How long does a siesta normally take, anyway?"

She walked over to the window. Outside, the Spanish countryside was an indistinct orange color. It looked uninhabitable in the heat.

"An hour or two, but he's been drinking." Henry was sitting sideways in his chair, with his legs hooked over the arm and a guitar resting on his lap. "Knowing Bunny, he'll be asleep until dinnertime."

Megan moved to the drinks cabinet and examined the bottles, carefully turning each one until all the labels were facing outward. Henry took the cigarette from his mouth and held it up in front of his right eye, pretending to watch her through it: a mock telescope. "You're breathing through your shoes again."

She'd been pacing back and forth for most of the afternoon. The lounge, with its white tiles and wipe-clean surfaces, reminded her of a doctor's waiting room; they could have been in a redbrick hospital back home, rather than a strange Spanish villa at the top of a ragged red hill. "If I'm breathing through my shoes," she muttered, "then you're walking with your mouth."

A few hours earlier they'd been having lunch at a small tavern in the nearest village, a thirty-minute walk through the woods from Bunny's house. Bunny had stood up at the end of the meal and they'd both immediately noticed how drunk he was. "We need to have a conversation," he'd slurred. "You've probably been wondering why I asked you here. There's something I've wanted to discuss for rather a long time." It was an ominous thing to say to his two guests, both entirely dependent on him in a country they'd never been to before. "When we're at the villa, just the three of us."

It had taken them almost an hour to walk back to the house— Bunny struggling up the hill like an old donkey, a gray suit against the red earth—and it felt absurd now to think of the three of them in Oxford together, all those years ago, when he'd aged seemingly ten years more than they had. "I need to rest," he'd drawled, after letting them into the house. "Give me some time to sleep, then we can talk." So while Bunny had gone upstairs to sleep away the heat of the afternoon, Megan and Henry had collapsed into armchairs on either side of the staircase. "A brief siesta."

That was almost three hours ago.

• • •

Megan was looking out of the window. Henry leaned forward and counted the number of squares between them: She was standing diagonally across from him, a distance of seven white tiles. "This feels like a game of chess," he said. "Is that why you keep moving about—you're putting your pieces in place for an attack?"

She turned to face him, her eyes narrowed. "Chess is a cheap metaphor. It's what men use when they want to talk in a grandiose way about conflict."

An argument had been building between them all afternoon, ever since Bunny had brought their lunch to a sudden end. *The three of us need to have a conversation, away from Spanish eyes.* Megan looked out of the window again and there it was, as inevitable as the weather: the impending argument, a black stain layered over the blue sky.

"Chess is all about rules and symmetry," she continued, "but conflict is usually just cruel and dirty."

Henry strummed the guitar as a way of changing the subject. "Do you know how to tune this thing?" He'd found it hanging on the wall above his chair. "I could play this if it was tuned."

"No," she said, and left the room.

He watched her walk deeper into the house: successively smaller versions of her framed by further doorways along the corridor. Then he lit another cigarette.

"When do you think he'll wake up? I'd like to get some fresh air."

She was back, the biggest version of her standing in the nearest doorway.

"Who knows," said Henry. "Right now he's sleeping the sleep of the just-had-lunch." She didn't smile. "You can go ahead and leave. I think anything he has to say can wait."

Megan paused, her face as pristine and unreadable as it was in her publicity photos. She was an actor, by profession. "Do you know what he's going to say to us?"

Henry hesitated. "I don't think so."

"Fine. I'm going outside, then."

He nodded and watched her leave. The corridor led away from the lounge in the direction he was facing, and he saw her walk down it and through a door at the end; the stairs were to his left.

He continued toying with the guitar strings until one of them snapped and the flailing metal cut the back of his hand.

At that moment the room darkened, and he automatically turned to his right: Megan was at the window, looking in, the red hills behind giving her outline a demonic glow. She didn't seem able to see him; maybe the day outside was too bright. But he felt like a creature in a zoo anyway, with the back of his hand held over his mouth as he sucked the slight cut and his fingers hanging from his chin.

• • •

Megan took shelter on the shaded side of the house.

Standing in a clump of wildflowers, she leaned back against the building and closed her eyes. From somewhere nearby came a soft, percussive sound: dip, dip, dip. It seemed to originate from behind her. She thought at first it was the carried sound of the guitar, coming through the walls, but it wasn't melodic enough for that. It was very faint—almost not there at all—but she could still hear it, as unmistakable as a stone in her shoe.

Dip. Dip. Dip.

She turned around and looked up. Through a wrought-iron grille she could see a fly repeatedly hitting itself against the closed window of Bunny's bedroom. The one next to hers, on the top floor of the house. It was just a tiny fly, trying to escape; then she saw that there were two of them. Three, in fact. Now four. A whole swarm of flies, trying to get out. The corner of the window was dark with them. She could picture the dead ones littering the windowsill. She found a small stone on the ground and threw it at the window; the black cloud scattered at the audible clunk, but no sound came from inside. She tried again but couldn't rouse her sleeping host.

She grew impatient and picked up a whole handful of stones,

throwing them one by one until her hands were empty. She walked back around the outside of the house, in through the door and along the corridor to the foot of the stairs, where Henry, surprised by her sudden appearance, dropped the guitar with a clatter on the cold white floor. "I think we should wake Bunny."

He saw that she was worried. "Do you think something's wrong?"

In fact, she was angry. "I think we should check."

She started up the stairs. He was following closely behind her when she saw something that made her stop and cry out. Instinctively, he put his arms around her. It was an attempt to keep her calm, but it was done clumsily and it left the two of them locked together, unable to move. "Let me go." She elbowed him off and ran forward, and then with her shoulders out of his way he saw what she had seen: a pointing finger of blood reaching from below Bunny's door toward the top of the stairs, pointing straight at him.

● ● ●

Neither of them had ever seen so much blood. Bunny lay on the sheets, facedown. A knife handle emerged from his back, with a twisted red trail leading up to it from the lowest end of the bed. The blade was almost entirely hidden; they could just see a thin line of silver between his body and the black handle, like a glimpse of moonlight coming through a crack in the curtains. "That's where his heart is," said Megan. The handle itself could have been part of a sundial, the dead body unknowingly marking the passage of time.

She approached the bed, stepping around the puddles on the floor. When she was a foot away from the body, Henry stopped her. "Do you think we should?"

"I have to check." Absurdly, she pressed two fingers into the side of his neck. There was no pulse. She shook her head. "This can't be true."

In a state of shock, Henry sat down on the edge of the mattress; his weight caused the bloodstains to spread toward him, and he leapt up as if waking from a bad dream. He looked at the door, then turned back to Megan. "The murderer might still be here," he said in a whisper. "I'll search the other rooms."

"Okay," Megan whispered back, and because she was an actor she whispered in a way that was as clear as speaking. It was almost sarcastic. "And check if all the windows are locked."

"You wait here." And he left.

She tried to take a deep breath, but the air in the room was rotten already, and the few telltale flies were still tapping against the edge of the blisteringly hot day. They must have grown bored of the body. She walked over and lifted the window by a couple of inches. The flies shot straight out and dissolved into the blue sky, like grains of salt stirred into soup. As she stood there by the window, cold with shock, Megan could hear Henry searching through the nearby rooms, opening wardrobes and looking under beds.

He appeared in the doorway again, a disappointed look on his face. "There's nobody up here."

"Were the windows all locked?"

"Yes, I checked."

"I thought so," she said. "Bunny locked everything obsessively before we left for lunch. I watched him do it."

"What about those doors, are they locked?" He indicated with his hand the two doors to the balcony behind her. She stepped over to them and pulled at the handles. They were bolted from the inside at the top, middle, and bottom.

"Yes," she said. She sat down on the edge of the bed, ignoring the spreading blood. "Henry, do you know what this means?"

He frowned. "It means they must have left by the staircase. I'll lock all the doors and windows downstairs. Stay here, Megan."

"Wait," she began, but he had already vanished. She heard his bare feet thudding unmusically on the steps that were as white and hard as piano keys, heard him pause as he reached the turning in the staircase and slap one palm flat against the wall to steady himself, then heard the course of his movements around the floor below.

She opened a drawer in Bunny's bedside cabinet: There was nothing inside but underwear and a gold watch. Another held a diary and his pajamas. He'd fallen asleep in his clothes, of course. She took the diary out and flicked through the pages. The entries had stopped almost a year ago. She put it back. Then she looked at her watch.

How long would she have to wait here, indulging Henry's makeshift display of taking control, before she could go down and confront him?

. . .

With each door that Henry closed, the house became incrementally hotter, so while he'd started the process in a rush he was now moving slowly and methodically, breathing heavily and walking through each room multiple times to make sure he hadn't missed anything. The layout was confusing, and he wondered why Bunny had come to live alone in a house so large. None of the rooms seemed to be the same shape or size, and many had no windows. *No light, but rather darkness visible.* It's what you do when you have money, he supposed.

He walked back to the lounge and found her there, perched on the chair he'd been sitting in and smoking one of his cigarettes. He felt he should say something playful, to delay confronting reality at least for a moment. "All you need is the guitar and a haircut and it would be like looking in a mirror."

Megan didn't respond.

"They've gone," he said. "There are plenty of windows and doors down here, of course. They could have got out any way they wanted."

Slowly, she dropped the cigarette into an ashtray and picked up a small knife that she'd placed beside it. He hadn't even noticed it; just another slender object blending into the sparsely decorated room. She got to her feet and held the blade out toward him, the tip pointed at his chest. "Don't move," she said quietly. "Just stay right there. We need to talk."

· · ·

Henry stepped away from her. The backs of his knees touched the chair opposite hers and he crumpled into it. She jumped at this sudden movement and for a moment he felt powerless, gripping the arms of his chair in desperation. But she stayed where she was. "Are you going to kill me, Megan?"

"Only if you make me."

"I could never make you do anything." He sighed. "Can you pass me a cigarette? I'm worried that if I reach for one myself, I might lose a finger or two. I might end up smoking my own thumb, like a little cigar."

She took one out of the packet and threw it toward him; he picked it up and lit it carefully. "Well," he said. "You've been looking for an argument all afternoon, but I pictured something more civilized than this. What's the idea?"

Megan spoke with the confidence of someone who's outsmarted their enemy. "You're trying to act calm, Henry, but your hands are shaking."

"Maybe I'm cold. Is it me or is the Spanish summer a little nippy this year?"

"And yet the sweat is pouring off you."

"What do you expect? You've got a knife to my face."

"It's a small knife, you're a big man. And it's nowhere near your face. You're shaking because you're worried about being found out, not because you think I'll hurt you."

"What are you implying?"

"Well, here are the facts. There are five rooms upstairs. They all have bars on the windows. Thick black bars, the kind they have in cartoons. Two of the rooms have doors leading to balconies, and both of those were locked. The windows too. You checked them yourself, just now.

There's only one staircase leading up to the top floor, this one right here. Does that all sound about right?"

He nodded.

"Then whoever murdered Bunny must have gone up that staircase." She pointed at the shadowed hinge of the stairs, where they turned and briefly lost all their light. "And come back down by it. And you've been sitting here at the bottom ever since we got back from lunch."

He shrugged. "So what? You're not suggesting I had anything to do with this?"

"That's exactly what I'm suggesting. Either you saw the killer going up that staircase, or you went up there yourself, which makes you either a murderer or an accomplice. And I don't think you've been here long enough to have made any friends."

He closed his eyes and concentrated on her words. "That's nonsense. Somebody could have crept by me. I was hardly paying attention."

"Someone crept past you in a silent white room? Which was it, Henry, a mouse or a ballet dancer?"

"Then you really think I killed him?" Her whole argument clicked into place and he stood up in protest. "But, Megan, there's one thing you've failed to mention. I may have been sitting here since lunchtime, minding my own digestion, but you've damn well been sitting here with me."

She tilted her head to one side. "That's true, mostly. But I can think of at least three times I've stepped outside for some fresh air. I wonder if that's why you've been smoking so much, to drive me out? I don't know how long it takes to plunge a knife into someone's back, but I'd imagine it can be done pretty quickly. Washing your hands afterward probably takes up the bulk of it."

Henry sat back down. "My God"—he struggled to get comfortable—"you're actually serious, aren't you? We've just found our friend lying dead upstairs and you're really suggesting that I did it? Based on what?

The fact that I've been sitting near a staircase? When we've known each other for almost ten years?"

"People change."

"Well, that's true. These days I think Shakespeare is overrated and I don't go to church anymore. But I hope someone would have told me if I'd left the house without my sense of morality."

"Don't take it so personally. I'm just connecting the dots. You've been here the whole time, haven't you?"

"Don't take it personally?" He shook his head in disbelief. "Haven't you ever read a detective story, Megan? There's a million ways it could have been done. Maybe there's a secret passage leading upstairs."

"This is reality, Henry. In real life, if there's only one person with motive and opportunity, then they're usually guilty."

"Motive? And what exactly is my motive supposed to be?"

"Why did Bunny ask us here?"

"I don't know."

"I think you do. After five years of silence he sends both of us a letter inviting us to his house in Spain. And both of us come running. Why? Because he was planning to blackmail us. You must have known that?"

"Blackmail us? Over what happened in Oxford?" Henry waved away the idea. "It was Bunny that was driving the car."

"We weren't exactly innocent, though, were we?"

"That's nonsense. I came because he told me that you'd be here and he said that you wanted to see me. There was nothing about blackmail."

"Do you have his letter with you?"

"No."

"Then we only have your word for it?"

He stared vacantly at the floor. "I still love you, Megan, that's why I came. Bunny knew exactly what to say to get me here. I can't believe you'd think I could do something like this."

She was unmoved. "I wish I could live in your world, Henry. You're probably picturing us breaking into song any second now."

"I'm just telling you how I feel."

"And like I said, I'm just joining the dots."

"Except."

"What?" She looked at him suspiciously. The knife twitched in her hand. "Except what, Henry?"

He stood up again, one hand on his head and the other pressed against the solid white wall. Then he began to pace back and forth. "Don't worry, I'll keep my distance." She tensed; the tip of the knife followed his movements. "What if when you went outside for a few minutes of fresh air, I left too? I could have done. You wouldn't have known about it if I had. And then the killer could have struck."

"And did you?"

"Yes," he said, sitting back down. "I went to get a book from my bedroom. That's when the killer must have got by me."

"You're lying."

"I'm not."

"Yes, you are. You'd have mentioned this sooner if it was true."

"I forgot about it, that's all."

"Henry, stop it." She took a step toward him. "I'm not interested in being lied to."

He held out his hand; it wasn't shaking. "Well, look at that, I'm telling the truth."

She kicked the leg of his chair, and his hand became a claw as he steadied himself against the armrest. "This conversation has gone on long enough. I just want to know what you plan to do next."

"Well, there's no telephone here, so I was going to run down to the village and fetch the police and a doctor. But if you're planning to tell them I'm guilty, that makes it rather difficult for me, doesn't it?"

"We can worry about the police later. Right now I just want to make sure that if I put this knife down I don't end up lying on the bed next to Bunny. Why did you kill him?"

"I didn't."

"Then who did?"

"A stranger must have broken in and killed him."

"For what reason?"

"How would I know?"

She sat down. "Look, I'll help you out here, Henry. It's not inconceivable to me that you had some justification for doing this. Bunny could be cruel, we both know that. And reckless. I might even be able to forgive you for it, in time. But if you want me to lie for you, then you should stop testing my patience. Why now? And why like this?"

"Megan, this is madness." Henry closed his eyes. The heat was unbearable, with all the doors and windows closed. He felt that they were two specimens suspended in oil, being studied by someone.

"Then you're still protesting your innocence? Christ, we've been through this, Henry. You've been tried and convicted by the jury of twelve potted plants lining the hallway. You were here the whole time— what else is there to say?"

He buried his head in his hands. "Just give me a moment to think." His lips moved silently as he went back over her accusations. "You've given me a damn headache." Absurdly, he reached down and took the guitar from the floor beside him. He began to pluck at its five remaining strings. "Could they have been hiding upstairs when we came back from lunch?" His forehead was dripping with sweat. "There's no way they could have left. Unless it was right when we got back. In fact . . . In fact, I think I've got it."

He was on his feet again. "I think I know what happened now, Megan."

She tilted her head up toward him, an inverted nod of encouragement.

"Megan, you little spider," he said. "You little, conniving snake. It was you that killed him."

Megan looked distinctly unimpressed. "Don't be ridiculous."

"I can see you put some thought into it. Here we are, two suspects with the same opportunity and a motive broad enough to cover both of us, so that all you have to do is deny everything and it all gets blamed on me. That way it comes down to which of us is the better actor, and we both know the answer to that."

"As I pointed out, Henry, you've been sitting here all afternoon guarding your kill. So how could I have done it?"

"There's no need to frame me, to fake evidence. Not when you can just deny everything, until your throat dries up. That was your plan the whole time, wasn't it? When the police arrive, they'll find two for-eigners here and a dead body. One of them will be me, flustered and incoherent, trying to argue that someone might have crawled upside down along the ceiling to get up that staircase without being seen, and the other one will be you, perfectly in control, denying everything. The English rose against the brutish male. We both know who they'll believe, and how can I convince them otherwise? I can't even order a coffee in this damn country."

"That's your theory, is it? Then how did I sneak past you, Henry? Did I crawl along the ceiling, like you suggest? Or have you come up with something more convincing in the last twenty seconds?"

"I don't need to. It's the wrong question." He walked over to the window, no longer afraid of her. "It's true that the top floor of this house is locked up tight. And that staircase is the only entrance to it. And it's true that I've been sitting here all afternoon, since lunch, since Bunny went up to his bedroom. I haven't even used the toilet. But it's also true that when we first got back and I was hot and dirty from the road, I went to wash. And I left you sitting here all alone, right here. And when I returned you hadn't moved. It took me about nine or ten minutes to wash my face, neck, and hands; it was so brief I'd almost forgotten about it. But, then, how long can it take to plunge a knife into someone's back?"

"That was hours ago."

"Three hours ago. And how long do you think he's been dead? There's blood all along the corridor."

"We'd just come inside, he'd only just gone upstairs. He wouldn't even have been asleep by then."

"No, but he was drunk enough that it wouldn't have mattered. Once he was facedown on the mattress, he was totally defenseless."

"So that's it, is it? You're accusing me of killing him?"

Henry smiled, proud of his logic. "That's right, I am."

"You pathetic, gloating fool. He's dead and you want to play games about it? I know it was you. Why are you doing this?"

"I could ask you the same thing."

Megan paused and thought the matter through. The hand holding the knife relaxed. Henry was looking out of the window now, a halo of red hills visible through the smeared glass. He was taunting her with his lack of fear; it was a way of asserting his authority. "I see what you're doing," she said. "I see it quite clearly now. It's a matter of reputation, isn't it? I'm an actor. A scandal like this would ruin me. As long as there's the slightest fragment of doubt, my reputation will be shot. You think I have more to lose than you, so I'll have to cooperate?"

He swung around, suntanned by the bright daylight at his back. "You think this is about your professional reputation? Not everything is about your career, Megan."

She bit her lower lip. "No, I don't suppose you would admit it, would you? First you'll show me just how stubborn you're willing to be. And then what? When you've convinced me that I can't win, that my career will be ruined if I don't cooperate, you'll make your proposal. You'll come up with some kind of story and ask me to corroborate it. If that's really what this is about, you'd be better off telling me the truth."

He sighed and shook his head. "I don't know why you keep saying all these things. I've explained the circumstances of the crime. But even the best detective can't do anything in the face of outright denial. I could pull my hair out, that's all. But I don't think baldness would suit me."

She stared at him. Neither of them said anything for about a minute. Eventually she placed the knife on the table beside her and spun the tip of it away from him. "Fine," she said. "Pick up your guitar and keep playing. I'm accusing you and you're accusing me, that's obviously the situation we're in. But if you think that I'm the kind of woman who will crack and be convinced the sky is green just because a man says so, then you've underestimated me."

"And if you think you can just put your foot down and flutter your eyelashes and I'll sing like a bird, then you've overestimated your powers."

"Oh." Megan blinked. "But I thought you still loved me?"

Henry sat down in the chair opposite hers. "I do—that's what makes this so maddening. I'll forgive you for everything, if you'll simply admit that you killed him."

"Then let's talk about something we've never talked about before." She picked up the knife again; real fear showed in his eyes for a moment. "You have a violent side, Henry. I've seen you drunk. I've seen you starting fights with strangers because you didn't like the way they were looking at me. I've seen you shouting and screaming and smashing glasses. Are you going to deny all of that too?"

He stared at the floor. "No, but that was a long time ago."

"And did you ever see me behaving like that?"

"Maybe not, but you can be cruel."

"A sharp tongue never killed anybody."

He shrugged. "So I have a short temper. Is that why you wouldn't marry me?"

"Not entirely. But it didn't help."

"I was drinking a lot in those days."

"You were drinking a lot at lunch."

"Not a lot. Not like back then."

"It was enough, clearly."

Henry sighed. "If I'd wanted to kill Bunny, I'd have done it in a better way than this."

"Henry, I know it was you. We both know it was you. What are you trying to convince me of, exactly? That I'm going mad?"

"I could say the same thing, couldn't I?"

"No, you couldn't." She stabbed the small knife into the arm of her chair; it went straight through the upholstery and stuck in the wood. "Bunny is upstairs dripping like a tap, and we're just sitting here arguing. What are the police going to think when they find out how we've spent the afternoon?"

"This is like a bad dream."

Megan rolled her eyes. "Another cheap metaphor."

"Well, if this is the way we're spending the afternoon, I'd like to have a drink in my hand. Would you care to join me?"

"You're sick," she said. And he poured himself a whiskey.

• • •

Half an hour later, nothing had changed; they'd gone over the situation several times and come to no conclusion.

Henry had finished his drink; he was holding the empty glass up in front of his eyes, looking through it at the squashed and hollow room, moving his hand from side to side. Megan watched him, wondering how he could be so easily distracted.

Henry looked over at her. "I'll have one more and then I'm done. Would you care to join me?"

The doors and windows were still shut, and the room was stifling. It was as if they'd agreed to inflict it on themselves as a punishment.

She nodded. "I'll have a drink with you."

He grunted and walked over to the drinks cabinet. He filled two large glasses from the tall decanter of whiskey. It was warm, of course. He took one in his hand, swirled it rhythmically, and passed the other to her. Her eyes widened at the size of it, two-thirds full. "One last drink," he said.

"We need to discuss what to do next," said Megan, "assuming neither of us is going to confess. Do we need to involve the police at all? Nobody knows we're here. Maybe we can just leave in the night?"

Henry sipped his drink in silence. They sat like that for several minutes, Megan shielding her glass with her hand. When she finally lifted it to her mouth, she paused before putting it to her lips. "How do I know this isn't poisoned?"

"We can swap glasses," he said.

She shrugged. The conversation didn't seem worth the exertion. She took a tiny sip. "Tastes fine," she said. He was staring at her in silence, in a way that made her uncomfortable. "On the other hand, for the avoidance of doubt . . ." He sighed and handed her his glass; she took it and gave him hers.

He sat back in his chair, exhausted, and raised his glass. "To Bunny."

"To Bunny, then."

The whiskey was as orange and fiery as the impending sunset. Henry lifted the guitar again and picked out the same clumsy tune as before. "We're back where we started," he sighed.

"Like I said, we need to discuss what happens next."

"You want me to say we can just run away together and pretend we were never here? Like last time. That was your plan all along, was it?"

"Why are you doing this to me?" Megan put down her glass and shook her head. "Is it because I called off our engagement? But that was so long ago."

Sipping from his drink had become Henry's primary means of punctuating the conversation. But in response to this, he put the time in and lit a cigarette. "I'll say it again, Megan. I do still love you."

"That's nice to know." She looked at him expectantly. "Are you feeling dizzy yet, Henry?"

At first he was puzzled, then he glanced at his glass. He'd drained it all the way to the bottom, except for the final half inch. He reached for it and found that his left arm was almost asleep. His shapeless, clumsy hand knocked the glass to the floor, where it smashed, a brown circle on the white tiles. He looked back at her. "What did you do?" The cigarette fell from his mouth and into the body of the guitar, leaving a spiral of smoke creeping up between the strings. Her face showed no emotion, just a hint of concern. "Megan." He tumbled forward off the chair, half of his body frozen. The guitar bounced to one side. He lay facedown on the white floor, shaking without rhythm. Saliva pooled on the tile in front of his chin.

"That's the thing about lying, Henry." She stood up and towered over him. "Once you start, you can't stop. You have to follow it where it takes you."

2

THE FIRST
CONVERSATION

Julia Hart had been reading aloud for almost an hour, and her throat felt like it was full of stones. "*That's the thing about lying, Henry. She stood up and towered over him. Once you start, you can't stop. You have to follow it where it takes you.*"

Grant McAllister was sitting beside her, listening intently. He was the author of the story she'd just read out; he'd written it more than twenty-five years earlier. "Well," he said, when he realized she had finished, "what do you think of that one?"

She lowered the manuscript, angling her notes away from him. "I like it. I was firmly on Megan's side, until that last paragraph."

He caught the dryness in her voice and got to his feet. "Would you like another glass of water?" She nodded gratefully. "I'm sorry," he said, "you're the first guest I've had in a very long time."

His cottage was at the top of a short, sandy slope that led up from the beach. They'd been sitting on wooden chairs under its wide porch for the last hour or so, while she'd read the story out loud to him. He left her there now and disappeared inside.

A cool breeze was coming from the sea, but the heat of the sun was overwhelming. She'd had to walk from her hotel to his cottage that morning—fifteen minutes in the metallic Mediterranean heat—and she could feel that her forehead was already slightly burned.

"Here." Grant came back with a rough earthenware jug and placed it on the table between them. She filled her glass and drank.

"Thank you, I needed that."

He sat down again. "You were saying, I think, that you expected Megan to be innocent?"

"Not quite." She swallowed another mouthful of water and shook her head. "Just that I felt sympathetic toward her. I've met enough men like Henry, fragile and full of self-pity."

Grant nodded and tapped a few times on the arm of his chair. "Megan has her own failings, don't you think?"

"Oh yes." Julia smiled. "She killed him, didn't she?"

"She strikes me as"—he chose his words carefully—"untrustworthy in nature. She was suspicious from the start."

Julia shrugged. "We don't know what happened to them both in Oxford." She took out her notebook and placed it on her knee, holding a pen in her other hand. "When did you last read that story?"

"Before I lived here. As you know, I no longer have a copy of the book." Grant shook his head slowly. "Twenty years ago, probably. That makes me feel very old."

He poured himself a small glass of water. It was the first thing she'd seen him drink all morning. There was a pale wooden dinghy lying upside down on the beach below them; it looked like the abandoned cocoon of a giant insect. Maybe he crawled out of that, she thought, smiling to herself. An alien creature, immune to the heat and the need to eat and drink.

"So what happens next?" he asked. "I'm afraid I've never edited a book before. Will we go through it line by line?"

"That would take a long time." She flicked through the manuscript.

"There's not much I want to change. A few places where the phrasing could be more economical, perhaps."

"Of course." He pushed his hat back and wiped his forehead with a handkerchief.

"I did notice some inconsistencies in the description of the house, but I assumed they were intentional?"

He stopped for a moment and then hung the handkerchief from the arm of his chair, to dry in the breeze. "What kind of things do you mean?"

"Nothing serious," said Julia. "But the layout of the rooms, for example." She looked at him. He gestured for her to proceed, swirling his hand in a circle. "The room where the body is found is described as having its window on the shaded side of the house, but the knife is described as casting a shadow." Grant stared at her blankly, tilting his head to one side. "So is the sun shining through the window or is it in shade?"

He raised his chin to indicate comprehension and breathed in. "That's interesting. It's possible that I made a mistake."

"And the hallways on the upper and lower floors seem to extend in different directions. At one point we see Henry sitting on a chair with the stairs to his left and a corridor extending away from him in the direction he's facing, while the staircase turns once again to its left and then the upstairs corridor leads on from that. So does the upper floor actually fit on top of the lower floor?" His eyes flickered from side to side as he pictured the villa in his mind. She went on: "Then there's the sun. It seems to be setting, although the story takes place in summer, in the few hours after lunch."

He laughed softly to himself. "You're an extremely observant reader."

"I'm a terrible perfectionist, I'm afraid."

"But you think these mistakes were intentional?"

"I apologize if they weren't." She seemed slightly embarrassed and shuffled in her chair. "It's just that a lot of those details seemed extraneous. It's as if they were put there on purpose, purely to introduce these inconsistencies."

He wiped his forehead again.

"I'm very impressed, Julia." He touched the back of her hand with his palm. "And you're quite right. I used to add inconsistencies to my stories to see if I could sneak them past the reader unnoticed. It was a game I'd play. A petulant habit—I'm impressed that you spotted it."

"Thank you," she said, slightly unsure of herself. She was quiet for a moment as she checked her notes. "I'd thought perhaps that the story was supposed to be a depiction of Henry in hell, with the repeated references to heat and the red landscape. Is that not correct?"

"It's an interesting theory." Grant hesitated. "What gave you that impression?"

Julia ran her finger over a list that she'd made in the top corner of the page. "Swedenborg describes hell as a place that doesn't obey the usual rules of space and time. That could explain the spatial impossibilities and the weird chronology. When Megan's face appears at the window, she is described as having a demonic glow. And in the first line she speaks in the story, she says quite clearly: It is hell. There's even a quote from Milton, when Henry is searching the house."

Grant parted his hands in a gesture of capitulation. "Again, that is very well observed. You're probably right. I suppose the idea must have been at the back of my mind when I wrote it. But it was so long ago, I can't be certain."

"Well," she said, shifting the subject slightly, "if we treat all those discrepancies as intentional, then there's not much I'd like to change about the story itself."

He took off his white hat and twirled it in his hands. "Then let me explain how it relates to my mathematical work. That's the main reason you're here, isn't it?"

"It would be very helpful," said Julia.

Grant sat back, with a fingertip held to his chin, and thought about the best way to start. "All of these stories," he said, "derive from a research paper that I wrote in 1937, examining the mathematical structure of murder mysteries. I called it 'The Permutations of Detective Fiction.' It was published in a small journal, *Mathematical Recreations*. The response was positive, though it was a fairly modest piece of work. But murder mysteries were very popular at the time."

"Yes," said Julia. "That would have been the golden age of detective fiction, as it's now known. And you were a professor of mathematics then, at the University of Edinburgh?"

"That's correct." He smiled at her. "The aim of that research paper was to give a mathematical definition of a murder mystery. I think it succeeded, broadly speaking."

"But how?" she asked. "How do you use mathematics to define a concept from literature?"

"That's a reasonable question. Let me state it slightly differently. In that paper I defined a mathematical object, which I called a *murder mystery*, in the hope that its structural properties would accurately reflect the structure of murder-mystery stories. That definition then allowed me to determine the limits of murder mysteries, mathematically, and apply those findings back to literature. So we can say, for example, that a murder mystery has to meet a number of requirements to be considered valid, according to the definition. And then we can apply that same conclusion to the actual stories. Does that make sense?"

"I think so," she said. "Then it's almost like one of those lists of rules that various people have come up with for writing detective fiction?"

"Yes, there is some overlap. But another thing we can do with our definition is to work out every single structure that would count as a valid murder mystery. So I was able to list all of the possible structural variations, which you can't do with a series of rules or commandments."

"And those are the so-called permutations of detective fiction?"

"Precisely, which became the title of the paper."

In addition to being published as a research paper, "The Permutations of Detective Fiction" had formed the appendix to a book that Grant had written, comprised of seven murder-mystery stories. He'd called it *The White Murders* and had published it privately in the early 1940s, with a print run of fewer than a hundred copies.

Julia had contacted him on behalf of a small publishing house called Blood Type Books. She'd written to him, explaining that she worked as an editor at Blood Type and that her employer, a man called Victor Leonidas, had recently discovered an old copy of *The White Murders* in a box of secondhand books and was determined to publish it for a wider audience. After some correspondence by post, Julia had set out to meet with the elusive author—a man in late middle age now, living in solitude on a small Mediterranean island—to tie up the loose ends and prepare the book for publication. One thing that she and Grant had agreed on was that instead of including the research paper as an appendix, Julia should write an introduction to the seven stories that would serve the same purpose, covering the same ideas but in a more accessible format.

"There must be an awful lot of these permutations, though?"

"Strictly speaking there are infinitely many, but they divide into a small number of archetypes. In fact, the main structural variations can be counted on two hands. The stories were written to illustrate these major variations, including the one we've just read."

"Can you explain how?"

"Yes," said Grant, "I think so. The mathematical definition is simple. Disappointingly simple, I'm afraid. Effectively, it just states the four ingredients that comprise a murder mystery, with a few conditions applying to each one."

"Four ingredients." Julia wrote this down.

"They are necessary and sufficient, so that anything having them is a murder mystery and every murder mystery must have them. We should look at each one in turn."

"That sounds reasonable."

"Well," Grant began, leaning toward her, "the first ingredient is a group of suspects—the characters that may, or may not, have been responsible for the killing. A murder mystery will rarely have more than twenty suspects, but we don't set any upper limit on the number allowed. If you can have a murder mystery with five hundred suspects, then you can have a murder mystery with five hundred and one. The same argument doesn't apply to the lower limit. There, at the very least, negative numbers are impossible. So let me ask: If you were tasked with distilling the murder mystery down to its basic features, what is the minimum number of suspects you'd require to make the whole thing work?"

Julia thought about the question. "It's tempting to say four or five, because it's hard to imagine many detective novels working with fewer than that. But I expect you'll tell me the answer is two."

"That's right. If you have two suspects and the reader doesn't know which one of them is the murderer, then you have a murder mystery. Two suspects can give you the same essential structure as any other number."

"It's a bit limiting perhaps, in terms of characters and setting?"

"But as we've just seen, it's not impossible. So the first ingredient is a group of at least two suspects. And while usually there are three or more, there's something special about the murder mystery with exactly two."

Julia was making notes. Grant waited for her to catch up. The sweat from her palm left a print on the page, veined with red pen. "Go on," she said.

"It's a matter of simple logic. If there are only two suspects, then both of them know who the killer is. That stops being true when there are three or more—then only the killer can know for certain. But with two suspects the innocent party can work it out, by a simple process of elimination. I know I'm not guilty, so the other suspect must be. And then it's only the reader that doesn't know the truth. That's why I considered the two-suspect murder mystery to be significant."

"And that's why you wrote this story?"

"Both Henry and Megan know which one of them is guilty. And we know that both of them must know. But they're still both denying it. The idea amused me."

Julia nodded and wrote this down; it seemed simple enough.

"That's very helpful, thank you." She stopped to take another drink, then turned to a new page. "I'd like to include some biographical information in the introduction too. Just a few sentences about you. Where you were born, that sort of thing. Does that sound all right?"

Grant looked uncomfortable. "Isn't that rather self-indulgent?"

"Not really. We do it with all of our authors. Just an interesting fact or two. Your readers will want to know who you are."

"I see," said Grant. He was leaning forward in his chair, fanning himself with his hat. He looked down at his twitching hand as if it was something unknown to him, and the movement ceased. "I'm not sure there's anything interesting I can tell you. I've lived a very simple life."

Julia cleared her throat, then lowered her notebook and pen. "Grant, you used to be a professor of mathematics. Out of nowhere you produced a single volume of murder mysteries, but you never published anything else. Now you live alone on an island, thousands of miles from where you were born, in almost total seclusion. To most people, that sounds terribly exciting. There must be some kind of story behind it?"

He waited a moment before replying. "Not really, only the war. I served in North Africa. I found it hard to go back to a normal life after that. But that's not uncommon for a man of my age. I had no commitments, so I came to live here."

Julia made a note of this. "Forgive me for getting personal, but when Victor asked me to track you down, I wrote to the department of mathematics in Edinburgh. I spoke to one of your colleagues there,

Professor Daniels. He remembered you. He told me you were married once."

Grant winced. "Yes, that's right. It was a long time ago."

"And that you left for this island in something of a hurry. There must be a reason you chose to come here. It's beautiful, but it's a strange place to end up."

He looked away from her, toward the sea. "I wanted to be a long way from my previous life, that's all."

"But why? Did something happen?"

"I'd rather not explain my reasons, not in print."

"We don't have to include this in the introduction if it's too personal. But I can't help you make that judgment unless you tell me the truth."

Grant's expression was stern. "I didn't ask for your help."

"All right, then." Julia allowed the moment to pass. "Perhaps I can describe you as a misunderstood artist, living apart from the world. That always sounds suitably romantic."

Grant nodded, a little embarrassed at his incivility. "I live alone on an island, where my hobbies are mathematics and fishing."

"Thank you, that's very useful." Julia closed her notebook. "I tried to get in touch with your wife, but I couldn't locate her. It didn't matter in the end, of course. The professor had an address for you, here on this island. Twenty years out of date, but my letter still reached you. And you have no other family?"

He began to fan himself with his hat again. "Forgive me, but I'm feeling rather tired. That was a more engaging conversation than I'd expected. Please, may we take a break?"

Julia smiled; they had plenty of time. "Of course," she said.

And he put the hat back on his head.

3

DEATH AT
THE SEASIDE

Mr. Winston Brown was sitting on a green bench in a shabby charcoal suit, staring dreamily at the sea. His gloved hands were resting on the head of a wooden cane, just below his chin, and a worn black bowler hat was perched above the thinning crescent of hair on his head. While his face was almost a perfect pink circle—a face drawn by children—the rest of his body seemed to be built solidly and exclusively out of dark-gray rectangles.

A woman sat down beside him, placing a heavy bag of groceries on the pavement. A tenacious gull turned its head and began to waddle toward the two of them, but a sharp tap from Mr. Brown's cane sent it running in the other direction.

He turned to his companion. "I've always said that seagulls and squirrels are the highwaymen of the animal kingdom. It's something about their eyes."

The woman next to him nodded warily; she hadn't sat down to make conversation.

"Tell me," Mr. Brown continued, smiling at her in his childlike way, "do you live in this delightful place?"

They were in the picturesque town of Evescombe on the south coast, which had a small harbor and a handful of houses laid out around a circular bay, like a wreath. It was early in the morning and the sun had just risen above the water.

"Yes," she said briefly. "I've lived here all my life."

He took off his hat and balanced it on his knee. "Then perhaps you can tell me something about the murder that happened here. A week ago, wasn't it?"

Her lips parted automatically and she leaned forward, and Mr. Brown recognized in her a fellow collector of gossip. "Four days ago." She spoke in an exaggerated whisper, which was no quieter than her normal voice. "It was in all the papers. A young man pushed a woman from the cliffs. He claims it was an accident, of course. But he's lying. His name is Gordon Foyle and he lives in that last white house on the left there." She gestured toward the distant end of the town, where the buildings thinned out rapidly as the coast separated into a scrawny slim beach and the steep cliffside rising above it, where a bulbous white house stood as the last visible dwelling of the town, near the top of the hill.

Mr. Brown lifted his cane with one arm and used it to point malevolently across the bay. Like a lightning rod, it seemed to introduce the suggestion of a storm into the picture. "That house there? Why, it wouldn't hurt a fly."

"That house there is Whitestone House, where he's lived his whole life. Not that anyone around here really knows him. He keeps himself to himself, mostly."

"How extraordinary." Mr. Brown tapped his round glasses up to the top of his nose. "And you think he's guilty?"

She looked around to make sure they weren't being overheard.

"Everybody does. The victim was well known in this town, Mrs. Vanessa Allen. She knew those cliffs like the back of her hand. It's inconceivable that she could have fallen, unless she was pushed."

"They knew each other, then? The victim and the suspect?"

"They were neighbors, of sorts. She lived in the next house along the cliff, which you can't see from here. There's a footpath that passes by his house and runs along the top of the cliffs until it reaches a bright-yellow cottage, a five-minute walk away. That's where she lived, with her daughter, Jennifer."

"And what was his motive?"

"That's simple," said the woman, who had forgotten her initial reticence and was now speaking freely. "He wants to marry Jennifer. But Mrs. Allen never liked him and she was set against it. So he wanted her out of the way, that's all. Four days ago they were both walking along that path. Mrs. Allen was coming to town and he was heading in the other direction. As they passed each other he saw his opportunity and pushed her to her death, then claimed she slipped. It's the perfect crime, when you think about it. There was no one watching except for the sea."

Mr. Brown smiled at her confidence and leaned back, seemingly satisfied with the sordid nature of her tale, then tapped his cane twice against the ground as punctuation. "In even the most innocent scenes, there is darkness to be found at the corners," he said, "from the way the light falls on the frame."

She nodded. "And there is his house, at the corner of the town."

"Where he waited like a spider, pinned to his white web. But spiders are often harmless creatures, no matter how sinister they might appear. Maybe the young man is simply misunderstood?"

"Nonsense," she muttered, suddenly quite indignant.

"Then you're certain it couldn't have been an accident?"

The woman shrugged. "There aren't a lot of accidents in this town."

Mr. Brown stood up and tipped his hat to her, after putting it back on his head. She gasped; he'd seemed so small, sitting down, but in fact he was over six feet tall.

"My dear, that was a most interesting discussion. Let's hope the matter is laid to rest soon. Have a wonderful day."

And he walked off toward the white house on the hill.

• • •

In fact Mr. Brown had found Gordon Foyle quite pleasant and sympathetic when they'd sat down together the day before, at a small table in a cell of the local police station.

The young man had looked at him with pleading blue eyes. "They're going to hang me."

Between them was a piece of paper and a pencil. Gordon Foyle's movements were slow and ponderous, partly due to his nature and partly because his hands were chained to the table. He straightened the paper and started to draw. "I'm frightened."

"Why do you think they'll hang you?"

Gordon continued to sketch as he talked. "Oh, because I keep to myself. Though that makes it sound like a selfish thing to do. It's not really, I've just never been very good at making friends."

"Nevertheless, they'll need some evidence."

"Will they?"

An uncomfortable silence filled the room. Mr. Brown chose his words carefully. "If you're innocent, there is reason to be hopeful."

Gordon waved his right hand dismissively. There was a cascade of metal as the chain fell from the table. "There was actually a witness, you know." The young man was looking directly at Mr. Brown now. He turned the piece of paper around; he'd drawn a yacht, floating on the straight line of the sea. "A boat, about two hundred yards out in the bay. It was painted red. That's what it looked like. It was too far away for me to get the name, but if you can find whoever was on that boat, they would have been able to see everything."

Mr. Brown closed his eyes, as if he were breaking bad news. "But only if they were looking."

"Please, Mr. Brown, you have to try."

• • •

"There's only one unusual thing about this crime, and that's the unflinching ruthlessness with which it was carried out. A quiet young man kills the mother of the woman he loves, and all it takes is a gentle push."

After his visit to the police station, Mr. Brown had been met by his old friend, Inspector Wild. They were discussing the case over sherry at the bar of Mr. Brown's hotel.

"We have no real evidence," the inspector continued. "But what evidence could we possibly have? It's the perfect crime, in that sense. With no witnesses except for the birds."

"If it leaves him as the only suspect, I would say it's rather imperfect. Wouldn't you? How can the poor man ever prove his innocence? People have been hanged on less evidence than this, and you can't tell me that's not a possibility here."

Inspector Wild brought finger and thumb together along the length of his pointed beard and cocked his head back. He let out a long sigh. "I damn well hope it is. I think he's as guilty as a louse."

Mr. Brown lifted his glass. "Well, then. Here's to the inquisitive, open minds of our police detectives."

Inspector Wild narrowed his bright-green eyes. "I would be glad to be proved wrong." And he finished off his drink.

They ordered food and the hotelier brought them some disappointing sandwiches, tinted pink by the red lamp behind Inspector Wild's head.

"Then he lives alone," asked Mr. Brown, "our friend Gordon Foyle?"

"It's rather a tragic case, really. You can see how he'd get out of line. Both his parents died seven years ago, when he was eighteen, in some kind of motoring accident. But they left him the house and enough to get by, so he's come out of it all right. I don't believe he's done a day's work in his life."

"But he must have help?"

"Yes, a lady comes up from the town every day. He says he likes it that way, rather than having someone living in. But the whole thing happened before she was due, so instead we know about his movements from a local woman named Epstein."

"I see," said Mr. Brown. "And where can I find her?"

• • •

Whitestone House sat in its surroundings—a neat green lawn and beyond that a brownish expanse of heather and gorse—like an egg snug in a nest. At present there were no signs of life, and each of the dim windows showed only a dusty white leg of curtain, running seductively down the side of the frame.

All of the rooms inside were dark.

Mr. Brown knocked his hat back with the head of his cane and took in the whole scene at a glance. "An empty page," he muttered to himself.

He carried on walking and came to a wooden bench just beyond the house, before the start of the footpath. It had a charming view of both the sea and the town. A woman was sitting on it, facing away from him: He could see only the deep-red shawl covering her back and a sweep of long white hair hanging down from her head. Two bruised-orange butterflies hovered around her shoulders.

Mr. Brown approached her and removed his hat. "What a wonderful view."

She hummed and turned her head toward him. "You're with the police, aren't you? I can always tell."

"Actually, I'm afraid I'm not."

She nodded. "Then you're a journalist?"

"I'm conducting my own inquiries, on a private basis."

A small, fluffy brown dog was running around her feet.

"The police all think he's guilty. And so do the newspapers. But I've always liked him. The people around here are rather judgmental when it comes to outsiders. Where do you stand on the matter?"

"Only where you see me, Mrs. Epstein."

She blinked at him, her smile unbroken. "How do you know my name?"

"It's written on the diary that's poking out of your bag."

"You're very observant."

"I should hope so," he said. "That's why I'm here. I understand you were present on the day Mrs. Allen died?"

"I'm here every day, from nine to half past. I sit here from one strike of the church clock to the next. Jacob gets upset if we don't follow our routine to the minute." She reached a hand down and placed it defensively on the dog's back, as if she was testing a radiator to see if it was warm.

"And what can you tell me about that day?"

"I'll tell you what I told the police. There was a strong wind that morning. Gordon left the house and set out along the path at about ten minutes past nine. He came running back in this direction three or four minutes later, shouting something about an accident. I don't remember his exact words, but he was awfully upset. I followed him inside and we rang for the police and a doctor."

"And you heard nothing during the few minutes he was gone?"

"Nothing at all. The poor boy was in a terrible state."

"Thank you," said Mr. Brown. He had no further questions. He checked the time: It was five minutes past nine. "I do hope you have a lovely day."

She watched him walk off. "Be careful," she called out, pointing to the ground.

He'd already seen it. Three telltale fingers of dog feces lying on the grass; like the rotting hand of a corpse, rising from its grave.

"Of course," he said, and stepped around it.

• • •

To enter the path, Mr. Brown had to go through a little wooden gate, which was padlocked shut. There was a battered sign tied to the middle of it: THIS PATH IS CLOSED FOR REASONS OF PUBLIC SAFETY.

"Well," he said to himself, "I imagine the police would consider me an exception." And he climbed over it without difficulty.

The path formed a thin line between two impassable types of nature. On the left was a thick verge of sharp gorse and soft heather—yellow and purple flowers playing out a kind of puppet show of good and evil, their heads bobbing in the gentle breeze—that led to the edge of the cliffs and the sheer drop beyond, where the polished ocean seemed to wink in the sunlight. And on the right was a steep rise leading up five yards or so to the brow of a hill, which was itself crowded with vegetation and covered sporadically with trees.

Mr. Brown was unable to see the cliff face to his left, but he could see its twin a hundred yards ahead of him, where the path turned out toward the sea. There the broad expanse of white stone was dappled with gray and stained almost red in places, leading down to a tuberous growth of furious black rocks. An unpleasant place to land, he thought.

He'd asked Wild about the state of Mrs. Allen's body: Her neck had been broken and her eyes were bloated and black. A chunk of flesh on her right arm had been gouged out, and four ribs on that side had been crushed by the impact with a rock, presumably one below the surface, as they'd found no traces of blood on anything.

They'd had to row along the cliff in a small wooden boat and fish her body out with an oar and a net. "In Foyle's defense," Inspector Wild had said, "we might never have found her if he hadn't raised the alarm so quickly. But, then, to do otherwise would have made him look guilty, wouldn't it?"

Mr. Brown followed the path at a very careful pace. The brush-covered verge and the shadowed slope were littered with oddments—handbills, cigarette ends, various food wrappers—but he was unable to find anything incriminating among the mute pieces of illegible litter. And the ground wasn't soft enough for footprints.

Nonetheless, he stopped every few yards and examined the path thoroughly on both sides, using the head of his cane to raise and lower the brim of his hat as he turned between the silent shade of the slope and the sudden loud blue of the sea.

After a couple of minutes he came to a small dark stone of irregular shape, sitting in the middle of the path. He stooped down to look at it, then shook his head. It was an uncharacteristically dry piece of canine excrement. He flicked it into the sea with the tip of his cane and watched it fall to its death, then turned back to look for Mrs. Epstein, wondering if her dog had been on the path at the time of the incident.

That's when he realized how severely, and yet imperceptibly, the path had been twisting and turning since he'd clambered over the gate. Whitestone House had vanished from view and so had Mrs. Epstein; he could see nothing of any interest behind him or ahead. The path here was truly isolated.

It was the perfect place to murder someone.

And yet there was a witness, Gordon Foyle had said: that yacht, out in the bay.

"I wonder," said Mr. Brown, squinting out to sea.

• • •

A hundred yards farther along, he spotted a white shape swirled through the innards of a heather bush, almost glowing against the dark-green background. It was hidden deep enough that he doubted anyone else would have seen it, but Mr. Brown's powers of observation were nearly supernatural, and he was justly famous for them. He poked his cane into the bush, and through patient, skillful manipulation he managed to twist the white material around the end of it.

Then he pulled it out.

He extracted what turned out to be a white scarf, coiled through the bush like a tapeworm. He ran the length of pale fabric through his gloved hands. It clearly belonged to a woman and had recently been worn. There was no blood on it, but there was a boot print at one end in the shape of a slender heel.

Most illuminating, thought Mr. Brown.

Vanessa Allen had been wearing a scarf when she died, according to her daughter. But they hadn't found it with the body. They'd assumed it was lost in the sea.

He folded it into a small rectangle and put it in his pocket, then wiped his cane on the grass.

• • •

It was Miss Jennifer Allen that had brought him into this affair. She'd called on him at his house in London, two days after her mother's death. "I hear you have a record of solving problems where the police have failed?"

Her eyes were still red from crying, but she seemed a very calm and levelheaded young woman. Mr. Brown showed her through to the parlor. "Oh, I've managed it once or twice. What can I help you with?"

She told him the facts of the case, including her own version of events. She'd been having breakfast at home that morning, with a view over their front garden. She could see the footpath from there and she watched her mother set out along it, struggling into the wind. "And that's all I saw, until the doctor appeared. About half an hour later. To tell me the news."

"I am sorry," said Mr. Brown. "This must be a very difficult time for you."

She stared down at her shoes. "Poor Gordon. The police are determined to hang him, of course."

Mr. Brown nodded. "And you're hoping I can prove his innocence?"

She reached up and wrapped her fist around the silver locket she was wearing. "I don't know what I'd do if they hanged him."

· · ·

After a few more steps, Mr. Brown stopped again. Here the heather on the left side of the path was visibly disturbed: Its normally resilient branches were trampled down and torn aside.

"We found some signs of a struggle." So Inspector Wild had told him. "He claims that she was ahead of him on the path. He saw her slip and fall and pushed through the heather to the cliff edge to see if she'd managed to save herself. But by that time she was just a splash and a smear of clothing on the rocks."

Mr. Brown lifted one of the broken branches with his cane. "The green incarnation of urgency."

Thirty yards beyond that he reached the place where Gordon Foyle claimed the accident had happened, where the cliff edge came right up to touch the path—the result of decades of erosion—leaving a crescent-shaped indentation in it, like a bite taken out of a biscuit. The path here was still a generous three feet wide, but if you weren't paying attention you could easily fall.

"Maybe that's how it was done." Mr. Brown whistled to himself. "Death by distraction."

He took an absurd degree of care as he positioned himself next to the gap and leaned forward to look down. The sight of the sheer drop embraced him bodily, and he held tight to his cane to steady himself. Below him the buttressing rocks extended only slightly into the sea, while around them the waves showed their white teeth. It was a picture of pure terror.

He turned his back on it and continued on his way.

The rest of the path was unremarkable. It soon broke from the erratic shoreline and cut straight across the land. There were trees and a multitude of bushes on both sides of the path now, forming a quiet, secluded corridor; the light was green here, even on such a bright blue day. After that, the path led farther inland to twist around a row of pastel-colored cottages that had originally been built for coast guards.

The first of them, a pleasant yellow, had been the home of Mrs. Allen and her daughter. It was set back from the path in a garden overflowing with flowers. A stark contrast to the white walls and plain grass of young Gordon Foyle's house. The front door was a deep, dark red.

Mr. Brown knocked on it twice.

• • •

A young woman answered the door. She was rather small, with her hair tied back in a plait; she looked startled to see someone standing there. "Can I help you, sir?"

She must be the maid, thought Mr. Brown. "I do indeed hope so. May I speak to Miss Jennifer Allen?"

She frowned and looked tentatively behind her. "I'm afraid she's not in, sir."

"That is unfortunate. Would it be worth me waiting for her to return?"

"I'm sorry, sir. Miss Jennifer won't be home for a while."

"Of course." Mr. Brown smiled at the shy young woman. He removed his gloves, took a folded map from an inside pocket, and held it open before him. The thin paper rippled between his leathery hands. "I wonder, would it be terribly rude of me to ask to step inside and inspect my map in the hallway, out of the wind? Only I have a terrible memory for directions, and I would like to get my bearings."

She breathed in sharply at the audacity of it but stood to one side and nodded sheepishly. "Please, sir."

He smiled as he passed through the doorway.

Mr. Brown's shoes were slightly muddy, and he stepped carefully from the doormat onto a half page of newspaper, which had been placed in the corner of the hallway, next to a stained pair of Wellington boots. He stood in that pose for half a minute, with his tough, blunt thumb following the ancient line of the coast as he pretended to study the route.

"Ah, yes," he said. "I see where I am now. Thank you, I shall be on my way, then."

There was movement behind one of the closed doors leading off from the hallway. The maid flushed with embarrassment. The door opened and Miss Jennifer Allen emerged from the room. "Mr. Brown." She glanced at the maid. "Forgive me, I asked not to be disturbed. But I didn't know you'd be stopping by."

"That's perfectly all right. I'm just making my investigations."

She stepped closer to him and spoke in a whisper. "How is it proceeding?"

"I have a lot of things to think about." He noticed that she'd taken off the locket she'd been wearing. "Are you starting to have doubts?"

"No." She put a hand to her forehead. "I don't know. People have been telling me stories. Have you found anything yet? Anything that proves his innocence?"

He felt that he should say something comforting. "I'm afraid it's too early to tell."

Then he left the house and made his way back to the path.

• • •

His walk back to Evescombe went fairly quickly: The case was a simple one, after all, and he considered it almost solved. He even went so far as to light his pipe and trundle along with one hand held aloft, the smoke tangling itself in the trees and the glowing bowl announcing his passage through the undergrowth to anyone watching.

He arrived at the wooden bench by Whitestone House just as the church clock was striking half past nine. He sat down to take in the view. The sky was dim now and the day was curiously quiet. He looked down at the dark water, riddled with white reflections, and thought of the terror she must have felt tumbling into it. "An unpleasant way to die."

He sat and smoked in solitude, watching the waves, wondering if Mr. Foyle's secret boat had really existed. Then he tapped his tobacco ashes into the deep and set off again for the train station.

• • •

The following evening Mr. Brown and Inspector Wild were reunited in the restaurant of the Palace Hotel. Both were smoking—Mr. Brown with his rustic, twisted wooden pipe, like a claw in his cupped hand, and Inspector Wild with a thin cigarette—and their corner of the room was crawling with curls of tobacco smoke. The two demonic figures sat in this dark haze, drinking brandy, after a heavy meal of red meat and vegetables, and their talk turned to the Foyle case.

"Well," began Inspector Wild, "it seems we've wasted your time. Through no fault of our own, at least. But now we know exactly what happened on that cliff in Evescombe. Would you believe it: The boat he saw really does exist? It's called the *Retired Adventurer*. It arrived in Southampton yesterday."

"I've believed more outlandish things, I have to say."

"But rarely with as much consequence as this, I'd wager. The owner and his wife crossed the Channel last week. They didn't hear anything about the case until he happened to glance at an English newspaper in Guernsey. His name is Symons. He seems a respectable type. It turns out that his wife had seen the whole thing and told him about it, but she'd been at the bottle and he hadn't believed her. When he saw the newspaper, he put two and two together. Then sailed back immediately, feeling terribly guilty. His wife's still in Guernsey, but she told him all the details."

"That sounds like quite an ordeal. He'll make a sympathetic witness, at least." And both men exhaled smoke in lieu of laughter.

"Anyway," said Inspector Wild, "let me enlighten you."

He struck a match and was about to light another cigarette, when Mr. Brown leaned forward and blew it out. "Wait just one second," said Mr. Brown. "I wouldn't want to give you the satisfaction. I already know what happened."

"But you can't possibly know. We agreed there was no evidence."

"Well, I found some. Enough to give me a good idea, at least."

Inspector Wild looked at him suspiciously. "I see. Let's have it, then."

The large sallow man sat back in his chair. "There were only two options in this case. It was either an accident or Gordon Foyle was guilty. All it would take to decide between these two possibilities was one definitive clue."

"Yes, I can see that. And did you find such a clue?"

"I did." And here Mr. Brown took the folded square of white, stained material from his jacket pocket and handed it to the inspector, who spread it open on the table. "I present to you the victim's scarf."

"Where did you find this?"

"It was caught in a heather bush. Your lot must have missed it."

"And what is it supposed to tell us, exactly?"

"Here, you'll see, is a footprint from a Wellington boot. Slim, in a woman's size. It matches the prints on a half page of newspaper in the victim's cottage. You'll be able to tell me, no doubt, that she died in a pair of Wellington boots?"

Inspector Wild nodded. "Yes, she did."

"Very good. Then answer me this: How does a woman falling suddenly to her death manage to put a footprint on her own scarf? On a windy day, the ends of the scarf would be behind her. And then the only way to make a print on it, and a heel print no less, would be by walking backward. Or by being pulled backward."

Inspector Wild was hesitant. "Go on."

"What I think happened on that cliff is this: Gordon Foyle and Mrs. Allen passed each other by; some impolite words were exchanged. And then it must have occurred to him that he could put an end to the whole situation. So he turned back, approached her from behind, and took her by the neck. She resisted, of course. But he pulled her backward. That's when she trod on her own scarf and it came off and was blown into the bushes. He wrestled her through the heather and threw her off the edge of the cliff. That dip in the path was a mere convenience: The murder happened where the heather was disturbed." He took up his drink. "Well, Inspector, now you can enlighten me."

Inspector Wild looked slightly bemused. He gave his friend a wry smile. "What can I say? It seems like you got a lot of that from guesswork, but you're exactly right. The wife of the man with the boat saw everything that you've just described. Gordon Foyle is as guilty as a louse. The only thing I don't understand is why he told us about the boat in the first place, if he was guilty the whole time."

Mr. Brown touched his fingertips together. "I suppose he saw it out in the bay and thought it added a nice bit of color. The implication that his story could in theory be corroborated lent a kind of credence to it. He probably presumed there was no chance at all that they'd actually seen anything. The odds were against it, weren't they?"

"Undeniably."

"It was just bad luck for him that they did." He pictured the young man's pleading blue eyes. "Well, then, he'll hang?"

The inspector nodded. "Most likely. By the neck until dead."

Mr. Brown shook his head in sympathy, and it was as if his tired, wavering face were a marionette suspended on strings from his skull. "That is a shame, I rather liked him. My only solace is in knowing that I've saved Jennifer Allen from marrying a murderer."

He thought of her words. *I don't know what I'd do if they hanged him.* And he smiled at the credulity of youth.

"Death is always messy," said Inspector Wild. "It's for the culprit, not us, to bemoan the consequences." And the two men lifted their glasses in a half-hearted toast, then faded back into their bright-red armchairs.

• • •

That night Mrs. Daisy Lancaster, of Station Road, Evescombe, woke in her bed and went to the window. The sea was there before her, as calm and comforting as the glass of water on her nightstand. She had dreamed that the face of the man she'd met on the seafront the other day, the man whose photograph was in the papers as an "assistant to the police," a Mr. Winston Brown, was rising above the water like a pale moon, his probing eyes fixed on her window, and his impossibly long cane reaching across the bay to bang against her front door, with an expression as cold and uncaring as the waves.

She shivered and closed the window.

4

THE SECOND CONVERSATION

Julia Hart couldn't help speeding up as she reached the last page. "*. . . with an expression as cold and uncaring as the waves,*" she read. "*She shivered and closed the window.*"

She placed the manuscript on the ground beside her, then poured herself a glass of water. That story reminded her of the Welsh coast, where she'd grown up. Grant sat tapping his foot, seemingly deep in thought.

"Is everything all right?" she asked.

His head jerked upward, as if he was surprised by the question. "I'm sorry," he said. "I forgot myself for a second. That one really takes me back."

"Then is it based on something true?"

He shook his head. "It reminds me of something that happened to me once, that's all. It brought back some memories."

"It reminds me of Wales," said Julia. "My family moved there when I was very young."

Grant smiled at her, trying to appear interested. "Then where were you born?"

"Scotland, actually. But I haven't been back there since."

"And I've never been to Wales," he sighed wistfully. "Do you miss it?"

"Sometimes. Do you miss Scotland?"

Grant shrugged. "I hardly ever think about it now."

Julia felt she should change the subject. "So Gordon Foyle was guilty all along? I suppose there was no other way it could have ended. If it had turned out to be an accident, the ending would have lost its impact. Don't you think?"

Grant pushed himself up with his fists and turned his back to the sun. "I don't approve of happy endings in crime stories." Now his head was in silhouette. "Death should be shown as a tragedy, never anything else." He picked up a lemon from the ground and started to spin it between his fingers. It was as if all these frantic movements formed a sort of apology for letting his attention drift earlier.

Julia tapped the manuscript with her pen. "You also seem to dislike the idea of the heroic detective. Mr. Brown is a sinister creation. And he seems to be improvising. There's not much method to his madness— even his colleague acknowledges that."

"Yes." Grant shrugged. "I suppose I was pushing back against the idea that detective stories are about logical deduction. As a mathematician, I can tell you they're about nothing of the kind. Inspired guesswork is all that most fictional detectives do. And seen in that light, there's something fundamentally dishonest about the detective character. Don't you think?"

They were sitting in a grove of lemon trees, a short way up the hill from his cottage. Grant had left her there alone after they'd eaten lunch together. "I'd like to take a short walk," he'd said. "Would you care to join me?"

But Julia wasn't used to the heat yet and the skin on her face felt tight from the morning sun, so instead she'd stayed with the lemon trees, where there was plenty of shade and the cooling breeze could still reach her. She'd sat down on the sloped earth and made some annotations on the story they'd just read.

Grant had returned thirty minutes later. She'd watched him approach from the direction of the cottage: Perspective had shown him first the same size as a leaf, then as a lemon, and finally as one of the diminutive trees. He'd been carrying a carafe of water—it seemed he would take one everywhere now—and had placed it at her feet. She'd poured herself a glass and started to read.

"Are fictional detectives fundamentally dishonest?" She thought about the question. "That could be the title of a doctoral thesis." He waited for her to answer, the silence punctured by birdsong. "I would say no. No more than fiction itself."

Grant closed his eyes. "That's a wise answer."

She poured herself another glass of water. She hadn't relished reading out loud again, not with the day as hot as it was; her throat had dried up by the end of the first page. But Grant had confessed to her that morning that his eyesight had grown very poor in the last few years. There was no optician on the island, and he'd broken his glasses some time ago.

"I read rather slowly as a result. Painfully so, I'm afraid."

"You don't write anymore, then?"

He'd shaken his head. "I neither write nor read. Except when I have to."

So she'd felt she had no choice; she'd indulged him and read the first two stories out loud. Now she was exhausted.

The breeze picked up, bringing with it the faint smell of the sea. It was invigorating but ever so slightly putrid. It was the smell of life being renewed. Against this the lemons gave off a cloud of sweet scent, like lamps glowing in a mist.

"I'll fall asleep if we sit here too long," said Grant, getting to his feet and hopping from one foot to the other. He was wearing a blazer over his white shirt, again showing no sign of being troubled by the heat. "Let's get started, shall we? Is there anything you'd like to change about that story?"

Julia looked up at him. "Nothing substantial. A few phrases. But I did notice another inconsistency. Again, I think it's an intentional one."

He turned toward her, the hint of a smile on his face. "Are you going to tell me that the town in this story is another depiction of hell? Damnation could start to sound quite appealing in that case, like a holiday park."

"No," she laughed. "It's near the end. When Mr. Brown returns to the bench by Whitestone House, after his walk along the cliff tops, the church bell is tolling half past nine, but he finds the bench empty. And yet Mrs. Epstein has just gone to great lengths to tell us, a few pages earlier, that she should be sitting there at that time. Do you see what I mean? Why mention her routine at all, if not to highlight the discrepancy?"

Grant paced back and forth, still in silhouette. "Then the implication is that she's been abducted or something like that?"

"No," said Julia. "I think the implication is that it's actually half past nine at night when he returns from his walk. If you read the surrounding sentences very closely, they're clearly describing moonlight on a dark sea. Then there's a clue in the name of the town itself."

"Evescombe?"

"Evening has come."

"Ah." He clapped his hands together. "That's just the sort of joke I would have enjoyed when I was younger."

"Then what did Mr. Brown do with the rest of his day?"

"That's a mystery, I suppose." Grant stood with his loose clothes rippling in the breeze, his eyes wide with excitement. "But you're right, I must have added that on purpose. To see if the readers were paying attention. I don't remember it, but, then, I barely remember writing these stories at all." He sat down again. "You ought to be explaining them to me, not the other way around."

She raised an eyebrow. "Well, here's something you can explain to me." Grant took off his hat and leaned toward her. "You told me this morning that a group of suspects is the first requirement for a murder mystery and that there must be at least two of them. But this story appears to have only one."

He tilted his head back and grinned at the sky. "Yes, it's made to look that way. But it's just sleight of hand. I've always liked the idea of a murder mystery with a single suspect—it's a sort of paradoxical take on the genre. But to explain how it satisfies the definition, I first have to explain the second ingredient."

Julia held a pen in one hand and had her notebook open on her lap. "I'm ready," she said.

"The second ingredient of a murder mystery is a victim or group of victims. Those characters that have been killed in unknown circumstances."

Julia wrote this down. "The first ingredient is a group of suspects, the second a group of victims. I might be able to guess what the others will be."

He nodded. "I told you it was simple. The only requirement we make of the group of victims is that there must be at least one of them. After all, without a victim, there can't be a murder."

"Not a successful one, at least."

"So in this particular story, we have a victim, Mrs. Allen, and a suspect, Gordon Foyle. And it turns out that he did kill her, but there were other alternatives. It could have been an accident; the victim could have lost her footing."

Julia made a note. "Death by misadventure. I've always enjoyed that phrase. I like the implication that adventure is something you can do correctly or incorrectly."

Grant laughed. "Certainly. My prolonged sojourn on this island, for instance. That was an adventure once. But as I grow old I wonder if it hasn't, perhaps, been done incorrectly."

My time on this island too, thought Julia; she was tired and her throat was still sore. She smiled at him. "It could also have been suicide, though the possibility is never mentioned."

"That's true," said Grant. "And in both of those cases, accident and suicide, who would we consider most responsible for the death?"

"I don't know. The victim, presumably?"

"Yes, Mrs. Allen herself. Which means that either Mr. Foyle was responsible for her death or she was responsible for it herself."

"Then she is the second suspect?"

"That's correct. Our definition requires a group of two or more suspects and a group of one or more victims, but it doesn't say that they can't overlap. So she can be the second suspect, even though she's the victim."

"Wouldn't it be a little strange to call her a murderer if she'd slipped and fallen?"

"That particular word would be inappropriate, of course. But it doesn't seem unreasonable to say that of all the characters, she would have done the most to cause her own death. She went for that walk along the path to begin with. And therefore it doesn't seem unreasonable to consider her a suspect. It simplifies things."

"I see," said Julia, as she wrote this down. "Then this is another example of a murder mystery with two suspects?"

"Yes, with the qualification that one of them is the victim. So it's a murder mystery with a single suspect, except for the victim herself."

"That seems to make sense." Julia took a lemon from the ground and inhaled its sweet smell. "There's one other thing I wanted to ask you."

Grant nodded. "What's that?"

"You called this collection of stories *The White Murders*. I've spent some time over the last few weeks trying to work out why."

Grant smiled. "And what conclusion did you come to?"

"Well, here we have Whitestone House."

"And the previous story took place in a whitewashed villa in Spain."

"And that theme continues through the rest of the stories. But I wondered if there might be something more to it than that?"

"What do you mean?"

"The name seemed familiar somehow. And then I realized why." She left a momentary pause. "Are you aware that there was a real murder, a number of years ago, that became known colloquially as the White Murder?"

"I was not. That's an interesting coincidence."

"Then you've never heard of it?"

Grant's smile had gone by this point. "It does sound vaguely familiar, now that you mention it."

"We've published several books on unsolved murders at Blood Type, so I'd read about it before. That's how I knew the name. It happened in North London, in 1940. It was one of those murders that the press likes to obsess about: The victim was a young woman called Elizabeth White. She was an actor and playwright and she was very beautiful. She was strangled on Hampstead Heath late one evening. The newspapers called it the White Murder. It was before I was born, but I understand it became quite a famous case at the time. They never managed to find her killer."

"How unpleasant."

"Yes, it is rather. But is it really just a coincidence?"

Grant put his hand to his chin. "What else? Do you think I named the book after the crime?"

Julia tilted her head to one side. "It would have been in all of the papers around the time you were writing."

"The London papers," said Grant. "But I was in Edinburgh. I'd have had to go looking for it. Certainly if I saw the name written down somewhere it might have affected me subconsciously. Either that, or it really was just a coincidence." He shrugged. "The truth is, I chose *The White Murders* because I found the name evocative. Poetic, almost." He spoke like a man reciting a quotation in a foreign language, adding emphases that weren't there: "*The White Murders*. But it could have just as easily been *The Red Murders* or *The Blue Murders*."

Julia wondered if he was telling her the truth. "It would be quite a big coincidence, given the timing."

Grant smiled once again. "That depends on what you're comparing it to."

"Yes, well." Her hand was tired from taking notes. "Shall we take a break?"

5

A DETECTIVE AND HIS EVIDENCE

A discreet gentleman, dressed smartly in a dark-blue suit, was passing through one of the three streets that formed the boundaries of a small square in Central London, when he had the misfortune to step in a puddle. It was five minutes before noon. For a man in his state of mind, both distracted and agitated, the incongruity of this was enough to bring him to a sudden stop. He looked down at his shoes in a sort of self-pitying disbelief; it was a pleasant late-summer's day, after all, and it hadn't rained for three weeks.

He watched his reflection take shape as the murky surface of the puddle renewed itself. There was his round face, floating above his shoulders. There was his dark hair and elaborate black mustache, squashed between his suit and the blue sky. There was his almost non-existent neck. His eyes followed the trail of wet pavement from the puddle up to its source: a display outside a florist's shop, where an audience of flowers in childish colors were nodding their heads at him in half-hearted sympathy. The man swore under his breath and turned and looked moodily at the neighboring buildings, as if searching for a way to get revenge on the street itself.

And that was how it all began.

• • •

The square was called Colchester Gardens. That was also the name of its vaguely rectangular private park, which sat at the intersection of two roads and was bounded by a narrower, more meandering third road, which linked the other two and cut off the corner. This third road was called Colchester Terrace, and the man in the dark-blue suit stood halfway along it, hidden from the two busier roads by the gardens themselves.

The residents of Colchester Terrace were the only ones supplied with keys to the park; the man in dark blue, like everybody else, could merely look at it through the bars of the black metal fence. He glanced to his left, then to his right. The street was deserted and the florist's shop was closed, with no explanation. There was a greengrocer's on the corner that seemed to be open, but nobody was coming or going.

On the other side of the railings were two young girls. They were struggling with a large paper plane that wouldn't take flight. It was made from a folded sheet of splendid purple craft paper and was the size of a small dog. Their laughter was the only sound he could hear as they took turns trying to launch it. Each time they tried, it flew for two or three yards, then seemed to meet a great wave of resistance and spiraled either haltingly into the sky or hastily down toward the ground, at which point they would both scream theatrically and try again, furious and hopeless and infected with laughter.

The man in dark blue watched them for almost a minute and then took a step toward the fence. He wrapped his hands around the railings and pressed his forehead between two of the sharp, ornamental fleurs-de-lis that emerged from the top of them. "Girls," he called. They both stopped laughing and looked at him. They must have been about the same age, and they wore similar blue dresses. "Girls, what are your names?"

One of them, the one with a reddish tint to her hair, was less shy than the other. She took a step toward him, while the other one sat down on the grass. "I'm Rose," she said. "And that's my friend Maggie."

Maggie looked down at the mention of her name.

"Well, girls, my name is Christopher. And now that we are no longer strangers, let me give you some help with flying that plane." He pointed. Rose looked down at the forgotten toy. It sat on the grass between her and Maggie, as forlorn as her friend. "It just needs a little weight at the front, then it will fly."

Rose stared uncertainly at the tangle of paper, reluctant to pick it up; it was an insult to be invited into the world of adult conversation by a serious-looking man and then immediately to be cast back as a child by being asked to hand him a toy.

"Here," he said. "Take this." He took a small card from the inside breast pocket of his suit and tore it in half. One half he placed back in his pocket; the other he folded three times into a small, stubby rectangle and held out through the railings. Rose took it automatically and stared down at it, a disappointing gift. "Tuck it inside the front of the plane, in the nose. Then try again."

She was ready to protest that they weren't really bothered about flying it, that they were just passing the time and really she was too old for such things. But there was something warm about his voice that canceled out these objections, a conspiratorial flavor that she found comforting. She slotted the card into the plane, as instructed. Then she ran a few paces with it. He watched her arms as she reached out to propel the plane forward: It flew for twenty yards this time before skidding to a graceful stop, like a large knife cutting through the sky. He smiled and then looked at the other girl, hoping for her approval.

But Maggie sat picking at the grass, looking rather bored. There is something not quite right about that girl, he thought. She glanced up at him surreptitiously, and he realized then that she was neither sulking nor bored but scared of him. He stepped back in a flame of self-doubt. He watched her for a few moments more, then made his decision.

"You girls have a splendid day, now."

He bowed briefly to Rose. She waved back enthusiastically.

And then he left.

• • •

At twenty minutes past twelve, Alice Cavendish was walking through the eponymous park of Colchester Gardens—toward the black gate that led out onto the street—when she saw her sister and the younger Clements girl playing with their dolls.

Alice was in a good mood, so she changed direction and headed toward the two of them. Tucked inside her light summer jacket was a letter from Richard, saying how nice it was to have seen her last week, that he'd got her the gift she'd asked for, and did she think they might go for a walk sometime? She'd stolen away to the darkest part of the park—to a shaded triangle between three stout plane trees, spaced a few yards apart—to sit down and open it in private. The grass had been slightly wet, since it was so well hidden from the sun, but his words had been sweet enough that she was able to relish every sensation, even the damp.

"Morning, Maggie," she said to her sister. "What are you two doing?"

Rose stood up. "It's afternoon, silly."

"Hello there, Rose."

"You must call her Mrs. Clements," said Maggie. "We're playing that we're widows and that these are our orphans." She indicated the two dolls. Alice laughed, unsure of whether to inform her sister of the semantic mistake or to inquire further about the nature of their game. She decided, in the end, to do neither.

"Where is the airplane I made for you yesterday? I thought you were going to fly it today if the weather was nice?"

Rose Clements, who always had to speak first, pointed at a nearby tree with a burst of energy, taking a few steps toward it as she spoke: "There!"

The purple plane, which was entwined with the leaves high up on a branch, looked like a shard of stained glass from this distance.

"Oh dear," said Alice. "That is unlucky."

"It was the man's fault," said Maggie. "Everything was fine until he changed it."

That cryptic comment seemed to fill Alice with a vague sense of apprehension, to the point where she wasn't even sure if she'd heard it correctly. But then Rose's previous statement came back to her suddenly and all her other thoughts faded away: "Did you say it was afternoon already?"

Rose nodded. "The church bell went ages ago."

Alice had been too busy daydreaming to notice. "I must take Mummy her tea."

And everything else was quickly forgotten.

She rushed over to the gate and out onto Colchester Terrace, then down a few doors to their house. It was when she reached for the door handle that she noticed how filthy her hands were. "Oh dear," she said to herself, examining them closely. There was a thick curved line of dirt under her thumbnail, like a pool of uneaten sauce along the edge of a plate.

She opened the towering red door and stepped into the hallway. Elise, the maid, appeared at the far end of the corridor. Alice took off her jacket and gave it to Elise, slipping Richard's letter from the pocket as she did so. "Elise, will you prepare Mummy's tea? I shall take it up to her if she's awake." Elise nodded, vanishing into the darkness at the distant side of the house.

Alice crept into her father's study, which was immediately to the right of the front door, and—being careful not to touch anything—sat down at his desk and read the letter again.

• • •

A few minutes later, Elise was waiting for Alice on the first-floor land-ing. She was holding a tray with a cup of hot copper-colored tea and a gaudy slice of lemon; Alice took it from her and carried it up to the top floor of the house. She entered the large master bedroom, announcing herself with a gentle knock.

"Good afternoon, Alice." Her pale mother had propped herself up in bed and sat like a bookmark between the flowing white sheets, wear-ing a crimson robe. Alice put the tray down and went to the window and opened the curtains; her mother winced and pulled the sheets up to her neck, as if the daylight itself would make her colder. The window looked out onto the square, and from this height Alice could see that insufferable Rose Clements chasing her sister from tree to tree with a chrysanthemum in her hand, like a kind of sword; she could also see her own hiding place between the three trees, just about.

"How are you feeling this afternoon, Mummy?" And she went to the bed and took her mother's hand in her own.

"Improving with your presence, as always, sweetheart. Though I slept poorly, and my lungs feel very sore." Her daughter smiled sympa-thetically. "Why, Alice darling, you're filthy!" Her mother's eyes wid-ened. Alice withdrew her hand, as if she'd been holding it too close to a candle, and rubbed her thumb against her fingertips.

"I know, Mummy. I got my hands dirty picking flowers."

"And then rubbed them all over your face, to look at it."

"Oh dear." Alice went to the mirror on her mother's dresser and saw that it was true. She'd been absentmindedly touching her hair while reading the letter from Richard, picking compulsively at the grass and anxiously tearing leaves into pieces. There were several muddy smudges around her eyebrows and chin. "Gosh. Mummy, I should go and have a bath. Will you comb my hair afterward?"

"Of course, my darling."

And she hurried down the stairs and found Elise on the first floor, dusting the children's old nursery. "Will you run me a bath, Elise?"

The maid nodded.

. . .

At seven minutes before one o'clock, Alice Cavendish entered the bathroom of her family home on Colchester Terrace and pulled the curtain across the window. There was no building directly opposite, so the gesture was unnecessary and merely darkened the room, but the added sense of privacy was precious to her. She wanted to read the letter from Richard again; it was currently tucked inside the waistband of her skirt.

She undressed and placed her clothes on a chair next to the door, then put the letter on top of them and moved it next to the bathtub. She held her breath as she stepped into the beautifully warm water.

"And how do you wash your hair in the bath?"

That is what her mind went back to, now that she was free from any interruptions: the memory of her friend Lesley Clements asking her this question one dreamy autumn day when they were playing together in the park, as she sieved handfuls of dry leaves from her long red hair.

"I mean the actual technique. I have my own, but I'm curious about yours."

"You tell me yours first," said Alice, fearful that she might embarrass herself.

"No, no," said Lesley. "I asked, so you have to tell first. Don't be shy, I'm just curious. You always have such neat hair."

Alice grew morose. "It used to be that Mummy would stand by the bath with a basin and pour the water over my head. But when she got ill she couldn't do that anymore. I suppose I'd be too old for that now, even if she could. Elise did it for a while, but it never felt quite right. Normally I sit there with a basin, bent forward, and pour the water over my own head."

"That sounds laborious," said Lesley, who was now miming the action to see if it felt natural. "I don't think I could do it. I've never found any way to wash my hair other than to take a deep breath and put my entire head under the water for about a minute. It's not very ladylike, but I find it almost exciting."

"I used to like doing that too," Alice laughed. "Mummy always told me off. She says it's dangerous to hold your breath, even if it's only for a few seconds."

Lesley Clements rolled her eyes. "Well, you can do it now and she'd never know, would she?"

And that was true: Ever since then, Alice had indulged herself, whenever she was feeling lazy, by washing her hair in the way her friend had described. And today was no exception. She pinched her nose with her right hand and submerged her whole head under the water, then ran her left hand along the length of her fair hair until it felt silky and untangled. She managed about twenty seconds before she could feel the lack of breath starting to bite; after that the feeling of coming to the surface was almost ecstatic, as Lesley had hinted. She took a few deep breaths and went down to do it again, closing her eyes and thinking of Richard while her shoulders sank slowly into place at the bottom of the tub.

When she dipped down into the water for a third time, somebody hurried over to the side of the tub and placed their hand in the water above her head. That was all. They didn't press down, not yet. They'd been watching from the doorway, slightly behind the bath, and knew that she would stay submerged until she ran out of breath. It would be wasteful to do anything before that happened.

When Alice had been holding her breath for fifteen seconds, with her eyes closed, running her fingers through a length of hair pulled over her left shoulder and across her chest, she raised her forehead slightly and felt something brush against her skin. It was almost imperceptible; at first she thought it was just her forehead touching the surface, so she didn't immediately begin to panic. But when she raised her head farther, she found that it wasn't the surface at all, that what she was feeling was the touch of warm wet leather, and when she opened her eyes, she saw only darkness where the gloved hand covered them. She tried to sit up. The hand closed over her face and pushed her back down. She reached up with both hands, but her right arm was seized and pinned against the edge of the bath and her left was powerless against the arm holding her head. She reached to where she might plausibly find a face, but she found only shoulders; the arm seemed to be made of iron, and her fingernails did nothing to it. Her legs flailed against the far end of the bath but found no purchase. Something seemed to be squashing her. She'd been underwater for about forty seconds by this point. She had roughly the same time again before her consciousness would start to get hazy and her body would start to weaken. That short amount of time was the only warning she had of her impending death; it was not long enough to wonder who might be murdering her or why, and instead she spent the whole of it trying her hardest to scream.

• • •

Shortly after three o'clock on that same afternoon, Detective Inspector Laurie and Detective Sergeant Bulmer approached the black bars of Colchester Gardens. To get their bearings they agreed to walk in opposite directions around the park, so that they seemed to converge on the house a few minutes later like two people meeting by chance. Bulmer was a big man with heavy hands and an ill-fitting suit, while Laurie was a man of slight build, with small round glasses and heavily oiled hair: One might be asking the other for the time, or for directions, but they didn't look like two men who would know each other.

Bulmer leaned back against the wall outside the house and looked up at the three-story building, with its cream-colored façade. "How bad do you think it will be in there?"

Laurie was looking at a flower bed, by the front door. There was an oval indentation in the soil. "Particularly bad, given that she was the favorite daughter." He waved his hand at the flowers as if he were reading this information directly from them.

Bulmer walked over and looked down; he gave Laurie the glance of playful suspicion that began so many of their conversations. "I don't understand."

"There were two girls playing in the park when I passed. One of them had a purple flower in her hair. The flower came from here." He looped his forefinger around a weeping green stem from which the head had been pulled. "So the girl most likely came from this house. Note the child's footprint here in the soil. And yet despite the fact that there has been a murder, that little girl has been left outside unsupervised. I would suggest that her parents have forgotten about her, caught up in their own grief."

Bulmer looked over at the two girls and nodded at the artistry of his colleague at work. "Though I suppose she's safe enough," he added. "There's an officer at each corner of the park."

"Nonetheless, you would expect the parents to want to keep her close at a time like this. Anyway, the room through that window there"—he pointed at the glass next to the front door—"appears to be the father's study. I drew the same conclusion from the photographs on his desk, which are almost all of the older daughter."

Bulmer stepped up to the window and quoted the line he'd heard Laurie repeat on many occasions: "Because theories are never facts. And each one must be confirmed by several pieces of evidence." He looked at his colleague and nodded, after seeing the photographs for himself.

Laurie knocked on the front door.

A few moments later a uniformed policeman opened it, his face deathly pale. A tiny white cigarette emerged from his mouth: the same color as his skin but somehow more solid, pointing up like a light switch set into a wall. It shook as he smoked.

"Thank God you're here," he said. "I don't like this house, and these people don't like me."

. . .

Police Constable Davis had been holding the pieces of the shattered household together for the last two hours all by himself. He sat down now and pulled a hip flask from his pocket. He unscrewed the cap, holding it carefully like a rare coin, and took a long, gentle drink. "My first, I promise."

Laurie waved away his concerns. The three men had gathered in Mr. Cavendish's study, their bodies propped against the furniture. Davis continued: "It's horrible up there. When she drowned she let everything go. Blood and bodily fluids, all throughout the bath. Believe me, you won't look at a blonde the same way again."

The body had been discovered at around half past one. Elise had knocked on the door to the bathroom and got no reply; tentatively, she'd pushed it open. Then she'd stepped forward onto the small emerald rug next to the bathtub, looked down into the water, and started to scream. The cook, who had just arrived at the house, hurried up the stairs, saw Alice's bloodless, submerged face from across the room, and ran to get Dr. Mortimer, a friend of the family who lived a few streets away. Dr. Mortimer called Constable Davis. Constable Davis phoned Scotland Yard.

Mr. Cavendish was sent for and came running from his office about fifteen minutes later. Things had remained relatively calm after that until Mrs. Cavendish had crawled, wailing, on her hands and knees down the stairs and demanded to see her daughter; Constable Davis, fearing that she might compromise the crime scene, had refused to allow it. She'd sworn and screamed at him. Overwhelmed by his first murder and now in a state of panic, he'd carried her roughly up the stairs and put her back to bed, while Mr. Cavendish howled at him that it was "all too much." After that, the fragile parents had locked themselves in their room in protest, the maid had disappeared downstairs, and Constable Davis had been left to walk the hallways and corridors of the house by himself, a doubtful jailer unsure of what to do next. He'd taken the opportunity to check on the body every time he passed by the bathroom door—at first the doctor had been hovering over it, then he'd been standing by the window, smoking, then finally he'd left—until it had become a compulsion, and Davis had found himself returning to it every few minutes.

Laurie offered him another cigarette. "It's our concern now. Just tell us everything you've managed to find out, then you needn't be here much longer."

"There's not much to know." Constable Davis took another drink. "There were three people in the house. The cook was out at the time it happened. She'd gone to the market, which we've confirmed. The father was at work, at his office nearby, seen by his colleagues. And the younger sister has been outside playing the whole time. The mother was upstairs, in bed. She's not well. And the maid, Elise, was cleaning downstairs. A few rooms away from where it happened."

"And she didn't hear anything?"

"Nothing."

"How close was she? Would she have heard if the victim had cried out or screamed?"

Constable Davis shrugged. "Said she heard nothing and saw nothing."

Laurie frowned. "Then it sounds like we need to talk to her."

"I sent her to bring the doctor back, in case you wanted to ask him any questions. She'll return soon."

"Very well," said Laurie. "Then let's go up and see the body."

• • •

The three men went into the bathroom; there was no steam now and the condensation had dried. The water in the tub was perfectly still and Alice's head was fully submerged. A towel had been laid over her body, to preserve her dignity, and had sunk down into the water and settled asymmetrically. It was such a cold and unsubtle picture of death that for a moment it seemed impossible that she could have been alive earlier that day.

Bulmer whistled. "Man, beast, or devil?"

Laurie walked up to the bath and knelt down. A chair to one side held a pile of neatly folded clothes. He searched through them briefly, as if he were flicking through the pages of a book, but there was nothing of interest. He held his glasses in place as he peered over the edge of the bath and, with his other hand, touched a fingertip to the top of the water. It was stone cold. "She was a beautiful young woman," he said. "The motive was most likely sexual."

Constable Davis spoke up: "I assumed so too, but it doesn't make sense to me. She hasn't been touched, before or after. Someone came here, crazed with desire, just to kill her and leave immediately?"

Laurie turned and stared at him, with the slightest hint of a patronizing smile. "Some men have strange fascinations. Maybe he just wanted to kill something beautiful."

Bulmer, who had never relished the examination of crime scenes and was waiting patiently at the back of the room, took a step closer. "Do we definitely know it was murder?"

Laurie plunged his arm into the icy, filthy water and turned the dead girl's wrists upward. "The left hand is beaten bloody—this was no quiet death. It could have been a seizure of some kind, but the right arm is bruised with four finger marks, as if it was clamped tight in somebody's hand."

From his vantage point farther back, Bulmer could see a little way under the bath. "Laurie, by your left foot. There's something there."

"We saw that earlier," said Constable Davis. "But I didn't want to touch it."

Laurie laid his head against the wooden floor; kicked a little way under the bath was a wet black glove. He pulled it out and picked it up; it lay across two of his fingers like a small dead animal. Constable Davis and Sergeant Bulmer both came closer to examine the find. "That's the murder weapon, then," said Bulmer.

Laurie held the glove up high and sniffed it; it was still dripping with water and smelled of nothing. Then he tried it on. It was neither too big nor too small. "A man, of average size. Assuming this isn't a false lead." He gave it to Bulmer. "Here, you try."

Bulmer pulled it over his fingers but couldn't move it past the ball of his thumb. "Well," said Laurie, "we can rule you out as a suspect." Constable Davis wasn't sure if this was meant as a joke or not and held his breath while the moment passed. Bulmer didn't react.

There was a knock at the door behind them. Laurie opened it to find an old man with a head as smooth as a pebble. "I am Dr. Mortimer," he said, holding out his hand. "I was asked to return in case you had any questions for me." Behind him, the maid was hovering in the shadows.

"I am Inspector Laurie and this is Sergeant Bulmer." The three men shook hands. "There is one thing I must ask immediately. How long would it have taken? For someone that size, I mean?"

The doctor flinched. "That is an unpleasant thought. I've known her since she was a child." He looked down at his hands. "About two minutes for immobility, I suppose. Five for certain death."

"Thank you. We will have more questions, I am sure. Constable Davis, would you kindly show Dr. Mortimer to Mr. Cavendish's study. We will be down shortly. First we must speak to the maid, if you'll show her in."

The doctor left with the uniformed policeman, and Elise stepped hesitantly into the dim room; the curtain was still drawn across the window. She tried to avoid looking at the body in the bathtub, though the twist of off-white towel kept drawing her attention.

"There's no need to be nervous." He closed the door behind her. "We just need to ask you some questions. My name is Inspector Laurie."

There was something menacing about the sight of these two

men in suits standing beside a dead young woman in a bathtub, and Elise swallowed audibly. Bulmer moved back against the wall. Laurie continued: "You ran this bath for Miss Cavendish?" Elise nodded, a glimpse of terror in the unnatural tilt of her head, as if they were implying this tragedy was her fault. "And where were you while she was taking it?"

"I was cleaning the children's old nursery."

"And that room is?"

"Down the corridor from this one." The maid winced, aware of the implications. "Three doors down," she added weakly.

"But you heard nothing? No screams or sounds of a struggle?"

A silent shake of the head. Then an unnecessary clarification: "I told the other man that."

"And he may have believed you. I'm afraid I find it difficult to do so."

She shook her head again, as if he'd asked her a question. He went on: "The problem is—it's Elise, isn't it?" She nodded. "The problem, Elise, is that murder is not a quiet event. It's not a quick event either. It strikes me as very unlikely that you could have been so close for the two minutes it was happening and heard nothing at all." A stronger shake of the head; Laurie's neutral stare had that hint of a smile again. "You are young and unmarried, Elise?"

She was glad of this change of direction and answered eagerly. "That's right, I'm eighteen."

"But you're an attractive girl. There must be a man."

Her face fell again. "I don't know what you mean."

"I can't help but notice that you're wearing a bracelet that is both new and a gift. Is that how he paid for your silence?"

She looked at her wrist. "How did you . . ."

"It's expensive, beyond your means, I'd suggest. But you wouldn't wear something so pretty to clean in—it might get damaged. You must have put it on in the last couple of hours, which suggests that it's new and the novelty hasn't worn off." He shrugged, as if it was obvious.

She shook her head again, softly this time. "It's new, but I saved for it myself."

"You haven't met my colleague, Sergeant Bulmer." Laurie gestured to a mirror on the wall opposite the window, and Elise turned to face it. "Bulmer has his own methods, quite different from mine." She watched through that backward window as Detective Sergeant Bulmer left his place against the wall and approached the two of them from behind, his face as big as a Halloween mask; her fear held her in place as if she was watching it all happen on a cinema screen, to somebody else. His right hand came slowly up to the back of her head, and he guided her to the edge of the bath. A hook of his leg unbalanced her and she found herself falling forward onto his heavy left arm, then she was lowered face-first toward the frigid, death-filled water and held there, shaking, scratching with her hands against the enamel and trying to push back but without any success.

"One minute," he said. "That should be long enough. There won't be any permanent damage."

Faced with this threat, her head jerked up in horror and she began to talk. "I left the house," she said hurriedly, almost screaming each word. "I'm engaged, he lives near here. I left for an hour while Cook was out. I do it every day, you can check. Please, don't tell them. I could lose my position. This wasn't my fault. I didn't know." Bulmer dropped her and she huddled into a ball on the rug. He looked at his partner—Laurie seemed slightly amused.

"The man who did this will do it again," Laurie said, "if my experience counts for anything. That blood will be on your hands if you hinder our investigation any further." He opened the door. "Give your fiancé's name to Constable Davis and we'll have him check your alibi."

Bulmer said nothing, just watched as she scrambled from the room.

• • •

"There are no witnesses, then."

"And no credible suspects."

After quickly comparing notes, the two men climbed the stairs to knock on the door of Mrs. Cavendish's bedroom.

She sat up in bed as they entered. "Oh, and who are you?"

The doctor had buried her in sedatives; her puffy head emerged from the flowing white sheets like a cake decoration. Mr. Cavendish sat at the end of the bed, slumped forward and silent in his mourning, facing away from the door. Hearing the men, he leapt up and turned around. Laurie greeted him warmly with a pat on the shoulder. "Mr. and Mrs. Cavendish, I am Inspector Laurie, and this is my colleague Sergeant Bulmer."

Bulmer nodded; Mrs. Cavendish waved half-heartedly from the bed.

"You'll understand that we need to talk to both of you separately. Mr. Cavendish, I wonder if you wouldn't mind leaving us and waiting downstairs in your study. You'll find your friend Dr. Mortimer there, so you won't be alone."

"Of course," the silent man muttered. He made his way down the stairs, shuffling sideways with both hands on the bannister.

Laurie closed the door and approached the bed; Bulmer moved to the window and stood staring at the street outside. "Mrs. Cavendish," said Laurie, "I'm afraid we must ask you a few indelicate questions."

"Delicacy is no longer a concept in this world, Inspector Laurie. Not now my little girl is dead."

"I am very sorry for your loss."

Mrs. Cavendish reached out and clasped Laurie's hand like a cat striking at a mouse. "I want you to kill him. Either with your own hands or have him hanged. Your colleague downstairs gasped when he heard they were sending you. He told us your reputation. They all pretended abhorrence. Men suddenly grow a conscience when they're faced with cruelty in the abstract. But I defended your methods. I want you to torture him until he confesses and then kill him."

"Mrs. Cavendish, do you have any suspicions as to who did this?"

"I only know that it was a man. This is a man's crime, through and through."

"But there's no one that you personally suspect?"

She frowned hopelessly. "If I thought that anyone I knew was involved, I would want them hanged just the same as a stranger. But I'm afraid I can't think of anybody."

"Where were you at the time it happened?"

"Inspector Laurie, before today I hadn't left this bed in almost three years." And she peeled back the duvet to display her emaciated frame.

"Were you asleep?"

"I close my eyes when I want to rest. I am rarely capable of sleep. But I heard nothing, I'm afraid."

"Well, that is helpful in itself. The second indelicate question, Mrs. Cavendish, is whether your daughter had romantic relations with any young men that you know of—did she have a sweetheart?"

Mrs. Cavendish thought about it for a long time. "I don't believe so. Several years ago she was close to a young man called Andrew Sullivan. They were childhood friends; we've known his parents for years. But he wasn't quite Alice's quality."

"Were they still acquainted?"

"Yes. But we haven't seen the Sullivans for a year or so. I don't suppose that's much help, is it?"

"It's worth looking into."

"If it was him, I want you to castrate him."

"Well, let us start with his home address, shall we?"

• • •

They found Mr. Cavendish waiting for them in his study at the bottom of the stairs, alone. Bulmer followed Laurie into the room like a muscular shadow. Mr. Cavendish had stood up when the door opened, but now that he saw himself surrounded, he sat back down, newly apprehensive about this meeting. "Where is your friend, the doctor?"

Mr. Cavendish cleared his throat. "Our maid, Elise, came in to see him. She was in quite a state; he took her out to get some air."

There was a chessboard placed on top of a drinks cabinet in one corner of the study; idly, Laurie began to play with the pieces. "We spoke to her quite briskly, but only because she was hiding the truth from us. Mr. Cavendish, do you disagree with our methods?"

The quiet man didn't seem to care. "Oh, I suppose so," he replied, shrugging. "Philosophically, I suppose, I would have to say that I do."

"But you want us to find your daughter's killer?"

Tears formed at the corners of his eyes. "Of course. This must never happen to anyone else."

"Then do me the favor of indulging my explanation. You read a lot of detective novels, I see." Laurie waved his hand toward a shelf full of cheap paperbacks.

Mr. Cavendish looked into the darkness beneath his desk. "Those books belong to my wife. She likes me to read them to her. I enjoy them too, I suppose." This picture of his domestic arrangements, now changed forever, overwhelmed him. He slipped out of his chair and sat down on the floor with his hands covering his face.

"I enjoy them myself," Laurie went on. "But it concerns me that people focus so much on the big denouement, where the murderer is revealed, and never on what happens next, which is usually that the criminal confesses or is caught in the act of repeating their crime. The author puts that in, you see, because they know that the evidence is never enough: When you stand back from it, what do you have? An ink stain, a cigarette end, the corner of a letter in a fireplace. You can't hang someone with all that. So they concoct this elaborate scene of confession, to cover over the cracks. Do you follow?"

The bloodshot eyes blinked, and the man nodded slowly.

"Good. The only problem is that it never happens in real life. Nobody confesses of their own volition, and an elaborate trap doesn't ever work out. So if we have a great deal of evidence that points in one way, and we need a confession to confirm it, our only recourse is to violence. Do you see?"

"I just want my daughter back, Mr. Laurie. Torture whoever you want. Just get me my daughter back."

Bulmer had waited until this moment to push the door fully closed. It gave a loud click as he did so.

"Do you know anyone that might have done this to your daughter?"

Mr. Cavendish frantically shook his head. "Of course not. I wouldn't associate with such animals."

"Your office is a short walk from here, I understand? People must be coming and going all the time—it must be difficult to keep track of who is in and who is out."

Mr. Cavendish looked up at Laurie from under his crimson, swollen eyelids. "I see where you're going with this. Why are you suggesting such a thing? I was at my desk the whole time."

"Then let me ask your advice: If I told you that we'd found the killer's left glove, that we'd turned it inside out and noticed that the fabric was scratched about a third of the way along the second finger from the end, what should we do next? My deduction is that the killer was wearing a wedding ring, one with a protrusion. A simple jewel perhaps, like yours. Let's say that only one of our suspects is a married man. Well, what would you have us do?"

Mr. Cavendish swallowed, shaking his head. "I don't know, I assure you."

"Don't worry, then, this won't hurt a bit." Laurie bent down and took Mr. Cavendish's hand. Meeting no resistance, he pushed the sleeve of his jacket up toward the elbow, then undid the buttons of his cuff. He rolled the shirt up and examined the hand and wrist, then did the same with the other arm. He found nothing worthy of note and dropped the arm as if it were nothing more than a newspaper, not a part of a man's body; it hit the floor with the same slap.

Laurie got up and left, signaling for Bulmer to follow him.

"Not guilty?" said Bulmer, when they had closed the door behind them.

"He was never likely to be. I was just being thorough. But there are no scratches on his arms or signs of a struggle; I can't see any way he could have killed her. Frankly, I've never seen such a well-kept pair of hands."

Bulmer nodded. "And that stuff about the wedding ring and the glove?"

Laurie shook his head. "There were no marks on the glove. I was just trying to frighten him."

"I thought as much."

• • •

The house had begun to feel like a dreary old cupboard, full of forgotten objects; with relief, the two detectives stepped outside into the perfectly temperate afternoon. They approached a policeman, a man they knew called Cooper, who had been knocking on doors along the street. "Found anything?"

Cooper shook his head. "Very few people have even been outside today. It seems like they hide from the sun around here. The florist's has been closed since this morning. The greengrocer thinks he saw a man in a long black coat hanging around at lunchtime, but he couldn't describe him."

"Nothing at all?"

"He only saw him from the back. Just said he wore a hat and was of average height."

Laurie looked over at the park, where the two girls were still playing. "What about the sister? Has anyone spoken to her?"

"Not yet. We've been keeping an eye on her, of course. But we didn't think it was our place to tell her what has happened."

"She must be wondering where her lunch is."

"I gave her an apple; I got the impression she's used to this."

Laurie frowned. "Well, they're younger than I'd like, but we have to talk to them. If they've been playing here all day, they may have witnessed something."

He began to walk over to them.

• • •

Maggie and Rose were still playing in the gardens; a kind of intoxication had come over them with the lack of parental attention, and they were now pulling up flowers and rearranging them to their tastes. Rose noticed Laurie and Bulmer walking toward them and nudged her friend; they dropped their flowers and pretended innocence.

"Girls," Laurie called, as he grew near. "What game is that you're playing?"

"I'm the florist," said Rose, pointing at the shop over the road, which was still closed.

"And I'm the customer," said Maggie.

Both were so tired they'd entered a sort of daydreaming state, and the edges of everything seemed soft to them. "Well, girls, I'm Inspector Laurie."

"And I'm Sergeant Bulmer."

"And why don't we play a game of being police detectives for a few minutes? You see that house over there, the one with the red door? I believe one of you lives in that house?"

"She does," said Rose, and Maggie sat down on the grass, her heart beating quickly.

"What's the matter with it?" she asked.

"Nothing is the matter; we just need to ask some questions. Have you seen anyone that you don't know go into your house today? While you've been out here playing?"

Maggie shook her head. "Not today. Why?"

Rose put her hands on her hips. "No, we have not. It has been very quiet around here."

"Well, have you seen anyone at all hanging about the square? Someone suspicious perhaps?"

Rose put her finger to her mouth and thought about it. "Yes," she said finally. Maggie was sitting silently now, picking at the grass.

"A man? Can you describe him to me?"

Rose considered the question. "He was a normal-looking man, but he had a large mustache. And he was wearing a dark-blue suit."

"But he didn't go into the house with the red door?"

"I don't think so. He just walked along the street and waved to us."

Maggie looked up as if about to add something, but Rose talked over her. "That's all, and then he left."

"I see. Well, girls, thank you for your help."

Laurie turned to Bulmer and shook his head, then together they left the gardens. They stopped just outside the gate, and Bulmer spoke: "A man in blue and a man in black."

"And you in gray and me in brown: What a rainbow of men's fashion this case contains."

"You joke, Laurie, but this is serious. Isn't it? We've no tangible suspects, and time is passing. What do we do next?"

"We take it one step at a time, that's all. I would say that next we should pay a visit to"—he took the note he'd scribbled earlier from one of his pockets—"a Mr. Andrew Sullivan, in Hampstead."

Bulmer grunted: "The childhood sweetheart."

• • •

They took a cab to the address in North London, where Andrew Sullivan lived with his widowed mother in a house at the top of a hill. They asked the driver to wait for them.

It was a modern house, opposite a church: all white walls and large windows, with a flat roof. The garden in front was overgrown with bushes, which concealed a number of sculptures—large, twisted lumps of rock in various shades of gray. It was the end of the afternoon and the light was beginning to fade.

Laurie knocked on the door. Thirty seconds passed, then a towering German maid opened it; they asked to see Mr. Sullivan. "I am afraid not," she said, in a frayed accent. "Mrs. Sullivan and Mr. Sullivan are not in the country."

They got the story out of her: Young Mr. Sullivan had fallen into a black mood about a month or two before, and his mother had suggested a trip to Europe to take his mind off whatever was bothering him. He'd reluctantly agreed, and they'd left ten days ago.

They confirmed this with the neighbors; no one had seen the Sullivans for over a week. Disappointed, they returned to the cab. "Well, then, where now?"

Laurie sighed. "Scotland Yard, I suppose. We can look through our notes and see if we've missed anything."

"It feels like a long shot."

Laurie gave him a look. "God wants justice, remember that."

• • •

The next morning, after knocking on every door along Colchester Terrace, they met back at the crime scene: It had become a kind of center of operations, quiet and confidential. The body had been removed by the police doctor, late the previous night.

Bulmer was looking out of the bathroom window. "The greengrocer was not forthcoming about the man in the black coat. He couldn't tell me anything more, except that he also wore a black hat and black gloves."

Laurie sat with his back against the wall, his eyes closed. "Do you think he's lying?"

"He has no cause to do so. I think he just sees a lot of people. The reason he remembers this particular man is because he was inside the gardens themselves, which ought to be reserved for residents only, but the man wasn't familiar to him."

"I see. Well, black gloves are hardly uncommon. Does the green-grocer have an alibi himself?"

"Only his customers, but there seem to be enough of them." Bulmer looked at the street below. "Do you think this could have been done by a stranger? If she were standing here, preparing for her bath, someone could have seen her from outside."

"Opportunistic, you mean? A frenzied fit of madness? It's possible, but that kind of thing is unusual. Normally it takes longer than that to form the desire to kill."

"But if they were watching the house and saw the maid leave, they might have concluded it was safe."

Laurie shrugged. Bulmer didn't see him; he was still looking out of the window, and now his eyes had drifted to the gardens, as if they were the heart of this whole affair. Laurie stood up and joined him. The effect was of two shutters being closed over the window, leaving the room behind them in darkness—a brown suit and a gray suit blocking the light. Laurie spoke: "One question that we haven't answered is why she took a bath in the first place."

"The mother said her hands were dirty from picking flowers."

"And yet she brought no flowers inside with her; there are empty vases everywhere."

Bulmer looked at his colleague, thought about it, and concluded he was right. Then nodded, disappointed with himself. Deduction, the detective's art form, was a skill he could never grasp, and yet every time he saw it happen it seemed so simple. Just a case of making self-evident statements, the right one for each occasion. He looked at his swollen fists self-consciously. "How else might she have got her hands dirty?"

"That's just the thing: We have to explain her dirty hands, but we also have to explain the fact that she lied to her mother. Maybe she was hiding something in the gardens."

The big man nodded. "Let's go and look, then."

• • •

They spent the next hour searching the gardens, carefully bending flowers and bushes over with gloved hands, stepping on untidy patches of grass, and probing the bases of trees. They had the gardens to themselves for the duration of this work, though an audience of curious children formed along the edge of the fence farthest from Colchester Terrace. None of them were permitted to use the park, though they lived nearby, and this solemn spectacle seemed to rectify that injustice slightly; they'd already passed the gossipy details of the girl's death between themselves like a rare and valuable marble.

Bulmer ignored them. He was staring in puzzlement at the garish paper plane caught in the branches above his head, wondering both what it was and whether some deduction was possible here, resisting the urge just to shake the tree with his huge fists and see what fell out, when he heard Laurie calling his name.

"Bulmer, over here. I've found something." Laurie was crouched in a close gathering of plane trees, three of them forming a sort of natural tent. It was dark inside; Bulmer approached and saw that Laurie was scratching at the ground with his fingers. "The grass is flattened— someone has been sitting here. See all this torn-up grass and the bark peeled off the base of this tree? That might be how she got her hands dirty." He pushed the soil around in circles. "But what was she doing here? Something that made her feel anxious, clearly."

But Bulmer was following a hunch and looking upward at the three trees; he saw what his shorter colleague had missed. There was an old, damp envelope slotted between two branches of the tree to Laurie's right, just above head height. It was pushed all the way to the back.

He leaned over and took it; Laurie had stopped digging and stood up. Bulmer opened the envelope, took out a sheet of paper, and read. His eyes lit up with secret pride: "It's a love letter. From a Richard Parker. To Alice Cavendish. There's no date on it."

"Does it have an address?"

"It does indeed."

"Then I would call that a clue."

•••

Richard Parker lived in his family home at the foot of the Surrey Hills, outside of London. The two detectives traveled there together. The house came into view as the car crawled haltingly through fields of lavender, like a bead of water trickling down a windowpane. Behind the house—a modest palace—the hills sat on the landscape like a crown. It was early in the morning and they could see their breath on the air.

Bulmer was driving; he'd begun the day with great enthusiasm but was now having doubts about the outcome of this trip. Laurie was right: The letter was a clue. It was so obviously a clue that it seemed it had to be a coincidence, a red herring. Besides, he'd been over it from all angles and there was nothing to be inferred from it: The man was in love with her, that was all. And that gave them nothing, not even a motive.

•••

They parked at the edge of the grounds and decided to walk the rest of the way; you could not observe anything through the window of a motorcar, said Laurie. Yew trees had been carefully placed along the gravel driveway so as to form no discernible pattern; it was supposed to give the approaching visitor a sense of delight, but the effect was disorienting. They looked like the carriages of a derailed train. "This reminds me of something," said Laurie. But Bulmer didn't reply; he had grown sulky, feeling this was all a waste of time. So far out of London he couldn't even use his hands; they wouldn't stand for such things out here. Or better not to risk it, at least. "I can't for the life of me think what it is," Laurie continued.

The whole episode seemed staged, from finding the letter to approaching the estate, an impression compounded when the first figure they came across—a man in oil-stained overalls, fixing a motorbike, with a towel spread over the gravel and a selection of tools laid across it, like a dentist's tray—turned out to be the person they were looking for. "Richard Parker. How do you do?" He was implausibly good-looking, Bulmer noticed.

He wore a leather glove on his left hand; he showed them his uncovered right hand, filthy with engine oil, to illustrate why he couldn't greet them properly. "Forgive me, I would shake hands otherwise."

"But you are Richard Parker?" asked Laurie.

"I am indeed. How can I help you?"

"You weren't what we'd pictured."

The young man smiled. "This machine is a hobby of mine. I can change before we talk, if it makes you feel more comfortable."

"That won't be necessary."

"Well, then, how can I help you?"

"We need to talk to you about Miss Alice Cavendish."

Richard nodded. "What about her?"

"She's dead," said Laurie.

Richard Parker fell to his knees. "Oh God. That can't be true."

Was it just an act? "She was murdered yesterday afternoon."

The fallen man let out a cry and brought his hands up to his face. Bulmer and Laurie both noticed something that seemed incomprehensible at first: The glove on his left hand seemed to crumple against his head, as if the hand had passed into his skull. Laurie saw the truth at once. Not unkindly, he took the man's arm and pulled the glove from it. He was missing three fingers and a thumb. "What happened to your hand?"

The shock of the question, coming out of nowhere, brought Richard back to himself. "The war, of course." He wiped his eyes with the back of his wrist. Laurie and Bulmer looked at each other; they were both thinking of the row of intricate bruises along the arm of Alice Cavendish, where her assailant had pinned her down. This man was innocent.

They spent another forty minutes answering his questions and taking notes on his relationship with Alice and other related matters. Then they left, just as it was starting to rain.

They were both wet when they reached the car. Bulmer fumbled the keys from his pocket and let them in. Laurie took off his hat and shook the water from it onto the floor of the vehicle. "It struck me, as we were talking to him, that there is one relative of Alice's we haven't been very thorough with. The sister."

"The little girl?" Bulmer looked at him. "But we spoke to her."

"We tried," said Laurie, "but her friend did all the talking. I think she was keeping something secret. Perhaps if we talk to her alone?"

"Don't ask me to use my fists on a child."

Laurie shook his head. "I wouldn't dream of it."

They drove back to London in silence.

• • •

At two in the afternoon they returned once again to Colchester Terrace, where the cream-colored house welcomed them like an old friend. They found Maggie lying in bed with her sickly mother, the two of them sleeping peacefully.

Bulmer picked up the child and carried her gently into another room—an unused bedroom, next to her mother's, where the two men could be alone with her—and propped her up in a corner. Laurie knelt in front of her: "Maggie, it's very important that you concentrate on helping us. We are going to find the person that hurt your sister. But we need to know if you can tell us any more about the man you saw in the square yesterday. Was he wearing a long black coat?"

She was crying already, half from sadness and half from the feeling that she'd done something wrong. She shook her head. "No, his clothes were dark blue."

"Dark blue? You're sure?"

"Yes. And brown shoes. And the left leg was wet where he'd stepped in a puddle."

Laurie glanced back at Bulmer. "You watched him quite closely, then?"

She answered in a barely audible whisper, the sound of raindrops in flight: "He was a nasty man. He wanted to look at us and ask us horrible questions. That's why he helped Rose fix the airplane."

"The airplane?" asked Laurie; she nodded again.

"That airplane?" asked Bulmer softly. He was looking out of the window at the pointed purple shape that was still stuck in one of the trees.

Maggie went to the window to join him. "Yes, that one. He put something inside it."

Laurie turned her toward him and took out a pen and paper. "Tell me anything else you know about him."

• • •

Twenty minutes later the purple airplane dropped artlessly to the ground. Bulmer had tried shaking the whole tree, but in the end Laurie had climbed along a branch, proving himself to be surprisingly nimble for such a serious-looking man.

Neither of the two men was expecting very much as they unfolded the elaborate paper construction and found their prize weighting the nose: a torn calling card, folded into a small white rectangle. Laurie actually laughed at the audacity of it.

The tear left a first name, an initial, and two letters of a surname printed on the card: MICHAEL P. CH. Underneath that was the one word: THEATER. It was printed in black on a white board. Laurie held it up to the light. "Well," he said. "This is a promising line of inquiry."

• • •

It took half a day to locate the careless man in the dark-blue suit, with his ruined brown shoes. His name was Michael Percy Christopher, theatrical agent; they found him at the New City Theater in London's West End.

Laurie and Bulmer didn't return to Colchester Terrace after that; the rest of the case was worked out in a dank cell in Scotland Yard, where the man's distinctive blue suit grew stained and dirty against a background of cold gray bricks while his fair hair grew matted with sweat and blood. They'd cornered him at his place of work: a small office above a dimly lit hall behind a shop, the walls loud with laughter and the floors wet with spilled drink. He had begun by denying he'd been anywhere near the gardens at all on the day in question, then had refused to explain when shown the card he'd inadvertently left there. That stubborn attitude was enough to justify an arrest, and they'd left him in darkness for five hours while the two of them went over his background.

He'd been in trouble with the police before: There were numerous reports of him exposing himself to women and young children. Nothing had ever been proven, but the suspicion alone was enough for some members of the public, and his body was covered in scars from the times he'd been caught and confronted. Everyone who knew him—and they talked to as many as they could find—would nod in acknowledgment of these rumors. They returned to his cell and found him lying on the damp, hard ground, his narrow head cushioned by a small patch of moss.

"Mr. Christopher, isn't it time you told us the truth?" He had no specific alibi for the time of the murder. He just said that he liked to take walks around London, tipping his hat to all the people he passed. Bulmer laughed in his face.

They considered bringing the young girl in to identify him but decided that was unnecessary. His presence at the scene of the crime was irrefutable. All they needed was one more thing to link him to the actual killing. They brought the black glove into his cell and forced it on him, after Bulmer had bent each finger back in turn to keep him from balling his hand into a fist: It fit well enough. "I'm being framed," he cried. They searched his home for the second glove but concluded he must have disposed of it. There were a multitude of scratches and bruises on his arms.

Laurie was dissatisfied. "The evidence is overwhelming. But I find I want a confession."

Bulmer agreed. "We still don't know why he did it or how it happened. All we have is an evil little man making very little sense."

"I think it's time, Bulmer."

"Because theories are never facts."

The two detectives shook hands. Laurie unlocked the cell, the key slippery with his nervousness, and took a deep, doubtful breath, as if he were letting a lion out of its cage. Bulmer stepped into the cell, pulling on a pair of brown leather gloves.

Laurie watched through the bars of the cell. Bulmer lifted the alleged killer up against the wall and limited himself to his fists; bloodstains bloomed like flowers from the cracks between the bricks. After ten minutes he stepped outside for a break, leaving the suspect to contemplate his options.

"He's held out so far," said Bulmer to Laurie.

"It's only been ten minutes."

"That's often enough. I might have to try more-extreme measures."

"If it's necessary, I will back you up. This is a murder case, after all, not a simple robbery."

Bulmer smoked a cigarette and then stepped back inside. This time he carried a razor blade.

Over the course of the next thirty minutes, Michael Christopher lost successively and to varying degrees of permanence: the sensation of taste in his mouth, two front teeth and one back tooth, the unobstructed use of his right eye, a mass of hair, an eyebrow and his slight mustache, a single fingernail, a quarter of an inch of his lower lip, and the ability to lift anything with three of the fingers on his left hand. As Laurie watched this unfold between the black strips of shadow, his face showed no compassion, only calculation. After half an hour of screaming, the accused was ready to confess. He slumped to the ground.

"It's true, I killed her."

"How did you do it?"

"I drowned her in the bathtub."

"You saw her at the window."

"I saw her at the window; I'm a weak man." He spat out a lump of blood. "I watched the maid sneak out and knew the house was empty. I crept up the staircase and killed her."

Bulmer stared down at him, satisfied. As the big man left the cage, Laurie patted him warmly on the back. "We have saved lives today, Sergeant Bulmer. I think you and I deserve a drink."

Later that evening, Michael Percy Christopher tied one arm of his dirty blue suit jacket around his long neck and threaded the other through a gap in the wall bracket holding the bars of the cell in place. He hanged himself with his knees bent and his toes touching the floor, which was an effort that required a constant renewal of willpower—like trying desperately to sleep when not at all tired—and took twenty painful minutes to accomplish.

. . .

One of the uniformed officers that haunted the building knocked on the door to Laurie's office to deliver the news; it was almost midnight. Detective Inspector Laurie bowed his head, made the sign of the cross, and thanked the man for informing him.

Bulmer had left already, tired from his exertions. He would find out in the morning and would probably be pleased. It was the best outcome, all considered. There was enough evidence now for the murder to be treated as solved, without the need for a tedious trial, and it had taken less than a week. Justice was swift, in the right hands. He lit a cigar to celebrate and poured himself a whiskey.

All alone, he looked around his office: austere and secretive, like himself. On a shelf on the opposite wall stood his collection of detective novels and stories: fifteen tattered volumes in total. On the far right was the one he'd taken from Mr. Cavendish's study—a little sleight of hand, that was all it took—as a souvenir of the case. He raised his glass to the electric light, the liquid a sickly, satisfying orange.

"To justice," he said to himself. "To finding the perfect suspect."

And thank God for that, he thought. Mr. Christopher had come along just at the right time. What a damn fool. A donkey, just asking to be loaded with guilt, laden with blame. And, frankly, deserving of it too. The perfect person to accuse. Because in a detective story, Laurie knew, you sometimes had to suspect the detectives. And he didn't want that to happen, not at all. Not when he'd put so much time into it. Covered his tracks so well. He'd chosen that square so carefully. Somewhere that nobody really lingered but where several people passed through each hour. The long black coat so that if remembered at all he was remembered simply as a man in black. The hat and brown scarf to hide his face. Nobody had even noticed the scarf. And Alice Cavendish herself, selected carefully and patiently. An astonishingly beautiful girl, who went to the gardens every day. And sat down in secret, hidden between three trees. That was where he would have done it, moving quickly before she could cry out. But her little sister and that other girl had been there. He believed he'd lost his chance. Then he'd seen her by the bathroom window, closing the curtains. And that's when the maid left, so there it was. One quick, thrilling glimpse of her naked body in the bath and then the act of drowning. Leaving the glove was a masterful touch. Its sinister implications would be recognized immediately. Here was a random, meaningless, and repeatable crime. One of great horror. Which he would be called to investigate. His reputation practically guaranteed it. And so it had happened. The letter too. He thought hiding that would make it easy to blame the love interest. But that didn't work out. Then Mr. Christopher came along. With a wealth of evidence against him. And so she was Laurie's now. On a slab in the cold police morgue downstairs. For him to visit at will.

6

THE THIRD
CONVERSATION

Julia Hart drank from her wineglass and finished reading. "*And so she was Laurie's now. On a slab in the cold police morgue downstairs. For him to visit at will.*"

The sun had finally set, and the evening sky was almost black. The bright, early moon was duplicated in three white plates that lay across their table like an ellipsis. With a look of pain, Grant removed an olive stone from his mouth and placed it on the edge of his plate. "That was an unpleasant story," he said. "I don't care for that one."

They'd both had mussels, and the middle plate was scattered with mismatched shells, the long black fingernails of mythical creatures. Grant had left half of his food unfinished, after becoming distracted several times and letting things congeal, so out of politeness Julia had left a small amount of hers to match. Now the three plates sat between them, a testament to their strange new relationship as author and editor.

Julia took the napkin from her lap and wiped her mouth. "The description of the murder makes for slightly uncomfortable reading, that's true. And the torture at the end is brutal."

Grant snorted sarcastically. "I found it all quite distasteful. Not just the violence. There were no likable characters, and the setting was tawdry. London, of all places."

Julia smiled. "You almost sound offended, but it was you that wrote it."

"That is true, but I was young and foolish at the time." He laughed and prodded the air with a toothpick, to emphasize his point. "Some of these stories seem frivolous to me now. Doesn't that one strike you as rather sordid?"

"Not really. I think that when you're reading about death as enter-tainment, it should leave you feeling slightly uncomfortable, even slightly sick. I thought that was perhaps the point."

"That's a generous interpretation," said Grant. "Isn't it more likely that I was just a morbid young man?"

"You would know better than me. But I can understand, after that one, why you had to publish the book privately."

"It was both too explicit and too academic for mainstream publi-cation."

"An unusual pairing." Julia took another sip of wine. "And you never wrote anything else after that?"

"If no one was willing to publish the work, what was the point in continuing?"

"Times have changed, at least."

"Well," he replied, shrugging, "I will take your word on that."

Julia picked up her glass and offered a toast. "To a productive first day."

He raised his wineglass and touched it to hers. "And may tomorrow be the same."

After concluding their work on the second story earlier that afternoon, Grant had told her that he usually slept for an hour or two while the day was at its hottest. He'd offered her a spare room, if she was inclined to do the same. But she had felt the weight of work pressing down on her, so instead she'd walked out along the sands and hidden from the sun in the shadow of a slight cliff. There she'd worked on the next few stories, until he'd woken up a couple of hours later. By then it was late afternoon and they were both hungry. She'd offered to buy him dinner. "We can read the next story while we eat."

So they'd walked for fifteen minutes to a nearby restaurant, ending up not far from Julia's hotel. They'd sat outside on a terrace overlooking the sea. There were two other guests, sitting a few tables away from them, so Julia had read the story quietly, almost in a whisper.

"I suppose I'm desensitized to the violence," she said, draining her glass. "I must have read about three hundred crime novels in the last few years."

Grant's eyes widened. "Three hundred crime novels?" He swirled his wineglass anxiously, as if he found the number intimidating. "That is a lot."

"It's not such a surprise, surely? You knew that this was my job."

"I suppose," he said, "but I can't say I'd really considered it. You probably have more to say about these stories than I do."

The uncomfortable heat of the morning had put her in a drowsy mood for most of the day. Now she was feeling slightly guilty about it, so she was trying her hardest to appear enthusiastic. "Your explanations have been very helpful."

He took another drink. "Thank you."

She picked up her notebook. "And now you can continue to help me, by explaining the structural significance of that story. I assume it lies in the fact that Inspector Laurie is both detective and suspect?"

"Yes, that's right. He's an evil little man, isn't he? In the story we read earlier, the victim was also a suspect. In this one the detective is also a suspect. And that brings us to our third ingredient."

Julia nodded. "A detective?"

"Yes, or group of detectives. Those characters that are trying to solve the crime. I considered this one to be optional, which is to say that the group of detectives can have nobody in it. That's why I usually talk of *murder mysteries* over *detective stories*. Sometimes there simply isn't a detective. So we make no restriction on the size of the group—it can even be zero. And we allow it to overlap with the group of suspects, as it does here. It can also overlap with the group of victims, though it's harder to make that work."

She was writing all of this down, her hand steady despite the drink. "Suspects, victims, and detectives. The first three ingredients of a murder mystery."

"Yes." He cleared his throat; the wine had made him bold. "And now it's your turn."

She looked up from her notebook. "What do you mean?"

"To explain something to me. That's our routine, isn't it? I talk about the theory and then you talk about the little details I've forgotten." She looked down again and continued writing. "Surely, Julia, you've spotted an inconsistency in this story?"

She didn't look up from the page, but the side of her mouth drew back in amusement. "It's as if you're testing me. Did you plant the puzzles in these stories as some kind of trap for me to fall into?"

"Not at all." He grinned. "I would have put them there as a joke, nothing more."

"They're testing my observational skills to the limit, I have to admit. Luckily, I'm an obsessive taker of notes."

"And what did you notice this time?"

Julia stopped writing and looked up at him. "Well, since you mention it, there is something that I noticed about this story. A discrepancy, let's call it."

He took the toothpick from his mouth. "Let's have it, then."

Julia tapped the table as she spoke. "The description of the man in blue at the start is contradicted in every single detail by the description of the man in blue at the end."

"Ah," said Grant. "That is interesting, isn't it?"

"If you go back and read carefully, you'll see. He changes from a round face with dark hair, an elaborate mustache, and a short neck to a fair, narrow face with a long neck and a modest mustache. And there's no explanation for it."

"Yes, I see," said Grant, looking out at the water. "That one could easily have been a mistake. But I think you're right. It probably wasn't."

Julia scribbled something in her notebook. "It pains me slightly to leave it uncorrected. But taken together with the inconsistencies in the other stories, it seems to fit the pattern."

"Yes, I think so too. What a wicked sense of humor I had in those days."

Julia sighed, suddenly exhausted. "Let's leave it there and call it a day, shall we? I'd like to put away my pen and pour myself another glass of wine, if you don't mind?"

"Please," he said, "finish it off."

And she emptied the carafe into her glass, thinking of the work she still had to do. Then she sat back and looked at the stars. "What is so special about this island, Grant?"

He seemed surprised by the question. "What do you mean? It's beautiful."

"Yes, but it's so quiet, so lonely. Don't you ever get tempted to leave?"

"Never. All my memories are here."

She swallowed another mouthful of wine. "You're a very mysterious man."

"I shall take that as a compliment."

"You're a spy, that's what I think. Working on some secret project. Or you're on the run from the law." She slurred this last word slightly so that it lasted for almost a second. "Are you willing to talk, now that you've had something to drink?"

"About what?"

"About the White Murder. The strangling of Elizabeth White, near the Spaniards Inn on Hampstead Heath in August of 1940. And why you named the book after it."

Grant raised his tired eyebrows. "I told you everything I know about that earlier. It's just a coincidence."

"Then the alcohol hasn't brought it all back to you?"

"I wasn't aware that was one of the side effects of alcohol."

Julia shrugged. "It stimulates the mind."

"It stimulates the imagination, clearly."

"It's true that I'm a little drunk," she admitted, lifting her glass, "but it didn't take much to spot the juxtaposition. This morning I asked why you'd run away to this island. You wouldn't tell me. And this afternoon I pointed out the link between your book and an unsolved murder. So are those things all related? Is that why you're here?"

He almost laughed. "You think I'm the murderer?"

"I don't know what I think, I'm just asking the obvious question."

"Then you ought to reconsider your detective work. You're suggesting that I killed someone, then wrote a book with a name just like the one given to the murder. And several years later I went on the run?"

"Well, do you have an alibi?"

Grant smiled. "Not off the top of my head, no."

"Then you can prove your innocence by telling me the real reason you came to this island. You left your wife and job and came to live as a hermit out here, but why?"

His smile straightened. "That got very personal very quickly."

Julia noticed that his hand was clenched tight around the stem of his wineglass, shaking slightly. "Yes," she said, "but I'm not just making small talk. In a sense, by publishing this book we're going into business together. I have to be able to trust you."

Grant shook his head. "I don't want to talk about things that happened more than twenty years ago." He lifted his hands defensively, his wineglass in one of them. "You can ask me about anything else."

He dropped his hands to the table, but the movement was clumsy, and a shard broke off from the base of the glass where it hit the hard surface. It spun across the tablecloth and came to a stop in front of Julia, visible only as a tangle of translucent lines on the white material.

"You haven't remarried in twenty years—can I ask about that?"

Grant put down the broken glass and began to tear open the few remaining mussels with his fingernails; a useless compulsion. "No, you cannot."

"Why don't you write anymore?"

"It's late. These questions are making me tired." The last shell refused to open, so to add the final full stop to the conversation, Grant picked up the middle plate from the table in front of him and emptied it over the railing, sending the mussels spinning toward the sea. There followed the scattered sounds of the shells raining on the rocks and a loud clunk as he dropped the plate back on the table.

Julia closed her notebook.

7

AN INFERNO
IN THEATER LAND

At first the fire was just a string of smoke drifting from a second-story window, with a few passersby pointing at it and commenting. It looked like somebody was flying a kite. Then it thickened to a single perfect curl that could have been taken straight from a shampoo advertisement. It soon spread beyond that one window, and the whole top half of the building appeared to grow moldy with smoke. After that it moved quickly: Complex, branching trees of dense black smoke began to emerge, blossoming in the fertile, sweltering heat. The building was one of London's largest, grandest department stores—with thousands of people inside, and a fortune in clothes and furniture—and it seemed about to be crushed by a huge demonic hand, the slim fingers scratching at the sky.

Helen Garrick, sitting alone at a table for two, had watched this progress over the last half hour; the slight twist in the road meant that although the fire was on the same side of the street—and about two hundred yards away—she could see it quite clearly from her seat by the window.

To begin with it was a kind of entertainment, a welcome distraction from dining by herself, but when the first body crawled from the building after the initial evacuation—an elderly man in a porter's uniform, who had been trampled in the rush—she found herself feeling terribly guilty and ashamed and barely able to eat her main course. A few noodles, that was all. But as grotesque as that sight was, it was nothing compared to the horror toward the top of the building, where the last two rows of windows showed the looping, ineffectual activity of people coming to realize they were trapped. They were screaming and smashing the glass, and repeatedly leaning out and looking down, but there was nowhere for them to go. And Helen realized then that although the fire had initially looked quite harmless—a string of colorless bunting, blowing about in the wind—there must have been people trapped inside from the start, as soon as the single staircase filled up with smoke. Any lingering excitement turned to shame at that point, and she ate the rest of her meal with tears in her eyes.

· · ·

The crackle of conversation inside the restaurant provided a fitting soundtrack to the fire outside, a mix of loud voices and the low continuous hum of chaos, while the repeated tapping of a spoon against a wineglass gave a good imitation of an alarm.

The tapping continued until the sounds of the restaurant died down and the manager was left standing in a silent room with everybody staring at him, like a circus performer about to eat a giant glass egg.

"Ladies and gentlemen," he said, gesticulating with the glass and spoon. "Do we have a doctor dining with us this evening?" He was needle-thin, with a strong accent and an impish beard; nobody stirred. "Or an off-duty policeman?" There was an evasive swell. "A man of military rank, perhaps?" A gentle muttering, but nothing conclusive. "Someone who holds an unspecified position of responsibility in the community?" Still the room was silent. "Very good. Please inform your waiter should the situation change."

He bowed briefly and left them to their meals.

"Wants someone to help with an evacuation." A man at the table next to Helen's sat back and offered his judgment. "In case it comes to it."

That can't possibly be right, she thought. The fire was still two hundred yards away. If they evacuated here, why not the whole of West London?

A waiter was passing by her table; she held her hand up to catch his attention. He leaned down to her. "Is everything all right, madame?"

She'd felt a great deal of sympathy for the restaurant manager. She knew what it was like to ask for volunteers and not receive any; it was a boulder that you'd pushed to the top of a hill rolling back down to the bottom, leaving you standing at the blackboard about to cry. And behind that was the knowledge that you'd now have to pick on somebody and spend the rest of the day feeling mean. Was it the sympathy that inspired her to put herself forward or the guilt she'd been wallowing in for the last twenty minutes? Or was it that wicked impulse to do the thing least expected of her, which overcame her sometimes? Perhaps a mix of all three.

She spoke discreetly. "You might let your colleague know that I'm a teacher at a girls' school in Guildford, if that's any use to him. I assume he wanted a man."

• • •

She was led to the restaurant manager, Mr. Lau, feeling like a sacrificial victim or as if she was thirteen again and being sent to see the headmistress. Since she was new to her profession, she often spent her time weighing her behavior against her own experiences of school—which, after all, weren't so far in the past, with the sisters still haunting the edges of her infrequent nightmares—and she definitely felt the same apprehension now as she had done on those occasions. And the same underlying embarrassment, which always came with the vague sense that she wasn't wearing the right clothes.

He stood waiting for her in a hidden corner of the restaurant, at the bottom of a staircase richly carpeted in deep red, like a tongue hanging down from the floor above.

"Mr. Lau?"

The staircase disappeared into darkness behind him; he drew her up a few steps so that they could talk more privately, leaving her standing slightly beneath him, with his willowy figure floating against the red background; it gave him the look of a preacher or a judge.

"Madame." He bowed, his gesticulations filling the width of the staircase.

"Helen, Helen Garrick." She offered her hand; he kissed it.

"You would hope to find at least one honorable person in any crowded restaurant, but I must admit I was doubtful."

"You're welcome," she said, relieved to find him speaking to her as an equal, forgetting her daydreams of being disciplined. "How may I help you?"

"I must ask you to perform a rather delicate task." He seemed hesitant. "You will have the eternal gratitude of this establishment."

"Is it to do with the fire down the street?"

"The fire? No, not directly. The fire is smoke and mirrors, a distraction."

"Oh," said Helen, slightly disappointed.

He stared at the carpet with a studied look of concern, twisting his beard between his fingertips. "These are troubling times. I am sad to say there has been a death on the premises."

Helen gasped. "Oh gosh."

"We have a number of private rooms upstairs. One of them is in use this evening, for what I believe is a birthday party. A happy occasion. But the host has been killed. Murdered, to be precise."

The word sounded glorious in his decorous accent, with both syllables equally stressed.

"Murdered?" Her eyes widened; what exactly was he going to ask of her? "But then you must fetch the police."

"We have a telephone; I have just spoken to the police." He began to sound tense. "The situation is a little difficult. They will send somebody, of course. But every policeman in the area is currently busy with the fire outside. Closing roads and evacuating buildings, I understand. Something of an emergency."

She nodded. "Of course."

"Until that situation is under control, it is apparently unthinkable that they could spare anyone to secure our crime scene. I was asked to arrange that myself."

"Oh." She began to see where this was going.

"They told me it is not, strictly speaking, urgent. Since no one is in immediate danger."

"Well, that's for the best, at least."

"I do not have the staff to spare," he continued. "Several who would have turned up by now have been delayed by the fire. I explained this to the police. They told me that any doctor or teacher would suffice, just to keep an eye on things until they arrive."

She felt sure they wouldn't have said *teacher* but didn't challenge him. "Yes, I understand." There was no chance of her refusing now, even if it meant missing her train. "What exactly do I have to do?"

"Simply keep watch. Make sure that the crime scene is undisturbed, that none of the guests tamper with it or leave. It should only be for a short time."

"The guests are still there?" She tried to hide her disappointment; she'd had visions of herself drinking wine alone with a corpse, watching the sunset.

"Five of them. We will turn away any others that arrive. But I was asked to make sure that none of the five leave until an officer has recorded their details."

"And is the murderer one of them?"

Mr. Lau gave a long and thoughtful sigh. "It's possible, yes. But I wouldn't ask you to do this if I felt there was any danger. Just stick with the group and there will be safety in numbers."

"All right." Helen was suddenly nervous; in her head she was cursing herself for offering to help. She'd assumed it would be something that could be finished with quickly.

Mr. Lau took her hand. "Madame, I will, of course, invite you back here on a date of your choosing, to dine with us once again. To dine with me personally. And there will be no charge, as there will be none today."

"Thank you," she said weakly.

"I will be down here if you need me; all you have to do is call out."

And with that he led her up the blood-rich staircase and opened the door that faced them at the top. As they stepped side by side through the doorway, their combined shape contracted, like a hand forming a fist or a throat in the act of swallowing.

• • •

This time the sense of being led to a sacrifice was more apt; the five guests stood in a half circle around the room, a skyline of human flesh, and stared inquisitively at Helen, wondering who she was and what potential she provided. A few looks were exchanged between them, then there was a kind of click and the whole scene came to life.

Mr. Lau stepped forward to speak. "I have talked with the police, on the telephone." There was a swell of interest from the five assorted faces. "They will be here soon." He paced a little, like a man onstage. "They request that all of you remain here until an officer arrives. But the fire is slowing things down. Miss Garrick is here on their behalf."

He waved his hand; ten eyes looked at her.

"She will be taking charge in the meantime and ensuring that nothing is moved or interfered with. And that nobody leaves."

This handover—from a natural authority figure to a pretender—would have been more impactful if she hadn't been standing directly behind him, eclipsed by his slim form. She felt like a magic trick that had gone wrong. She stepped forward slightly.

The five guests consisted of a very glamorous man and woman—evidently some kind of couple—standing nearest to the door; another man and woman, standing slightly more awkwardly next to each other at the farthest corner of the room; and a third woman, leaning against the wall.

The glamorous woman spoke to Mr. Lau, ignoring Helen. "Can't we go outside for some air, while it's still light, and come back when the police have managed to find their way here?"

Mr. Lau smiled patiently. He took a step backward. "I am afraid that is impossible. I have been given instructions to detain you on the premises."

"It's absurd," said the same woman, her voice sultry and disbelieving, "it's obscene. To be trapped in here, with a dead body not ten yards away."

The woman standing in the corner—weak-looking, with large blue eyes and a dark-blue dress—cried out at this image and leaned for support on the man standing beside her. She hooked her hand over his shoulder and rested her head on her forearm; it was clear that they weren't romantically involved. The man wore a brown suit. He had dark bushy eyebrows and his hair was a wiry gray, though he couldn't have been more than forty.

This is just like a school trip, thought Helen.

There'd been a visit to St. Albans at the start of the summer. She'd had to march a whole crowd of young girls—twenty-five or so—from the train station out to the Roman ruins, their bobbing heads a mosaic of precocious haircuts. On that trip Helen had learned of and come to hate the various types of troublemaker that were endemic to such outings, and these people here were no different: The woman who had spoken was the calm, seemingly reasonable kind that would instinctively balk at authority and use her constant questions as a means of disruption. That type could never be argued with—it was like talking to the tide.

"I agree with you," said Helen. "I don't like being here myself. But we should do as we've been told."

The woman in blue, her eyes ringed with tears, spoke up at this: "You might say that, but you haven't seen the body. You haven't seen what it did to him."

The sultry woman smiled and looked at Helen. "And who are you exactly? You're not with the police?"

"I've just come up here to keep watch." Helen laughed and risked a joke: "I suppose I'm more sober than most of you."

There was no response.

A slight creak came from behind her. She turned around. Mr. Lau, evidently satisfied with the situation, was creeping out of the room. He bowed at an angle so slight it was almost invisible, then opened the door and departed.

• • •

Helen turned back to the room; the five faces were still staring at her.

The glamorous woman's partner—an attractive young man with a pile of soft blond hair above his well-defined features—stepped forward with a charming smile and extended his hand. "Where are my manners? My name is Griff, Griff Banks."

They shook hands warmly. "Thank you. I'm Helen." She turned to the others; this situation was familiar to her. "Perhaps you could all tell me your names."

Griff stepped back and put an arm around the woman beside him, who looked away. "This here is Scarlett."

Helen turned to the other couple, who were scruffy in comparison. The man in brown was staring out of the window, presumably looking at the fire, with the daylight tangled in his thinning hair. He turned slowly toward Helen, as if dragging himself away from the critical moment of a boxing match, and seemed for a few seconds to have forgotten his lines. "Oh. My name is Andrew Carter. I'm pleased to meet you." He gave a smile that showed off his bad teeth and squeezed his weeping companion as if she were an overripe fruit. All the sadness seemed to spill out of her as her blue dress crumpled. "This is my sister, Vanessa. I'm sorry, she's taken this very badly."

"Oh, that's nothing to apologize about," said Helen. She was, in fact, wondering why the others hadn't taken it worse. Shock, she supposed. Vanessa dried her eyes and walked over to shake Helen's hand, moving with a slight limp.

"Nice to meet you."

Helen turned to where the third woman was standing nervously in a green dress—the bookend of the group, drinking a glass of cold black wine in the shadows. She put down the glass on one of several small tables scattered around the room, and cleared her throat. "Hello. My name is Wendy Copeland." Not knowing what to do next, she waved indistinctly at the other guests. "Hello, everybody."

"Thank you," said Helen. "And might someone tell me where the body is? I'm afraid I've been given very little information."

Griff raised his hand. "He's in the lavatory."

"Will you show me? If you don't mind."

He frowned. "Are you sure? It's not pleasant."

Helen was guided mostly by morbid curiosity. But she also felt that, if pressed, she could argue that she had to know the extent of the crime scene to be able to keep a watch on it, so she was unusually insistent. "Yes, please. I am sure."

Griff looked her up and down. "Well, then," he said, and turned to the wall that was on her left. He opened the small door there. Helen went to join him. Scarlett, left alone by the window, watched the two of them suspiciously.

•••

The room was larger than she'd expected, with a sink and mirror opposite the door and the toilet against the right-hand wall. Between the two was a small broken window. There was a shelf stocked with miniature towels to the right of the toilet, and a bin next to the door. Underlining all of these features was the body itself, lying diagonally across the floor with its head at the end nearest to them.

It was the body of a man lying on his back with his face covered by a black suit jacket, which had been removed and placed back to front on top of him. A channel of lumpy blood ran down it from roughly where his chin would be, as if he'd recently eaten something indigestible and spat it all back up again.

"Who is he?" she asked.

"That's our host, Harry Trainer. The playwright. Today is his birthday."

She knelt down to lift the jacket and saw underneath it a man in his late thirties, his pale, unmarked face ringed with a neat beard and sideburns. He was looking slightly to the left, with his whole head turned that way; the back of his skull had been beaten in and now sat against the ground at a slant. A pool of thick blood gave him a dark, bitter halo. She put a finger and thumb on either side of his forehead and tried tilting it in both directions, noting the uneven way it rolled over the tiles.

Surrounding the body was a wide pattern of bloodstains.

"You found him like this?"

"We found him lying on his front. The wound at the back of his head was unbearable, so we took his jacket off to cover him and rolled him onto his back. Then we checked his pulse. But everything else is untouched."

None of his clothes were undone. "He doesn't look like somebody about to use the toilet."

"No. The murderer must have struck quickly."

"Unless he'd just finished." She stood up. "Poor Harry."

"I think that's everything," said Griff, moving toward the door.

Helen was wavering on whether to leave it there or to ask him more questions. Her instinct was to indulge his impatience, but she also knew that if she could absorb as many details as possible now, it might help her later, when the witnesses themselves had grown hazy. "So this was his birthday party?"

Griff sighed. "A small gathering. He wasn't an easy man to get along with, but a few of us liked him."

"May I ask which one of you discovered the body?"

"All of us, I suppose. Harry had excused himself. At some point we realized he'd been gone quite a long time. We knocked and there was no reply, so I broke open the door."

She turned round and examined the lock. It was a simple bolt. A metal bracket that was nailed to the doorframe had been forced out of the wood by about an inch; it now hung precariously from the ends of its two nails, like something walking on stilts.

"So all five of you were here when the body was discovered?"

"Yes." He shrugged, as if he hadn't given it much thought. "I believe so."

"But there were no restaurant staff present?"

"No. We'd only just arrived. I think some food was due to be served later, but while people were coming in, they'd just left us alone with a lot of wine."

She stepped over to the window. At first glance it seemed like it overlooked a yard hidden behind the street, but in fact it was set into the side of the building and opened onto the flat roof of the neighboring shop.

"If the door was locked from the inside, the killer must have left through the window."

"Yes, and come in that way too."

She pictured the culprit waiting on the rooftop, in full view of the buildings opposite, peeking into the loo whenever they heard a sound from inside.

Griff went on: "Harry had his share of detractors, like I said. I don't know who else he invited to this gathering, but lots of people must have known about it. It would have been easy enough for one of them to climb up onto that roof and lie in wait for him. He'd have to use the toilet eventually."

She thought the image was slightly absurd. "But you didn't see anyone?"

"I'm afraid not."

She inspected the window. Most of the glass was gone from it, and the sharp fragments covered the sill and the floor below. It had been smashed in from the outside. With her handkerchief, she picked out a triangle of glass that was still in the frame: There was blood on the tip. "Somebody cut themselves."

"Be careful," he said.

She lowered her head and peered outside. There was a rusty-looking hammer at the other side of the roof, but she felt that it was beyond her remit to climb outside and retrieve it. A black cat sat next to it, licking its paws, its fur darkened with ash.

The day was warm, and the sky above the rooftops was covered with wispy black clouds.

"I wonder if he suffered much."

Griff became agitated. "This conversation is getting too morbid. Harry would want us to be celebrating his life, not picturing his death."

"I'm sorry," said Helen. She had little interaction with men in her day-to-day life, and it made her anxious when their moods shifted like this, though she supposed that she had spoken insensitively. She took a last look around the room, trying to take in all the details. The cramped space was beginning to smell of smoke. "Do you think we should block that window? All of this will be covered in ash before long."

"I know just the thing," said Griff. He left and returned with two large rectangular wine lists: They slotted perfectly into the frame, and the few lingering fragments of glass held them in place.

She smiled demurely. "Thank you for all of your help—Griff, isn't it?"

"Please. Harry was my friend, if there's anything I can do to help . . ." They shook hands again. He squeezed her fingers as he let go. "And now that I've transferred all of that knowledge to somebody else's brain, I can finally have a drink."

· · ·

When Helen emerged from the toilet with Griff, she found Andrew Carter—the man in the brown suit—waiting for her. "My sister is feeling faint. Can you help her?"

"Of course," she said. It was a common occurrence at school. He led her to a table where Vanessa Carter was sitting; Helen tilted her forward, then poured her a glass of water.

Andrew watched her work. "She's not normally like this, you know."

Helen wasn't used to people justifying themselves to her. She found it embarrassing. "That's quite all right, really, it's a perfectly reasonable reaction."

"But, then, this isn't a normal crime, as you've probably noticed."

Helen sensed that he wanted to tell her something. "How do you mean?"

"Did the crime scene strike you as unusual?"

She tried to look thoughtful. "It seems the killer came in through the window. But it's hard to imagine how they could have taken Harry by surprise, that way."

"In other words"—Andrew was nodding with an enthusiasm he attempted to portray as weary resignation—"the crime is impossible."

"Or they could have reached through the window and hit him with something."

Andrew gripped the table, giving his slightly wild appearance its full effect: "There is something we must tell you, but until you'd acknowledged the impossibility of the crime, we didn't think we'd be believed."

Helen didn't know how to react to that; she laughed nervously. "I will try," she said.

"What Griff won't have told you," said Andrew, a quick look of contempt passing over his face, "is that just before it happened, there was a terrible, inhuman wail. It was quiet but lasted almost a minute. The sound was identical to the screech of a giant hound."

Helen tried to disguise her interest. "When was that exactly? Just before it happened, you said. But before what?"

"About three minutes before we all noticed his absence. Only Vanessa and I heard it."

Vanessa raised her head from her knees; color had returned to her face. "I saw it," she said. "It came from the fire. I was at the window, watching the first flames take hold, and suddenly it just jumped out: a giant black dog, indistinct and phosphorescent, as if it were made of smoke."

Her blue eyes were wide; she seemed to be speaking earnestly.

"Something ungodly has happened here today."

Helen spoke in a very neutral tone. "You think he was killed by a spirit?"

When she was at school, ghosts and spirits had formed a sort of currency with which the girls could buy one another's interest; they were rumored to be everywhere. But Helen had never seen anything herself, just occasional shapes in the darkness and, of course, the sisters prowling the dim corridors. And even at her most credulous, she'd never heard of a ghost doing something as direct as what they seemed to be suggesting: beating a man to death with a hammer.

"No," said Vanessa. "Most likely he was killed by a human hand, but one directed and assisted by something malign. The devil himself, perhaps."

"Harry," said Andrew, "was a thoughtful man. I'm in the theater myself. We would talk about the craft for hours at a time; I considered him a friend. But there was an immorality to the rest of his life that I could not abide; it was all about drink and women. Even my sister wasn't safe from it."

Vanessa looked at the floor, ashamed. "He was very charming when I first met him. I was young, and he was dazzling."

"What we believe to have happened," Andrew continued, "is that the fire down the road briefly became a doorway to hell, and the devil saw a chance to take back one of his own."

Helen nodded insincerely. She let a period of time pass, then dared to ask a question. "You mentioned women. Has there been a woman in his life recently?"

Andrew shook his head. He looked at Vanessa; she shrugged. "Not that we know of."

"What about her? She's here alone." Discreetly, Helen indicated the other guest, to whom she hadn't yet talked.

"We don't know her," said Andrew.

"Was she with you when you found the body?"

"Yes, she was," he said. "At least, I think she was."

· · ·

Helen moved a table in front of the toilet door and brought a chair over to it. She poured herself a glass of wine and sat down, then closed her eyes. She tried to picture the different ways the crime could in theory have been committed, in case Mr. Lau asked for her impressions later. The sound of soft voices almost lulled her to sleep.

She opened her eyes.

Wendy—the shy woman in the green dress—was still hovering at the opposite side of the room. Helen caught her attention and waved her over.

Wendy arrived at the table, smiling gratefully. "It's hard to be at a party and not know anyone."

Helen smiled back. "Should this still be considered a party with everything that's happened?"

Wendy gave no answer. "Well, I can imagine it's even harder with the responsibility you've been given. Keeping order, when everything outside is chaos."

"I'm Helen." She offered her hand.

"Wendy. Pleased to meet you. I've been wondering if I ought to come over for the last twenty minutes or so."

"I'm glad you did. How do you know these people?"

"Oh, I'm an actor." She looked embarrassed. "Well, as a hobby really. We're all actors, I think. The thing is, I don't know any of this lot; I just knew Harry."

Helen sat up straight, interested to learn that she wasn't the only one isolated here. Things had moved so quickly, it hadn't occurred to her that this small group were just the first few people at a party—thrown together by punctuality—and might not all know one another. "Please, do sit down."

Wendy pulled up a chair and joined her in a glass of wine. "I take it you don't normally play detective?"

Both women had been here before, sitting at the edges of a gathering and seeking solidarity with their fellow introverts. The feeling was comforting and familiar, and Helen laughed at the question.

"No, I'm a teacher."

"Oh, that must be nice."

She thought about saying that, no, it was often hellish and that the grid of girls seated in front of her every day, with their precocious attitudes and withering observations, felt like the bars of her cage. But she was no more capable of expressing any such thing than she was suited to the profession itself.

"Yes," she replied. "It can be very rewarding."

"Listen, I might as well tell you this, though I haven't told anyone else." Wendy took her hand and spoke in a strong whisper. "Harry and I were engaged to be married."

She held up a finger with an ill-fitting ring looped around the base. It was a minimal silver band, smeared with condensation and sweat. "It's too large, I know. It belonged to his mother. She was a much bigger woman than me. But men don't understand those things, do they?" She half-smiled, defeated by the implausibility of her own words. "Well, you're the first person I've told."

Helen looked at Wendy with a kind of awe, her mind brimming with questions and clichés. "I'm so sorry for your loss."

"Oh, that." Wendy frowned. "It's a little more complicated than that, I have to say."

Helen said nothing.

"I'm not from London, you see. I met Harry when he was in Manchester for a play, about two and a half months ago. It was a sort of whirlwind romance. It only lasted a fortnight. Then we got engaged. This was to be the glorious occasion where we told everyone. All of his friends, at least. But it seems I got here too late."

"Yes, I should say so. You have my condolences."

"Thank you." Wendy spoke tentatively, unsure of her own response. "I know it's awful, I should be a shivering wreck. The thing is, it was so quick that I've been having second thoughts for the whole two months since we made the engagement. That's four times the time spent on love spent on doubt, do you understand? Then whenever I told people about the engagement, it seemed every one of them had a horror story about Harry Trainer. I've been so anxious, it's just been killing me. I was looking for a way out. So when they found the body, some small part of me was glad. Isn't that awful?"

Helen gave her a look that was comforting but held neither approval nor disapproval. "It's not really for me to judge."

"I've just been telling this lot that I'm a friend of his from up north. I haven't said anything about the engagement."

"Well, thank you for telling me. Do you feel all right?"

Wendy's small nervous mouth creased in concentration. "Yes. It was hard, when they found him. But also a relief. I'm afraid I can't get past the relief. I was the last one here. I arrived after Harry had disappeared to the powder room, but before his body had been discovered. So I haven't even seen him today. I've mostly forgotten what he looked like, to be honest."

"Then you haven't seen the body?"

"Oh gosh, no. I couldn't bear it."

"May I ask, did you hear anything before the body was discovered?"

"Of course," said Wendy. "The sound of smashing glass. Lots of it. I think I was the only one that heard it, though, because nobody else reacted. But, then, they were all standing by the window, so they might have thought it came from outside."

"They were all standing by the window?"

"That's right. I believed I'd got the wrong room at first, because I didn't see Harry. I was standing in the doorway and they were looking at something outside. The fire, I assume. So none of them saw me. I wondered whether to knock or just to retreat. And that's when I heard the glass smashing. From where I stood, I could tell it was coming from the lavatory. Anyway, that man Griff must have sensed something, because he turned around. I told him I was looking for Harry, and he invited me in. That got them talking about how Harry had been a long time, and where had he got to, and so on. Just a minute after that, they were breaking down the door."

"And were all of them there, by the window? All four of them?"

Wendy looked around the room. "Yes," she said. "I think they were."

• • •

Another fifteen minutes had passed and the police were still absent. The initial comfort Helen had felt with Wendy had faded, and for the last few minutes an awkward pause had stretched out between the two of them like a kitten luxuriating before a fire: the inevitable heat death of two introverts in conversation.

An idea seemed to occur to Wendy; she stood up and said in a sweet, dignified voice, "I need to use the lavatory. Is that all right?"

Helen was taken aback by this; someone her own age was treating her like a teacher. "Yes, of course," she stammered. "Please do."

Wendy's smile was at a slant. "Well, should I go downstairs and use the one there, or should I make do with the men's?"

Helen turned and looked at the nondescript door in the wall beside her, a dead body behind it. A letter *M* was pinned to the middle. "Where is the women's toilet?"

"That is the women's toilet," said Wendy. "The men's is out in the corridor."

Helen looked again and saw that the *M* wasn't quite vertical. It was pinned insecurely by a nail through its center. She reached up and turned it easily, until it formed a perfect uppercase *W.* It was clear from the faded patches on the wood that this was its normal position.

Harry Trainer had been killed in the women's toilet.

Wendy was still standing there. "Use the gentlemen's, please," said Helen. Wendy thanked her and vanished.

The women's toilet, thought Helen, her mind whirling with ideas.

The image Griff had put into her head—of someone climbing onto the roof next door and lying in wait for hours, because Harry would have to use the toilet eventually—had seemed slightly absurd before, but if he'd been killed in the women's lavatory, then it simply wasn't credible. Why would he ever need to use the women's toilet? That left two options: Someone had either tampered with the sign or they had somehow compelled him to go in there. Both required the participation of somebody in this room.

• • •

More time passed as Helen tried to process the possibilities. She wondered if she'd be able to remember all her theories and conclusions. She closed her eyes and rested her chin on her palm.

"Let us have a drink with you," said Griff, sitting down across from her. Her empty wineglass was the only thing on the table, a lonely chess piece in a losing game. "We hate to see someone looking so forlorn at a party. This was meant to be a happy occasion. Harry would have wanted us to keep it that way."

Scarlett was standing behind him. She nodded, giving her consent to this one act of kindness, and sat down at the table. They struck Helen as an astonishingly beautiful couple.

"Thank you," she said. "That's very kind."

Scarlett filled their three glasses. "Do you have any update on how long we'll be kept here? The world is practically ending outside."

"No," said Helen, confused by the question. "I haven't left the room."

Scarlett shrugged off this practicality.

"Are you from out of town?" asked Griff.

"Yes, Guildford. How could you tell?"

"I always can," he replied, grinning. "What are you doing here?"

"Shopping," she said. "In fact, I was in that building before it caught fire."

He whistled in admiration. "That was a lucky escape, then."

"Yes." She saw herself deep in the burning building, dark and crowded with the cloth-like smoke, panicking children running around her. "Very lucky."

Scarlett put her elbows on the table. "And what do you do in Guildford?"

"I'm a teacher."

"Oh." Scarlett considered it. "Then a little underqualified to be playing detective?"

Helen took a drink; she was no longer sober, and the alcohol had given her a very restrained recklessness. "In fact," she said, "I have a theory. It might interest you."

Griff sat back with a burst of laughter. He slapped the table. "Come on, then, let's hear it."

"Well," said Helen. "You suggested earlier that the killer lay in wait for Harry on the rooftop outside the toilet window. What was unclear, at that time, is that this is the women's toilet." She pointed up at the door that towered over them: the fourth guest at their small table. "Harry was tricked into using it instead of the men's, which necessitates involvement from somebody in this room."

"Perhaps," said Griff.

"But that got me thinking," Helen went on, "if someone in this room was involved, perhaps a neater solution could be considered. What if the killer was inside the loo, behind the door? When Harry enters, they take him by surprise, a simple clean hit. Then they smash the window and move the pieces to make it look like it was broken from the outside. They wait until the rest of you break in, hiding behind the door again, and rejoin the group without comment. Would anyone even have noticed?"

"Yes," said Griff, "I think I would have. When I opened the door."

Helen took a dismissive sip of her wine. "Of course. Unless you were working with the killer." She put the glass down and grinned. Griff burst into laughter.

Scarlett hissed. "Is she actually accusing us, or is this just a strange sort of joke?"

Griff turned to her. "Oh, not you, darling. She knows you'd never get your hands dirty like that."

"This is infantile." Scarlett stood up and returned to the window.

"I'm sorry, she's very sensitive," said Griff. He shook gently with laughter, as if an underground train were at that moment passing beneath the restaurant.

He was still laughing as he walked away.

. . .

Helen's head was muddied, and the evening was growing long. She looked at the window, which ran almost the full length of the wall: Scarlett and Griff stood at one end, Andrew and Vanessa at the other. Helen got up and tottered over to the middle of it. Outside, everything was chaos. The fire was raging unashamedly now; there was no sign of movement inside the building, beyond the yellow flicker of the flames. The street was thick with smoke. There were no cars and very few people that weren't with the police or the fire brigade.

Have we been forgotten? thought Helen, suddenly fearful. Are we stranded up here, at the top of this restaurant? A thick cough came from her right. Vanessa was bent at the waist, her hand on the windowsill. "My sister is very sensitive to the smoke," said Andrew Carter, frowning. Maybe she shouldn't stand by the window, thought Helen, who said nothing. "It would be barbaric to keep us here much longer."

Helen moved toward them. "Have you seen anything else in the fire? Any other shapes?" Was it sarcasm or simply the wine?

"No," Vanessa sobbed, between coughs. "But if there was any doubt that it's the devil's work . . ." She pointed to a row of bodies that had been laid on the pavement opposite. "Some have fallen, some are burned. I don't think there could be a clearer message."

Helen disagreed. She squinted at the flames, trying to detect the outline of something. Anything, really. But it just made her eyes sore.

She was about to ask a further question when a loud squawking reached them from below. Vanessa jumped back, as if a panicked bird had flown into the room. Helen peered through the smoke and tried to locate the source of the sound. Across the road, two servants were walking calmly, their arms filled with cages of exotic birds. Parrots and cockatoos, even a crate of live quails. Behind them, a third servant was walking a leopard on a leash. It was an eccentric man's menagerie being evacuated from a house nearby; a neat microcosm of the disruption caused by the fire.

Helen watched them parade down the street, wondering where they would go. "It does look like the world is ending," she said, mostly to herself. And then she noticed movement in the room behind her, reflected in the window.

The distinctive green dress that Wendy was wearing left the spot where she'd been standing, spun carefully around, and proceeded swiftly to the door leading downstairs. The door opened and the dress disappeared.

Helen blinked at the audacity of it, then turned and hurried after her.

• • •

She found Wendy in the corridor outside; she'd made it as far as the second step. "Wendy, where are you going?"

The departing woman turned around and shrugged. "Oh, Helen, I was going to tell you. I have a train to catch. I feel I've contributed all I can here."

"But we're not allowed to leave."

Wendy shifted nervously; there was a pleading tone to her voice. "I don't know any of these people. I barely knew Harry. And by all accounts he was killed before I got here."

"But you were engaged to him, you're a key witness."

"I don't want to be rude, Helen, but you're just a teacher. Don't ask me to indulge your delusions of being a detective."

Helen flushed at such a remark from this previously polite woman. "The restaurant manager won't let you leave."

"No, but I was hoping he wouldn't notice."

"I'll tell him."

Wendy sighed wearily. "Yes, I thought you probably would." She walked back toward Helen and took off her engagement ring, defeated; it slipped off like a scarf from a melting snowman. "If I'm being made to stay, I may as well tell you the truth." Wendy gave her the ring to inspect. "I borrowed that from a friend—that's why it's far too big for me."

Helen looked down at the simple silver band; it was scratched in several places. "You weren't really engaged?"

"I really am an actor. And I'm from Manchester, that's true too. Harry really did meet me while he was there for a play. But there was no romance; it was all business. I was asked to come here today and pose very publicly as his fiancée."

"Asked by whom?"

"By Harry, of course. He wrote me a letter. Someone had been pestering him—another woman. Being a bit too persistent, even scaring him a little. He thought if I came to this party and we pretended to be planning a wedding, it would send her a message. Then he'd quietly cancel the engagement once she'd moved on to someone else. Not the most pleasant scheme, I admit. But frankly I needed the work."

Helen was intrigued. "But you don't know her name, this mystery woman?"

Wendy shook her head. "Harry didn't tell me."

"I don't understand, though. You lied to me. But why? Why did you go on with the act after he'd been killed?"

"I wanted to see how you'd react. Look, you're not the only one that can play detective. As soon as you were shown into the room, I wondered if it might be you. The one who's been pestering him."

"The other woman?" Helen laughed at the impossibility of it. "But I've never even met Harry."

"Well, you suddenly showed up, you were acting nervous. I realize now that I made a mistake." She crept up to Helen and took her hands, speaking conspiratorially. "None of these people know my real name.

Can't you just let me slip away before the police come? It would save us both a lot of hassle."

"I can't blame you for wanting to leave. But we have to do what we've been told."

. . .

The two women returned to the room; those inside looked up momentarily and then went back to their increasingly strained conversations. Helen sat at her table by the toilet door, and Wendy, as if slightly embarrassed, took a seat alone at a separate table. There was near silence in the room now; everyone was waiting for something to happen.

And something did. The door opened and a loud voice came from outside: "This party is harder to get into than Buckingham Palace."

A refined, energetic young man—in his late twenties and very good-looking—entered from the corridor. He was greeted by a stunned silence: They all stared as he spun the scarf from around his neck and hung it and his hat on a stand behind the door. "It's smoking like my nan outside—I should have dug out my uncle's old gas mask. But the fellows downstairs couldn't seem to decide if this thing was canceled or not, so I reasoned there must be something they weren't telling me. I had to wait until they were all busy with bowls of soup and then sneak up."

His hat on the stand and a head of shining black hair revealed, he turned to face the group. "Well, where's the birthday boy?"

Griff stepped forward. "James, this really isn't a good time. You should have listened to the chaps downstairs."

"Nonsense," said James, pouring himself a glass of red wine. He left the bottle on Helen's table. "No social occasion is ever a lost cause: If I didn't believe that, I wouldn't talk so much." Helen noticed Andrew roll his eyes and return to the window.

"James, there's something I need to tell you." Griff was speaking again. "In private."

The two men went to the corner of the room. But as clear as the smell of smoke, everyone could hear James speak: "Harry is dead? My God!" He turned to the room and raised his glass. "Well, here's to absent friends." The response was apathetic; James downed his drink. "How did it happen, then?"

Griff whispered, "He was murdered."

"Murdered, you say? Not by Rhonda, I hope?"

"Rhonda? Who is Rhonda?"

"Rhonda, Harry's latest flame. A pretty young thing, about nineteen years old. Getting a bit possessive, I understand." He tapped his forehead. "Marriage on the brain."

Andrew Carter looked pointedly at his sister. "But Rhonda is the name Vanessa uses onstage—"

Helen interrupted proceedings by toppling the bottle of red wine onto the floor. It landed with a concussive smash, leaving a stain not unlike the one in the toilet, all thin blood and fragments of glass. The group turned and looked at her; James was finally silent, twisted around in surprise. If there was any doubt that she'd knocked the wine to the floor on purpose, she dispelled it by nudging a wineglass over the edge with her fingertips. She sat in an island of smashed glass.

"I don't believe we've met." James approached her and offered his hand. "I'm James."

Helen was staring at him. "I've seen you before, James."

He was slightly taken aback. "In a play perhaps?"

"You could certainly say that." She turned to the others. "I've seen you all before. And I recognize you, I recognize all of you. I recognize this whole situation. The quietest one in the room being preyed upon by the rest." She turned back to James. "Don't they say that you should never let the audience watch you setting up? Once you've seen the actors smoking and bickering outside the theater, kicking the props around, the illusion is ruined."

Helen was drunk; James glanced at the other guests, unsure of how to proceed.

"I'm sorry, I don't understand what you mean."

"After arriving here later than everyone else, you should have at least pretended you didn't know where the hatstand was. It's quite hidden, behind the door."

He looked insulted but relieved to have a concrete accusation he could deny. "Well, I've been to this restaurant before."

Saying the first thing that came into his head, thought Helen; everybody reverts to childhood when they lie. He was no different than a five-year-old girl claiming that a bird had dropped the contraband item into the room through the open window.

"That is true," said Helen. "The entrance we all just witnessed was actually your return. You were here earlier."

James shuffled awkwardly, isolated by this accusation, while the others gathered around Helen's table. The broken glass kept them back. When they had formed a rough half circle—even Wendy had approached, drawn by curiosity—Helen looked from one to another in turn. Griff spoke: "What are you suggesting?"

"I now know who all of you are," said Helen, pressing her head back into the wall, trying to focus her sobriety, knowing that it was the intoxication that was compelling her to speak. "I see six extroverts. All of you, even the shy ones." She looked at Wendy. "Six extroverts who think they can manipulate someone more reserved than themselves, just by talking more forcefully."

"She's drunk," said Vanessa.

"A little, but it doesn't affect my judgment. You would be wise not to underestimate how well I know this scene. You see it with salesmen most often: They realize they're talking to someone quiet and thoughtful and their eyes light up. They think they'll be able to make your decisions for you, as if not being inclined to voice an opinion was the same as not being able to have one." Helen had a moment of self-doubt.

Why didn't she save this for a cozy conversation with a police detective, over a cup of tea? "So I've patiently listened to your lies all evening; it's been like an afternoon in school. But your plan, implausible as it was, was downright sloppy in one respect: It didn't occur to any of you that before I was asked to come and keep watch up here, I'd been sitting downstairs for about an hour. In this very restaurant, quite close to the door."

The room was darkening, with the sun in decline and the windows almost black with smoke. She was speaking to an audience of silhouettes.

"I must have been sitting there, eating a bowl of soup, while the murder took place. And I expect I was sitting there while every one of you arrived. I didn't pay too much attention, of course. But I couldn't miss the sight of one smartly dressed, fully grown man carrying another into a crowded restaurant."

A gasp filled the room. Somebody at the back of the circle dropped a glass.

She spoke to James: "If you hadn't made such a dramatic entry just now, that memory might never have come back to me, but it has. And so I can tie the threads together. What I saw earlier this evening was you escorting Harry onto the premises, the poor man so drunk he could hardly walk. I only saw the back of his head—in its original, unspoiled state, of course—but I'm sure that it was him. It was his build, his beard, his sideburns, and his signature black suit. You, on the other hand, I recognize without a doubt."

"It's true," said Vanessa. "Harry was inordinately drunk when we arrived. We suspected he'd been drinking all day."

Her brother nodded. "That's right, he was ghastly."

Griff stepped forward, crunching a piece of glass. "Anyone who knew Harry would expect him to be helplessly drunk by six o'clock on his birthday. I fail to see how that changes anything."

"You've all been lying to me," said Helen pointedly. "I've heard any

number of stories today—from demon dogs to fanatical women—but not one of them accounted for the fact that Harry was delivered here too drunk even to stand up. I can see what happened. When I entered this room for the first time this evening, you were all surprised. You'd been expecting the police, but instead you got me. Then one of you saw an opportunity. You thought that if you each told me a story, with no two stories the same, I'd be all in a muddle by the time I spoke to the police. I'd repeat all your lies and make a mess out of everything. I was just a way of adding some confusion to the crime scene, that's how you saw me. And why—because I don't assert myself much?"

There was an uncomfortable silence, as if the room had filled with water. "It's been said to me," Helen went on, "at least once this evening that Harry had a lot of enemies. It seemed a strange thing for his friends to insist upon. Unless you're not his friends. You're his enemies." Guilty looks were exchanged by the guests; then the six of them stared at their shoes. "I don't know what he did to you individually—engagements and abandonments would have played some part, I'd imagine, from the way that you've depicted him—but I would guess that each of you held some grudge against Harry. So you gathered together, shared your grievances, and decided the world would be a better place if you killed him. You arranged this party, on Harry's birthday, and you all came along to pose as his friends. Presumably he didn't have enough actual friends to object or to have made any other plans."

Nobody spoke. Helen stood up.

"Did it happen like this: James here runs into Harry somewhere around lunchtime and suggests a drink, making it look like a coincidence. He's the type of person that makes everyone feel wanted, so Harry goes along with it." James reddened. "You get Harry drunk and bring him here; he's in no state to object. The rest of you arrive. Then the seemingly intractable crime scene is prepared: All it would take is for one of you to lock themselves inside the bathroom and let another break the door down, with Harry in the corner here the whole time.

Probably taking a nap. Then one of you smashes the window and places the glass piece by piece on the floor and the windowsill, to make it look like it was done from outside. Then, once the last of you has arrived, the proceedings begin. He's bundled into the toilet and propped on the seat, with his forehead against his knees. One of you produces a hammer. It would be easy enough to smuggle one inside, under a man's suit jacket. A simple hammer, like the one that is soaked in blood and lying on the roof outside. The six of you passed this weapon around and took it in turns to strike the inebriated Harry on the back of the head. Six bold strikes. The poor man has hardly any skull left. What else? There's a telltale spot of blood on a piece of glass in the window frame; I assume that's just a distraction, to make it look as if the killer went out that way. None of you have any visible cuts, but, Vanessa, you're walking with a slight limp. Did you take off your shoe and scratch the bottom of your foot with that little glass triangle? A neat piece of misdirection. Then, James, you must have taken the rest of the evidence with you and sneaked out of the restaurant. What was it? A bloody rag, perhaps?"

James looked forlorn. "A tablecloth, stained with vomit." He gave a long, futile sigh. "I ran into the burning building and threw it into the flames, then ran out looking like a hero. I went home to change."

The six guests stood in silence. Helen looked at each of them in turn. "And then you all spent the rest of the evening telling me stories, not one of them the slightest bit true."

There was a loud knock on the door. It creaked open. The restaurant manager's head appeared around the door; Helen had had a feeling he would return for the final act. There was a grin on his impish face. "I am sorry to disturb you, madame, but we have been told we must evacuate the building immediately."

He disappeared; Helen turned back to face her accused. They stared at her. James broke the silence with a burst of laughter. "Well, we all heard the man. It seems we're free to go." The room relaxed. Andrew picked up his jacket, James his hat, and Vanessa took a good look at her black shoes as if wondering how to make them more comfortable, then the whole group proceeded toward the door.

"You might find," said Scarlett as she passed, "that your story seems less plausible once we've all left the room." The rest of them filed past her.

"Don't worry too much," said Griff. "Harry really was an awful man. We've done the world a favor."

He departed and Helen was alone.

Andrew had opened the window in a small act of sabotage, and smoke was pouring in through it. An appropriate metaphor, thought Helen. Then she picked herself up, put on her coat, and left. The restaurant was eerily empty as she passed down the stairs and out of the door.

She walked down the street and looked at the burning building. It was such horror: Who would care about their simple corpse in the toilet when it had happened so close to this abomination? And yet, for all its branching chaos, the fire was essentially an act of God, whereas the murder had been planned and carried out in cold blood. The two events seemed to cover all cases of maleficence, as if this simple West London street were a diorama on display in a Sunday school. She stared at the fire and felt the heat wash her clean.

8

THE FOURTH
CONVERSATION

The two events seemed to cover all cases of maleficence, as if this simple
West London street were a diorama on display in a Sunday school.
She stared at the fire and felt the heat wash her clean."

Julia Hart finished reading and poured herself a second cup
of coffee.

Grant knocked twice on the tabletop. "Well," he said sleepily.
"What do you make of that one?"

"Everyone's a murderer." She flicked through the pages with her
left hand, holding the cup in her right. "An apocalyptic story, with an
apocalyptic setting. I liked it."

"It's the case where all of the suspects turn out to be guilty."

Julia nodded. "The idea's been done before."

"Famously so." Grant yawned. "But nonetheless it's one of the permutations of detective fiction. The definition allows for it, so it can't
be ignored."

"I have to say, I didn't anticipate that ending."

"Good." He looked at her with bloodshot eyes. "Lying is often overused in detective stories. But if all of the suspects are guilty, they can lie about everything. With impunity."

"I thought Helen would be guilty, when I first read it. She seemed"—Julia searched for the word—"unsettled."

"The detective as killer, again?" Grant shook his head. "It would be a cheap trick to use the same ending twice."

"But not against the rules." Julia smiled.

They were sitting at a rough wooden table, facing each other. Between them was a large jug of water, with two halved and polished lemons bobbing rhythmically on the surface. Beside it was a glass canister of thick black coffee. At the far end of the table was a window, patterned with raindrops.

It was Julia's second full day on the island. She had been woken that morning by the sound of the rain; slightly hungover, she'd hurried to Grant's cottage, half walking and half running. Grant had been standing outside when she'd arrived, eating a pear and watching the rain spit at the sea, with a sour expression on his face. "I didn't know if you would come," he said, his white shirt soaking wet.

"We have work to do." Julia approached him. "Are you feeling all right?"

He smiled unenthusiastically and threw the white heart of his pear into the pebbles on the shore. "I slept badly."

Julia had barely slept herself, but she didn't say anything. She'd decided she would be patient with him. "I hope yesterday wasn't too tiring for you?"

He guided her inside without answering, and together they took shelter in his kitchen. "I should make some coffee."

Julia watched him, wondering whether to help. When the kettle had been placed on the stove and Grant had filled a jug with water, she spoke: "I'm sorry if I was being intrusive last night. I think the wine went to my head."

Grant was cutting a lemon for the water. "It's nothing," he said. He was looking out of the window; Julia caught a glimpse of his face in the glass. It didn't look like it was nothing.

"I'm sorry, it was rude of me. I won't ask any more personal questions."

Grant pressed down too hard, and the buoyant flesh of the lemon burst under the blade of his knife. A spot of lemon juice landed on Julia's wrist. She decided to change the subject. "Should I start the next story while you're doing that?"

Grant turned and nodded at her.

It was still raining when she'd finished reading, but only slightly.

"This weather is more what I'm used to," she said. "Yesterday I felt I was carrying the sun around with me, like a bullet hole in the back of my head. I don't know how you can stand it every day."

"Over time it becomes something less impersonal than a bullet hole. A tumor, perhaps." Grant laughed quietly to himself. "You get used to it eventually. I should warn you, the sun will probably be back this afternoon."

"Then I shall enjoy this while it lasts." Julia took her notebook from inside her bag, where it was wrapped inside a towel. The rain hadn't got to it. "Yesterday," she reminded him, "you listed the first three ingredients that a murder mystery must include."

"Yes. Two or more suspects, one or more victims, and an optional detective or detectives."

"Then the fourth component must be the murderer?"

Grant's mood had improved noticeably as he'd swallowed his first cup of coffee. Now he was grinning again. "That's right, this story demonstrates it nicely. A killer, or group of killers; those responsible for the deaths of the victims. Without that it's certainly not a murder mystery."

"Not a very good one, that's for sure." She made some notes. "And there must be at least one killer?"

"Yes, at least one. If the death was accidental or done by the victim's own hand, then we hold the victim responsible and consider them to be the killer. For that reason I used the term *killer* rather than *murderer*. It seemed to cover more cases."

"Pun intended." Julia took another sip of coffee. "But there's no upper limit on the number of killers, if this story is anything to go by?"

"Not as such. The only condition is that the killer, or killers, must be drawn from the group of suspects. In mathematics we'd call it a subset and say that the killers must be a subset of the suspects, but we'll come back to that later. What it means is that everyone who is revealed as one of the killers must previously have been one of the suspects."

"Then that's what allows the reader to have a stab at guessing the solution themselves, which seems to be a defining feature of the genre?"

Grant was nodding. "But aside from that, we set no further restrictions on the killer or group of killers. So we have seen already that the victims and even the detectives can overlap with the group of killers. We have also seen the case where just one of the suspects is a killer, and we can, of course, imagine the case where two of the suspects are killers. This story covers the limiting case where all of the suspects are killers."

Julia put the pen to her lips. "One thing, though . . ." She took her time, thinking as she spoke. "I agree that it's not unreasonable to say that the killer or killers must have first been suspects, but isn't it irrelevant unless the reader knows who the suspects are? The narrator of the story, for example, could turn out to be the killer. And it might never have occurred to anyone that they were a suspect."

"It's a good question," he said, "though it takes us away from mathematics. The only answer I can give is that every single character should be considered a suspect, unless it is made clear that the author intends them not to be. A modern-day detective investigating a centuries-old crime should not be considered a suspect."

Julia wrote this down. "Anyone the reader would accept as the killer should be considered a suspect, more or less?"

"That's correct." Grant was staring out of the window. "It's stopped raining, I think."

Through the murky glass she could see the sea and the hills, the two hands of the horizon that between them juggled the sun and the moon, waiting expectantly with their palms facing upward. The sky above them was overcast.

"Wait one moment," said Grant, "let me empty the coffee grounds." He took the beaker of coffee from the table and stepped outside to pour its contents into the weeds.

Julia looked around.

A silver cigarette case lay on the windowsill, out of place in the simply furnished room. Julia picked it up and looked inside. It was empty, but there was an engraving underneath the lid. *For Francis Gardner, on your graduation.* Julia frowned and put it back on the shelf.

Grant came back and sat down across from her. "Now, where were we?"

She wanted to ask him who Francis Gardner was but was afraid of his reaction, after last night. "I didn't know you smoked," she said.

Grant laughed, wondering what she might have seen through the window that she could have misinterpreted so wildly. "I don't, actually."

"But isn't that a cigarette case?"

He turned toward the flat silver container, which he'd forgotten was there, and she caught the quick look of panic on his face. "I used to, of course. When I was young. But that's been empty for a long time."

She nodded and took up her pen. "So is that the end of the definition?"

"Yes." Grant smiled, composing himself. "Those are the four ingredients. We can go into more detail when we're a bit more awake."

"And then the permutations of detective fiction—they cover the different cases where the ingredients overlap? So we have the case where the detective is also the killer, and so on?"

"That's right. The definition is simple enough that there's a relatively small number of structural variations. Overlapping ingredients account for some, different-sized groups account for some others. And then there's this case, where the group of killers is equal to the group of suspects."

The manuscript was on the bench by her side. Julia picked it up again and started flicking through the pages. "Did you notice that there were several points in that story where the word *black* was used, though the word *white* was clearly intended?"

He raised an eyebrow. "No, I did not."

"At one point it talks of black wine, for instance." She found another passage where she'd underlined a few words. "There's a description of a bright day with wispy black clouds."

"Then this is another intentional discrepancy?"

She continued to search through the pages. "There's a phosphorescent black dog. A signature black suit. And a black cat with its fur darkened by ash. As descriptions they're out of place, but they all fit perfectly if you replace *black* with *white*. Can you explain that?"

"No more than you can."

Julia looked pensive. "That's four now. I think at this point we can state the general rule: When you were writing these stories, you added something to each one of them that doesn't make any sense. A detail, a discrepancy. It's as if they might all fit together to form some sort of puzzle, spread throughout the seven stories. Do you think that might be possible?"

Grant frowned. "It's been more than twenty-five years since I wrote these stories. I've forgotten that time of my life almost completely. But I assure you, they're just jokes. There's no puzzle to be solved. I would have remembered something like that."

"Yes, I suppose so." Julia crossed out an entry in her notebook.

Grant rubbed his eyes. "Last night I had a nightmare. We published this book and the island became overrun with journalists. I couldn't get back to sleep after that."

"I'm sorry," she said. "I've disrupted your routine. Do you have many visitors out here?"

"Not many at all, actually. But I like it that way."

"It must be a nice change, then, to have someone to speak English to?"

"A few people here speak English very well."

"But none of them are British, I imagine?"

"That's true." Grant nodded. "You're a novelty in that respect. And it's nice to hear an accent similar to my own. Tell me"—he reached across the table and took her hand—"do you think *The White Murders* will sell?"

Julia took a long, deep breath. Her face was unreadable. "It's hard to say. It's rather different to most of what we publish."

"What does your employer think? He must believe it has potential, if he was willing to send you out here."

"Victor is a wealthy man. And crime fiction is his passion. He set up Blood Type Books out of love, not for money. But we can see this book getting a dedicated readership. It's certainly unique."

"I hope so," said Grant. "It pains me to say it, but I'm almost broke." He picked up his coffee cup. "Do you often get sent abroad for work?"

"Never," said Julia. "But I was particularly keen to meet you." She looked like she was about to say more, but Grant stood up and took his cup to the sink.

"I'm flattered," he said.

Julia scanned the dim kitchen. It was poorly kept, with dirt in all of the corners. "I hope you don't mind me asking, but how do you manage to live out here? Do you work?"

Grant sighed and shook his head. "Family money. My grandfather owned factories. The business is not what it was, but my uncle still sends me an allowance every month."

Julia put the manuscript down and massaged her writing hand. "Of course." She looked out of the window again. "If it has stopped raining, maybe we should get some fresh air while we have the chance?"

9

TROUBLE ON
BLUE PEARL ISLAND

Sarah's father was dying in a room upstairs. She watched him from the doorway. His head, bobbing above the bedsheets, looked alternately terrified, pained, and bewildered; it was like she was watching a swimmer floundering on the surface while unknown terrors attacked him from below.

"Sarah," he croaked, as she brought him his bowl of soup. "My little genius."

She spent most of her time tending to the garden, waiting for it to all be over. After dark she paced the rooms downstairs and tried to forget about him. She'd been playing three separate games of chess by post, posing as a man. The morning after her third victory, she climbed the stairs and found her father dead.

• • •

A month later she had discovered the extent of his debts, and soon everything was gone: the house, the furniture, the business. She was left destitute at twenty-five.

She spent an afternoon hunched over in the corner of a cold restaurant—still wearing her mourning clothes, an apparition in black—applying for a role as a governess. Aside from helping her father, she'd never worked before. "It will be just like Jane Eyre," she said to herself.

Her application was flawless; she spoke four languages, could play the piano, and knew mathematics, history, and English grammar. But nonetheless she was terrified as she dropped it into the post box.

• • •

Two weeks passed, and then she met her prospective employer in a room with diamond-patterned wallpaper. He had come to town for the day. "This is not an interview," he said, sitting down with a sheet of paper and a pen. "Just a friendly conversation."

She bowed, hoping to appear obsequious.

"I was in the army," the old colonel began. "Retired now. I have just the one daughter. My wife is no longer with us." He was the kind of man that could only be comfortable speaking if he was doing something else at the same time; he took his glasses off and started to polish them with his sleeve. "My name is Charles."

"Sarah," she replied, her head lowered.

He'd arrived after lunch, and throughout their meeting he picked at a piece of food that was lodged between his teeth, with a half-hearted attempt at discretion, as if his mustache might make an effective curtain. "If you come to live with us, we'd like to consider you part of the family. Henrietta is"—he chose his words carefully—"wanting for companions."

She bowed again.

When they'd finished talking, he looked up at her, terrified. "I think I've lost my glasses." Sarah took them from the table, where he'd placed them, and handed them to him.

He lived in an impossibly small village on a wild stretch of the coast. She'd never lived outside of the city before, but it was that or starve.

. . .

Her belongings fit neatly into a single suitcase.

She was driven to the house, the last along a wooded lane. Charles helped her carry her things inside, then gave her a tour of the residence. It was small and dark; the trees blocked most of the light. But it was his childhood home, and he swung enthusiastically through the rooms without noticing that she was taller than him and had to stoop, that with each step the ceiling loomed at her like a fist.

Her bedroom had a brown carpet, a desk, and a single bed. The window felt cold when she stood beside it, but the view was breathtaking. At the other side of the short garden was an overgrown area of cliff tops and then the sudden and deadly sea, shining like marble.

. . .

The daughter, Henrietta, was shy around Sarah for the first few weeks. But she never missed a lesson. They did three hours in the mornings and two in the afternoons—"There are no schools around here," Charles had said—in a room with rocking horses on the wallpaper. She was almost thirteen, though her knowledge was advanced and it was clear that she was unusually intelligent. She looked nothing at all like her father, with green eyes and copper skin, and Sarah wondered if she was really his child. Her mother had died of malaria, when she was very young.

Sarah knew nothing about children and spoke to her like an adult. Henrietta flourished, and the two women became close friends.

. . .

Charles spent most of his time working on a bulbous memoir of his years in India. The work was exhausting, and during the winter he contracted an unknown illness; Sarah nursed him as she'd done with her father, taking soup up to his cold room at the top of the house.

He became feverish. At his worst point he was capable of saying only one lucid thing, taking Sarah's hand when she brought him some water: "If I die, look after Henrietta." She found it surprising that this was his main concern when his consciousness was down to a whisper; she rarely saw them in the same room together and had taken to thinking of father and daughter as two unrelated entities. She was surprised too by Henrietta's reaction; the girl was almost silent, trembling as Sarah sat across from her at the dinner table.

A few days before Christmas, there was a shift in Charles's fortunes. He swallowed a whole bowl of soup, sat up, and declared himself healthy again. Sarah was there by his side. He thanked her for her kindness and devotion during his period of sickness, then—still unshaven and wearing his pajamas—he proposed marriage, as if giving her a gift.

"I'm sorry," she muttered. "I don't think that would work out."

Charles looked momentarily shocked, then gently lowered his head. "I understand."

The second proposal was indirect and came a few weeks later, when he was dressed and had composed himself; it came hidden in an act of humility. "Sarah, I must apologize for my indiscretion a few weeks ago. I was feverish. My thoughts were still unclear. It was inappropriate to put you under pressure like that."

A wash of relief came over her.

"However," he continued, "I must tell you that the sentiment itself was not a delirium but an honest expression of my heart." Her relief tightened to a knot. "I cannot deny that I do have a certain affection for you. You are really a remarkable woman."

He took out his pocket watch and started to play with it, moving the hands around as if they meant nothing.

"Let me give you some time to absorb what I've said." He licked a fingertip and ran it across the smeared glass face of the watch. "You must take as long as you need. My only concern is that one day your presence here will become too painful to me, like an unfulfilled promise. Then it might be better for both of us if we make alternative arrangements. And you find employment elsewhere."

She took that as a veiled threat, and it left her with little choice; a bad reference could destroy her prospects of employment. They were married in the spring, his graying hair neatly combed and hers tied back in a bow. He said the words of his vows out of order. She spoke them back to him like a somber parrot, dressed in a grayish blue. It's this or destitution, she thought.

· · ·

Summer came and Sarah and Henrietta took their lessons to the summerhouse, a squat structure of wood and glass at the highest point of their garden. It commanded a clear view of the sea. A telescope stood in one corner, a birthday gift for Henrietta.

One quiet morning in June, Sarah entered the summerhouse and found Henrietta crouched down by the telescope, scanning the line of the coast. The girl heard the door click behind her and turned around. "Sarah, come and look. There's trouble on Blue Pearl Island."

Sarah went to her side. "What do you see?"

"The front door is open. It's banging in the wind. There's a broken window and a pile of clothes on the grass."

Blue Pearl Island was a stubborn lump of stone, about three hundred yards out to sea, centered in a ring of sharp black rocks that lay just below the surface of the water, which made it almost inaccessible by boat. You could reach it when the tide was high enough, at two times during the day, but then only if you knew the route through the rocks. When the tide withdrew, the falling water filtering through those stone teeth appeared to be boiling, so it was known by some as Hell Island. But the colonel found this name distasteful and had always referred to it by the name he'd called it in childhood: Blue Pearl Island.

Twenty years ago an American millionaire, struck by the dramatic setting, had a house built on top of it. But the stone was unyielding, and the whitewashed house had settled with all its angles slightly out of alignment, like a melting block of ice. An expensive folly, it was later abandoned to its impracticality and had stood empty for years. But it must have been advertised somewhere, because occasionally someone would take occupancy. An artist had lived there one summer, working on a series of sea paintings. An austere family had managed a year before leaving. And the navy had taken it once as a base for some kind of training exercise. But most of the time its windows were dark.

"Is there a boat?"

Henrietta checked the small jetty where boats would usually tie up. "There is one half of a rope that's been cut, but no boat."

"How can you tell the rope has been cut?"

"It's tied to a post but isn't long enough to reach the surface of the water. That makes no sense unless it's been cut."

Sarah stroked the girl's hair. "You're right. This might be serious. The rest could all be down to debauchery, but if the only boat has been cut loose, that suggests something else is at work. May I look?"

She'd known there was something strange happening at the house when she saw the visitors arrive a few days before; usually it was taken by those seeking solitude or a communion with nature, not by large groups of people chatting breezily to one another. She'd wondered if they were a secret society or political party, though they certainly hadn't looked like either. It seemed, instead, to be some kind of social gathering.

It had begun on the Wednesday, when a Mr. and Mrs. Stubbs had arrived in time for that evening's crossing. A local fisherman was with them to teach them the route, a yellow dog following at his heels. Sarah was outside reading in the last of the day's light, on a chair in the garden where it bordered the wooded lane, which led down the hill. At the bottom of the lane was a small stretch of sand where many people kept boats. She'd greeted them—it was a rare sight to see anyone passing by so late—and they'd stopped to say how nice her house was. "Such a remarkable part of the world," said Mr. Stubbs.

"Quietly beautiful," said Mrs. Stubbs.

"Are you heading for the island?" asked Sarah.

The fisherman bobbed impatiently behind them—the dog circling his legs—while Mr. Stubbs explained the purpose of their trip. They were both in service; they'd been asked to arrive early and prepare for a large group on the following Friday. They couldn't say who was coming or who their employer was. But it would be a very important occasion. "I hope we'll see you on our way back home." And with that, they walked on.

The guests had arrived two days later, at various times throughout the day. They'd come in pairs, clutching yellow sheets of paper that Sarah assumed were written instructions. She was outside for most of the day, tending to the garden. She counted eight guests—men and women, old and young, though all relatively affluent. Together with the Stubbses, that made ten. A large number for such a small island.

The only clue she got to their identity was a single name:

"How do you know this man Unwin?"

One of them had said it to another as they'd passed.

"I don't, in fact," the other had replied.

They'd heard nothing of the party since then; it had rained the last two days and neither Sarah, Charles, nor Henrietta had even ventured into the garden, and from inside the house the view was blocked by rhododendrons. But now, looking through the telescope, it seemed a terrible wave had washed the occupants away.

• • •

Sarah found her husband in his study with a newspaper and a flask of coffee. His half-finished memoir teetered on the edge of his desk, casting a long shadow on the floor below it. "We must go to Blue Pearl Island," she said. "The people there are in trouble."

He checked his watch, then a chart on the wall. "There are two hours left of this morning's tide. What kind of trouble?"

"It's impossible to say. But the front door is open, and the place looks empty. At least one of the windows is broken."

"Perhaps the people that were staying there have left?"

"Their boat has been cut loose."

Charles looked at her as if her thoughts were written on glass, transparent and fragile. "Sarah, dearest, you always think the best of people. They probably had a party, made a mess of the place, and then ran away from their responsibilities."

She took a deep, dismissive breath. "Charles, no one runs away from a broken window."

"Then what are you suggesting?"

"They could be dead. A fire could have broken out. It's impossible to say. There are clothes strewn on the grass."

Henrietta appeared in the doorway behind her. "One of them could have fallen ill and spread the disease to the others."

Charles stood up and slapped down his newspaper with a rare burst of energy. "You too, Henrietta? I'll have none of this." His face fell. Charles had daydreamed of a second marriage as if it were the acquisition of another chess piece for his side of the board, but instead his new wife not only overpowered him in most arguments but encouraged his daughter to do the same. "Clothes strewn on the grass could mean all sorts of immorality." The colonel's thoughts turned dark, and he loosened his collar. "If something disreputable has happened, then we should send one of the local men to investigate. It's no place for a woman."

"There isn't time," said Sarah. "If we go up to the village, we'll miss too much of the tide. Charles, I'd rather you came with me, but I'm going to the island now. Henrietta will be quite all right by herself."

He sighed, once again checkmated by the women in his life. "Well, if we must go, then let us hurry."

"Thank you."

He took a revolver and a raincoat, though the day was bright and peaceful. They left Henrietta with a sandwich for lunch and a book to keep her amused, then the two of them hurried down to the sandy inlet at the end of the road, where they kept a small dinghy and two oars. Charles dragged it into the water and the two of them got in.

Having grown up locally, and having been an adventurous young boy, he knew the route through the rocks by heart; he'd learned it before the house was even built, when the island was safe for children's games. "What do you think we'll find there?" he said, taking the oars.

"Disruption," said Sarah, sitting by herself at the stern of the boat. "But, please, let me concentrate and memorize the route." Charles laughed gently, as he always did when it came to her constant efforts to acquire knowledge. "In case I need to come back alone."

At this distance, the effect of the black rocks lurking beneath the tide was to spread a thin white foam across the expanse of the sea. Their simple wooden boat cut through it like a knife cutting into a wedding cake. The colonel didn't turn his head but steered by the things he saw in their wake, with the treacherous fearlessness of a teenage boy.

Occasionally, Sarah thought, there are things to admire about him.

• • •

The route took them to the right of the island, as seen from the shore, and then behind it to land on the left side. At the back of it—the part that pointed out to sea, away from the sun—the clustered rocks rose to a surprising height; a section of them was cut away in a sudden sharp drop, forming a kind of cliff. That left a flat wall of dark stone overlooking the sea, like an eye patch. At the bottom of this cliff were a few yards of sandy slope leading down to the water, too steep to be called a beach.

Sarah, looking ahead, was the first to see it. That short gray patch of sand, scattered with coarse grass and seaweed, held two dead bodies: tilted forward for display. Charles glanced over his shoulder and wiped the sweat from his brow. He turned back to Sarah, his face crumpled into what was clearly meant as a question mark. "They're dead, Charles. We must hurry." He took the oars again. As they approached the beach, it became clear the bodies were a man and a woman, both twisted into impossible angles, as if they'd been picked up by some monstrous sea creature and wrung out like wet bathing suits, then left to dry on the sand.

Sarah leaned forward; she recognized them. "Oh God, that's Mr. and Mrs. Stubbs. He was so friendly, and she seemed so sweet." She made the sign of the cross.

The colonel was standing now in the center of the tiny craft, upsetting its balance with his usual casual confidence, his pistol pointed at the sky. "What happened? Have they been murdered?"

"They fell," she said. "It could have been suicide. Or an accident. Or they could have been murdered."

"Both of them?" He seemed confused.

"It looks that way." She didn't tell him the image that was forming in her mind, of the eight guests drunkenly throwing their servants off the cliff.

"Then it would be madness to continue. Their murderer may still be on the island."

"The house looked abandoned."

"This morning? But the killer could have just been asleep."

Sarah knew this was a possibility, but in truth the danger appealed to her. "The evidence suggests otherwise."

There was a loud scraping sound. The colonel promptly sat down again and tilted the oars up toward his chin. The boat had drifted. "The rocks! It's not safe to linger here. Should we go on or turn back?"

They arrived at the island's only landing place a few minutes later. No sign of life had shown itself in that time. Kneading his tired hands as if they were made of clay, the colonel looked up toward the house at the top of the grassy slope.

"Hell Island." The words shocked his wife, as if he had sworn.

He signaled for her to wait while he disembarked, with the gun held out before him. Then he tied up the boat, turned toward the house, and reached back to offer his arm. She took it just to please him, but the gesture ended with him holding her hand while she stood uphill and towered over him: a parent with a small child. He frowned and adjusted his glasses.

"Wait here, my darling."

He stepped forward tentatively, one pace at a time. There was a tang of excrement coming from a nearby patch of grass, and she hoped he would hurry up.

At the top of the slope, he cried out. A cry of disgust more than of fear or pain, with a slight stifled retch behind it. Sarah raced forward. He motioned for her to stay back, repeating the gesture until she was standing by his side, then he took a handkerchief out of his pocket and held it over his mouth. He was looking down at another dead body. A man, lying facedown on the ground.

Sarah spoke as the realization came to her: "The pile of clothes strewn on the grass."

Her husband looked up and confirmed that their own summer-house was just about visible, if you knew where to look for it, with a direct view of this spot.

"Henrietta," said Sarah, wondering if the girl was watching them now.

The colonel stepped in front of the body. "I wouldn't want her to see this. I'm not sure you should see it yourself. Perhaps you should wait in the boat, my daffodil. Where it's safe."

Sarah looked at him playfully. "Charles, you would get hopelessly lost in the house by yourself. Besides, there is no reason to think it's any safer in the boat."

He frowned. "There's a wire around his neck. Maybe that's what he died of?"

"A garrote, attached to a weight. It's been tricked to pull tight when the weight is dropped, with a catch so it can't be loosened. A painful death." She shuddered. "And a particularly nasty trap. The kind of thing you'd use to catch a rabbit."

The colonel examined the small metal clasp at the back of the body's neck and wondered how she'd inferred that whole mechanism. "Come away," he said. "This is a horrid sight."

She ignored him. "We have three dead bodies now."

"Killed by the same person, do you think?"

"Perhaps. Though the methods are very different."

She considered whether one of the guests had gone mad and tried to kill the others, then the rest had fled. Or whether they'd all turned against one another.

"More than one killer? A disturbing idea."

"It's possible." Sarah knelt down and looked closely at the body. She was thinking back to the faces that had passed her by along the lane on Friday, as she'd clipped the dead flowers from the rosebushes. Smiling, excited faces. Had he been one of them? She believed he had. She could see him wearing a brown suit, walking with a younger man, the yellow sheet of instructions folded into his top pocket. He'd worn glasses then. It was the younger man who had mentioned Unwin, and this man who had confessed to not knowing him. She stood up.

"His clothes are dry, though it's been raining for the last two days. He died recently."

Charles frowned. "This morning, you mean?"

"Possibly."

The door of the house banged shut behind them. The wind was picking up now, blowing a fine spray of water across the island, thousands of tiny droplets, like little fish. Charles approached the silent snow-white house with his gun held out and stood for a moment as a soft gray outline in front of its sharp black door, then the door blew open once again and he stepped inside.

• • •

"Hello? Is anybody there? I have a gun. Please, make yourself known."

The house returned a silence as unpleasant as a bowl of cold soup.

Sarah followed him into the main hall. It was an awkwardly shaped room that reached to the whole height of the house, with black and white tiles on the floor. A low bench, meant for changing shoes, was placed to the right of the door, but there was no other furniture. Opposite that was a wooden staircase that led to an upper story. An unopened can of beans sat on the bottom step.

A series of muddy paw prints covered the floor; something had entered through the opened door and walked in circles over the tiles.

Charles and Sarah searched the room, their footsteps echoing. All of the doors were closed, except for a small misshapen one: huddled under the staircase, slanted at the top and with a simple magnetic latch instead of a lock. The magnet had proved too weak for the wind, and now the door swung back and forth rhythmically, as if the house were breathing. From beyond it came a sound like the scurrying of rats.

Charles walked up to the door and nudged the barrel of his pistol through the gap, then worked it open with his left foot. The dim, windowless room inside was lined with display cases. A miniature museum. The cases were full of clocks. Clocks of different colors, different ages, some with elaborate mechanisms and some simple. Many of them were still ticking. And laid out on the floor beneath them, neatly and respectfully—the head covered—was a human figure. A woman, judging by the clothes.

Sarah knelt and removed the veil. A young-looking middle-aged woman, her face gray but her hair still colorful. She was wearing a red cardigan over a white shirt, which was spotted with blood toward the top. Her face had a slight, sad frown and wide, frightened eyes; two extravagant green earrings rested against her cheeks. Sarah remembered her walking past the garden two days before, the red cardigan in particular.

She'd been walking with an older man; they'd found something they disagreed on and were engaged in a passionate dispute.

The woman's body was slightly too long for the room, so she'd been placed at a diagonal with her head propped up in one corner. Sarah felt around her throat, touched the dried blood at the corners of her lips, and forced open her mouth.

Charles was keeping a watch on the hall behind them, occasionally turning to look around the room. "These clocks all show different times, Sarah. Do you think there is some kind of code?"

"I think the clocks are just decoration."

He gave a doubtful grunt. "Well, then. What killed her?"

"I can't quite tell. Something internal. She seems to have swallowed something."

He choked down a touch of vomit and put the back of his hand to his lips, leaving his fingers dangling absurdly from his face like some kind of tentacled sea creature. "Come," said Sarah, moving past him.

"Must we find all ten of them dead?"

"Perhaps," she said. "Though nine is more likely."

A quick intake of breath. "And the tenth?"

"Escaped, probably. Either that or hiding."

• • •

The two largest doors leading off from the entrance hall opened into a grand dining room with a high ceiling, its corners lost in cobwebs. The windows along one side reached three-quarters of the way up to the roof, giving a magnificent view of the frothing, furious sea. Once inside, they closed the doors and Charles made a crude barricade with a serving table and a chair.

The room itself was a mess. The table had been set for a large meal, used once and never cleared. The diners hadn't even reached dessert, so that plates of half-eaten savory food dotted the length of the table, the remnants of sauces dried into dusty and cracked crescent shapes, like sores from a particularly unpleasant disease. Charles counted them. Eight places. That would be the entire group, minus the two servants. Eight chairs were set back from the table, some neatly and some in disarray. Two had fallen over.

"An argument erupted at dinner," said Charles, scraping at a spot of blood, or possibly sauce, on the tablecloth.

"Something must have happened to the servants," said Sarah, "to prevent this mess from being cleared." Thrown over the cliff, she thought.

She was examining a knife and fork. One of the tines of the fork was missing, with a neat hole in its place. She put it down and lifted up a plate. A square of white cardboard was hidden underneath it.

There was a short printed message on one side. Sarah read it out loud: "*Mrs. Annabel Richards, a teacher, is accused of taking sexual gratification from the torture of young children.*" Charles winced at the choice of words. There was nothing printed on the reverse.

"I think that's her in the room with the clocks," said Sarah.

"How can you know?"

"Children, that's how. When they passed me two days ago, she and another man were discussing the education of children. He was a doctor, I gathered, and she sounded like a teacher."

"Look, here's another one." Charles lifted a handbag from the table, beneath which there was a bloodstained napkin and a clean white card. He read the message printed on it. "*Andrew Parker, a lawyer, is accused of killing his family.*" He held the card up to the light; there were no other clues. "Could that be the man outside, caught in the snare?"

"I don't know. Perhaps."

While Charles stood hypnotized by the brutality of the situation, staring at the single card in his hand, Sarah found two more of them on the floor beneath the table. The first read: *Richard Branch, socialist, is accused of hounding an old man to his death.*

The other: *Thomas Townsend, alcoholic, is accused of murdering his wife.*

"They make no sense," said Charles with a sigh. "The mystery only deepens."

Sarah shook her head. "These cards explain everything. These people were brought here to be judged."

"But why would they come, if they were to be judged?"

"I assume they were tricked into it. By someone with a corrupted sense of justice. Or someone with a need for revenge."

Charles grunted. "This was meant to be a kind of courtroom, then?"

He stared in astonishment at the very thought of it; Sarah patted his shoulder. "Something like that, Charles. And it seems that four of them at least were sentenced to death."

• • •

At the far end of the room, two doors led through to a decadent lounge, which ran along the side of the house at a right angle to the dining room. The windows here had deep-red curtains, like thick smears of blood. All of the furniture either looked out through them, over the waves toward the coast, or pointed at a fireplace in the center of the opposite wall. Blood-red upholstery was everywhere, like spilled wine.

The center of the room was covered in ash; a feathery semicircle of gray smudges spread out from the fireplace and covered the table-tops and cushions. Sarah followed the trail of burnt debris inward. She found animal hairs and charred splinters of wood scattered across the floorboards, pieces of coal and several small fragments of white card.

One of the accusations must have been thrown on the fire.

"Look at this," she said, taking a log from the basket beside the fireplace and holding it out toward Charles. A small opening had been drilled in one end and filled with a gritty black powder.

He touched it, then held his forefinger to his nose. "Gunpowder. I would know the smell anywhere."

"A nasty trick to play on someone. It would burn normally for a few minutes and then explode." Sarah ran her hand across the chair nearest the fireplace and felt a mass of wooden shards poking out of the cloth, only vaguely visible against the dark fabric. "There's no blood here; it seems that nobody fell for it."

"It's lucky the whole house didn't burn down."

"This tells us the violence wasn't necessarily targeted. Anybody could have been killed by this, which means they were all brought here to die."

"Then who was their accuser?"

She considered the question. "Let's keep looking."

. . .

A smaller door took Sarah back into the entrance hall. She waited there for Charles while he looked out of the lounge window, trying to spot their own house. When he was done, she opened the door to the next room.

"Careful," he cried out.

She stepped inside. It was a study, but one almost empty of furniture. There was a desk and a glass-paneled bookcase; inexplicably, both were covered with a thick black soot. She ran her finger over the desk, leaving a line in the sludge.

At one side of the bookcase was a small window, and underneath that were two more dead bodies. They were laid out like market produce, stacked sloppily in a shallow pile. They were both women, one of them young and one old. Sarah remembered them clearly; she'd been weeding the foxgloves as they walked past the house, two days earlier. An affluent lady and her traveling companion, that much was clear. The older one had been bossy, a bully even; it was obvious from the sheepish way the younger one would respond to everything with single, conciliatory words and the way the older one would keep talking regardless, her speech never once deflected by a lack of interest.

Charles shuffled into the room behind her. "It smells of smoke in here." He left the door open and hovered on the threshold; his manner had become that of a child who has spent too long in an art gallery.

The two bodies were both saturated with smoke. The young woman's hair was gray with it and the old woman's almost black. Charles stepped past Sarah and opened the window, reveling in the clean sea breeze. He looked down at the bodies and tutted. "I make that six," he said. "And the killer still unaccounted for. I think we've seen enough of this place—we should leave."

"There is more to find."

"It's not safe here."

Sarah didn't respond; she was examining a small hole in the wall on one side of the room. Its presence there was unexplained. A few tins of food, a Bible, a bottle of pills, and a pitcher of blackened water were concealed under the desk, but there was very little else in the room. She gave the two dead women a cursory examination, but their pockets were empty. They'd both been carrying handbags when she'd seen them before, but they'd presumably been lost in the panic somewhere.

She walked toward the door. "It might have been these two that burned the accusations against them."

"That could well be." Charles stopped her. "Sarah, I know you like to show resolve, but are you really all right with all this horror and danger? Maybe we should rest a minute before we move on?"

She sensed the pleading embarrassment at the back of his words. "Charles, darling, I'm perfectly fine." And with a hand on his shoulder she ushered him out of the room.

As they left, she ran her other hand down the inside of the door-jamb, which the soot had not reached. "Interesting," she said to herself.

• • •

The next room along was a small library. There was nothing notable inside except for a large desk, made from a combination of wood and metal. An incongruous iron shelf emerged from the wall above it, at head height, and seemed to be linked to the desk somehow. Sarah studied it carefully while Charles stood in the doorway.

The house was not excessively large and, aside from a closet, which was seemingly untouched, the rest of the rooms on the ground floor were all dedicated to the preparation of food. The black and white tiles from the main hall continued into this part of the house, where it was noticeably colder and their footsteps were noticeably louder. Charles led the way, his gun pointed before him and his other arm held protectively in front of his wife, while she walked patiently behind. Together they searched the kitchens and the few small storerooms but found nothing. No more bodies and nobody left alive, just chaos and mess.

It was clear that there'd come a time, during the convulsions the household had suffered, when the occupants had decided that it was appropriate to stockpile weapons and supplies, and the kitchens had been raided for both. The canned goods had all vanished, except where they'd fallen from desperately cradled armloads and rolled into corners or been kicked across the tiles. A tin of pears in syrup lay on a mat by the back door, next to a tin of corned beef and a pair of Wellington boots. Knives had tumbled from their hooks, and pans had been taken as containers for water.

In a small pantry the floor was swampy with discarded foodstuffs, spilled flour, and smashed pots of honey. Footsteps of frozen meat were defrosting along the length of the corridors, with teeth marks where they'd been chewed at the edges. Those meager supplies they had seen under the desk in the smoke-stained room, and whatever else they might find upstairs, had come at the cost of all this mess. In many ways it was a more horrifying testament to the ordeal undergone here than the bodies themselves.

"At some point, civility broke down," said Sarah. "And they must have taken to their rooms with supplies. It confirms what I've been thinking."

"And what's that, my darling?"

"The accuser was one of the ten guests. If it was someone else, the guests would have united against them. But instead they turned on one another. So the killer must have kept their identity secret."

"While he killed the other nine, one by one? So you think one of the accusations will be a fake?"

"Either a fake or a confession."

Charles swallowed uncomfortably. "Then there may be three more bodies to find. And where do you think the killer went once they'd finished?"

He held his breath while waiting for her answer.

"Maybe they took the boat and left. Or maybe they're still here."

• • •

The upper floor of the house was less imposing. The staircase twisted around to reach a landing with a large window, and from there two corridors stretched in opposite directions to the two ends of the house.

Every room on this floor was either a bedroom or a bathroom. The bedrooms varied wildly in size and opulence, and some had bathrooms of their own. "If there's anyone left alive," said Charles, "they're probably in one of these rooms."

He insisted that Sarah open the first door with her fingertips, standing flat against the wall beside it, while he stood in the doorway and gripped his gun with both hands. She indulged him, finding the method faintly comical; the door swung back anticlimactically to reveal the quarters of the two servants.

Inside were twin beds, the sheets a drab gray color. The rest of the furniture was minimal. It was close to the head of the stairs and had presumably been chosen so they could come and go early in the morning without disturbing anyone. Both beds were made and the curtains were drawn; except for an opened Bible, the Stubbses had left no trace of their occupancy.

Opposite that was another simple room, with a single brown bed.

The window above it was smashed. It was the window they'd seen through the telescope, though it was clear now that a lot of the glass had been removed by hand.

"Perhaps there was a fight," said Charles.

Sarah looked in the drawers of a small desk; they were empty. Beside that was a wastebasket, containing a thick green candle. "Or someone made themselves an escape route."

There were two more bedrooms along that side of the house: one exceedingly large, with its own bathroom and balcony, the other more modest and without any appendages. Both contained beds that had been slept in, though only one of them had been made, and both had dressers covered with a host of female accoutrements.

"The quarters of the two women downstairs," Sarah remarked. "Can you guess which is which?"

Charles grunted, half in amusement and half disapproval. "They are equal in the eyes of God now."

The last room along that corridor was unremarkable, with a toilet, sink, and shower. The shower curtain was torn down and the floor was covered with water, but there were no other signs of damage.

. . .

They turned back and crossed the landing to the other corridor. Five doors looked out at them from alternating sides of the hallway, all closed.

The first opened into a bathroom, with a tasteless olive-toned carpet. A cabinet above the sink had been searched through in a hurry, but there was nothing else of interest.

The next door was locked. Charles banged on it for several minutes with the base of his gun, but there was no answer. He searched for a key but found nothing. "This seems ominous," he said.

"There are three doors left," said Sarah. "And three bodies missing. We'll have to return to this one later."

The next door along was also locked. The one after that opened into a slim, light room with a single bed placed alongside the wall. On the bed lay a woman, dressed in her daytime clothes. She was still wearing her shoes. She seemed to be asleep, but they both knew she wasn't. The few other things in the room were a desk beside the bed and a book of Russian short stories left at an angle that implied it had recently been read. Her traveling bag was at the foot of the bed, but nothing was unpacked. A handful of other books were lined up on a shelf above the desk, a notable gap where one had been removed.

"I remember her," said Sarah, thinking back to the bright-blue eye shadow this woman had been wearing two days before. "She walked past me with a handsome young man. He was very quiet, and she was doing most of the talking. She was giving her opinions on the countryside."

Charles nodded. "It's very sad, she's only about your age. But I can't say I'm surprised."

He didn't clarify this cryptic comment and they both left the room.

Behind the last door they found the body of a young man, also lying dead on his bed, though he was wearing his nightclothes and was under the covers. The room was equally bare.

"The quiet young man?"

Sarah nodded. His bag was fully unpacked; she found the optimism of that touching, in light of later developments. "So sad," she said. "He seemed a very nice type."

"Well, certainly an attractive one." And Charles pulled the sheets up to cover his face.

Sarah knelt to retrieve something from under the bed; it was another book. *Tales of Mystery and Imagination.* She turned to the desk opposite the bed. A dark-green candle was placed there, half melted. She ran her finger carefully over the tumbling wax. "The room next door had a green candle like this, which had also been lit. These last two rooms are both without electrical lighting. I think the candle must contain something poisonous."

"That gets released when it's burned, you mean?"

"Yes. A poison mixed into the wax, which creates a deadly vapor. It must be what killed the two of them, this man and the woman next door; it's the only thing they have in common. They were probably the first to die. I saw a candle thrown away in one of the other rooms."

Charles looked skeptical. "How can you tell they were the first?"

Sarah pointed at the bed. "They've been examined and laid out neatly and respectfully. All the other bodies we've found have just been left where they died, except for the woman in the room with the clocks. All three of them must have died before the panic set in, before anyone knew what was happening. And these two must have died at the same time; the poisoned candle is too obvious a trick for it to work twice."

He took her hand. "That's very clever, my darling. But we can't stand here and theorize all day. There's a shed outside—it might contain an ax or something. To take down those two locked doors. Then we must leave."

"I will wait here." She wanted to investigate further.

He shook his head. "Heavens, no. It's not safe. The killer could spring from behind those two doors at any moment."

"It will be fine, Charles. Every movement in this house is announced by a loud creak. And those two doors are locked. If I hear a single footstep or a key colliding with metal, I'll immediately run out and find you."

"Very well," he sighed, "I suppose there's a logic to that. But do be careful, my petal."

"Besides," she added, "the killer is more likely to be hiding in the shed."

He paled, trying to look brave. "Well, then."

And he kissed her and left before she could push him away.

• • •

Sarah stood alone at the end of the corridor; the silence was like a warm bath.

She pressed her forehead against the wall. It was an unladylike habit—Charles would have disapproved—but it helped her to concentrate. No distractions, just her and her thoughts and the hot feeling in her forehead from the friction as it slid imperceptibly along the wallpaper. And then she had it: "Where is the best place to hide a leaf? In a forest. And where is the best place to hide a piece of paper?"

She entered the room with the dead young woman. "Russian short stories," she said to herself, taking the heavy volume off the desk. "Forgive me, but you didn't seem the type. This book was picked because of its size." She searched through its pages. "And yet in many ways you were the most astute."

Tucked inside were a folded handwritten note and a small white square of cardboard, netted with faint lines that indicated it had at some point been screwed into a ball. *Scarlett Thorpe, slattern, is accused of seducing a man and persuading him to suicide for her own benefit.*

The accusation seemed even more brutal in the silence of the bedroom.

The note was more welcoming in its tone. Sarah sat down on the bed to read it: *I find myself in the most extraordinary set of circumstances. I was invited here for the weekend by a man called Unwin, who got my details from a previous employer. He didn't specify which one. He needed someone to act as his niece while meeting prospective clients. He wanted to stress that his was a traditional family business. All I had to do was make a good first impression, appear competent, that sort of thing. So I followed instructions and found myself traveling with a number of other people, all of whom had been approached by this man Unwin. It wasn't clear to me whether they were the clients in question, so I introduced myself as his niece to be on the safe side. I didn't know that we were going to an island. That did seem odd, but I didn't think of turning back. The money was too good. Unwin's man Stubbs rowed us over. He told us Unwin was delayed and would be joining us later. There are eight of us, plus Stubbs and his wife.*

Sarah turned the page.

It was all rather strange from the start. There was far too much small talk and a general sense of confusion. Then at dinner Mrs. Stubbs gave us all envelopes with our names on them, only she hadn't learned our names yet and had to call them out like it was the register at school. Each of the letters accused its recipient of some undiscovered crime. That caused quite the uproar. One man read his out, and there was some squabbling about whether the rest of us should do the same. We all did, in the end. Except for two ladies who caused a fuss. An exotic old bird, Mrs. Tranter, and her caged companion, Sophia. She's one of those insufferable religious types who'll never admit to a flaw. I stood behind them, though, and could read most of it. Something about them traveling in Amsterdam and pushing a beggar into a canal. Fairly horrid. Then the doctor—a man I don't like the look of—did the very manly thing of assuming authority.

Sarah knew the man she meant; he'd walked past her house with the schoolteacher in the red cardigan. His wasn't one of the bodies they'd so far discovered.

He turned on Stubbs, but Stubbs insisted he was just following instructions and had never met Unwin. There was almost a fight. He's a wild one, that doctor. I got some awkward questions too, being the man's niece, so I came clean about the whole thing. The funny thing is, my accusation was mostly true. It basically said I seduced Benny and then talked him into killing himself. Well, the seduction was mutual, but it's true I gave him the pills and told him to use them. The world is better off without a man like that, too keen with his hands. Not many people knew about it, though. Unwin had certainly done his research. Then, in the midst of all this, as if it wasn't chaos enough, a shrewish lady along the table started to choke. We thought it was just shock at first, then it got serious. She was given water to swallow, but it came back up bright red. They tried patting her on the back, but that only seemed to make it worse. Then she was all around the room, flailing at the furniture and making the most horrible sounds. Eventually she collapsed into the curtains, dead. In a way, she's done the rest of us a favor. Whatever kind of blackmail Unwin had planned, the police will have to be involved now. Stubbs says he will row to the mainland at the first opportunity tomorrow morning. A lucky escape, all considered. I won't be able to sleep tonight. There is somebody coughing at the far end of the hallway.

The note ended there.

. . .

Charles returned a few minutes later. "My dear, you've moved. I thought the worst had happened."

She showed him the note. He was holding a small ax in one hand, the gun in the other; he put both down beside the book and read carefully. "So the death she describes at the end is the woman we found with the clocks?"

"It seems that way."

"Do you think she could have been poisoned, then? Something in her food?"

"I found a fork on the dining table that was missing a tine. I believe she choked on that. There was a hole where it might have slotted in. Once stuck in a tough piece of meat, it would have just slid right out and been swallowed." Charles narrowed his eyes and mimed eating from a fork. "The hole was wedge-shaped, as if the hidden end had been sharpened. A blade, designed to get stuck in the throat."

"That's abominable—the poor woman."

Sarah shrugged. "She was a torturer, apparently. Did you find anything outside?"

He drew back his shoulders. "I searched the whole island in the end. When I was in the shed I heard movement and went to investigate. It was only a seagull, but since I'd started, I decided to check everywhere. There's no trace of anyone alive, and no more bodies either. The only place I didn't look is the beach, where Stubbs and his wife are. There is a way to get down to it, but it's a precarious path and I wanted to get back to you."

"We know now that Stubbs and his wife died fourth and fifth. I was wrong, of course, about these two. They weren't the first to die.

That was the schoolteacher. Then when everybody went to bed—early, probably, after all the drama of the evening—they both lit candles and stayed awake. One to write and one to read. Both died, poisoned by the candle fumes. Three deaths: That's when the situation must have dawned on them all. One could be unlucky but not three. I assume that Stubbs and his wife were already dead by the time these two bodies were discovered. They must have been killed early the next morning, before the dining room could be cleared. The obvious explanation is that Unwin asked to meet them by the top of that cliff—perhaps to get their stories straight before telling the police about the little accident at dinner—and pushed them over while they were off guard."

"The note doesn't mention Stubbs—or his wife, for that matter—being accused of anything. Why bring them here at all?"

"To help with the preparations. After that they must have been seen as expendable. It would have been impractical, I assume, to try and find a servant with an undiscovered crime in their past who was also willing to work for a pittance."

"I see." Charles looked morose. "At least their deaths were relatively quick and painless. Maybe that explains it."

"Unwin has a heart, of sorts."

"We must check the other rooms; come."

• • •

Charles beat at the first door with the ax, hacking at the hinges until the whole thing came away in his hands. He lost his grip on the gun and started to panic, the tumbling door pushing him back against the wall—like a child building a fort of furniture—but no one came rushing out at him. Sarah stepped over the door and into the empty room. There were no bodies, just a bare bed and a bare lightbulb. Facing her was a small window. There wasn't even a candle. A lone mosquito watched from the ceiling beside the bulb.

Behind the door was a suitcase, neither locked nor fully closed, and a pile of canned foods. On the floor next to that was a fork, a large carving knife, and a basin full of water. "Someone made preparations," said Charles, "locked the room, and then never came back."

They took the door off the next room in a similar fashion. This time Charles moved back as soon as it started to topple and waited with his two weapons. "These rooms would have offered little protection, if push came to shove."

This room was larger, with a double bed and a bathroom at the back of it. They noticed a series of scratches, bloody and splintered, around the doorframe. "There was violence here," said Charles.

"Of course," said Sarah. "It's the safest room. It has a supply of water and no balcony or other entrance. They probably fought over it."

The bed was a mess: unmade, littered with tins of sweet corn. The contents of a suitcase were strewn across the floor.

"There's a shape in the bathtub." Charles stepped slowly toward the bathroom with his gun pointed. He reached the door and looked down. "Another one."

Sarah was approaching behind him. He turned. "Sarah, you mustn't."

She slid past him. The dead naked body of a man lay in the tub, which was still full of water. His body was covered in patches of singed flesh; his hair smelled burnt. There was water on the floor. "Come," she said. "This might not be safe."

They both sat down on the edge of the bed, where the blistered, skeletal figure was hidden from view. "I wonder if that was Mr. Townsend?"

Charles nodded. "Nine bodies, leaving just one guest unaccounted for."

Sarah looked concerned. "I remember the tenth. He was a doctor, I believe. He didn't seem very pleasant."

"Then you think he was Unwin? He killed the other nine?"

"That seems to be the only conclusion." She sighed. "It doesn't seem quite right."

"Why not?"

She shook her head. "There are missing pieces that I can't explain yet."

"Well, there is one place we haven't explored."

"The beach, where Stubbs and his wife fell."

"Yes," said Charles. "I used to play down there as a child. It's tarnished now." He looked at Sarah. "That man there, in the bath. How do you think he died?"

She answered abruptly, "He burned."

"You think perhaps the bath was tricked to give out boiling water from both the hot and cold taps?"

She shook her head. "You'd be able to sense that before you got in. No, he was electrocuted. The bath is porcelain, but the overflow outlet is made of metal. You could run a current through the center of that. It's a clever trick. He could have tested the water with his hand and found it perfectly safe, then only when he got in fully would the water level rise enough to reach the overflow outlet. That's when the electrocution would start. It would switch itself off too, when the outlet did its job and the level went back down. From the state of the body I imagine it took him a long time to die."

A barrier broke within Charles, and he rushed to the bathroom and vomited into the sink, the boiled corpse in the corner of his eye. Sarah came in after him and rubbed his back, sitting on the edge of the bath.

"Careful," he spluttered, pointing at the water.

"I am being careful." She sighed. "When you're ready, let's go and explore that beach."

• • •

It was the afternoon now. The tide was draining rapidly, and all around the island the water was scarred with rocks. They looked like a congregation of monsters, sleeping beneath the waves. It was a familiar sight to both of them, but Sarah had never seen it from this close before.

The sky was overcast, and a ceaseless wind blew in toward the coast. What a miserable place to die, she thought.

Charles led them over the few slight hills that formed the distant side of the island, and when they came to the cliff, both were fearful of getting too close.

"Here." Charles showed her a path leading between the bushes: It wound back and forth along the cliff and then, after a short scramble over a rock, came out on the sands at the base.

They proceeded one carefully placed step at a time. When they crested the rock, Stubbs was staring up at them, his dead eyes glazed with fear and his chin propped on a slight rise in the sand. The rest of his body followed the upward angle of the slope: His neck must be broken. Mrs. Stubbs looked more peaceful, facedown in a halo of wet sand. Both arms and both legs seemed to be broken.

"She must have landed like a cat," said Charles.

He lifted her body with one hand and found that the sand underneath was red. The impact had pulled her jaw upward, slightly away from her body; the soft neck was split open. Her clothes were wet. He searched through them and found a damp white square of card in a pocket of her apron. Mr. Stubbs had landed closer to the water; Sarah found a soggier version of the same card in one of his pockets, wrapped in a handkerchief spotted with blood. They looked the same as the accusations had, but printed on them were the words *You are no longer needed.*

"That's particularly cruel," said Charles.

"It fits my theory."

There was nothing else of interest on or about the servants' bodies, so they labored their way back to the top of the cliff. "We'd need equipment to move them," said Charles, prompted by nothing.

When he reached the top, he turned and looked at the cold expanse of sea, as if the sight was cleansing, though around the island the sea looked diseased. "It's been an unusually cold year," he said morosely.

This set something ticking in Sarah's mind; she watched the clock-work motions of the distant waves and sought connections. Color came into her face. "That's what we missed."

She raced off toward the house. Charles, uncomprehending, struggled to keep up with her.

As they passed the body in the grass by the front door, Charles caught hold of her and slowed her down. "That man there, strangled by the wire," he said between breaths. "You said you thought he'd died recently, possibly this morning. Could he have been in on it, with Unwin?"

"We'll come back to him." She shook his hand off her shoulder and pushed through the front door, up the stairs, and along the corridor to the left, into the empty room they'd found locked earlier.

"Tell me what's wrong here, Charles."

"The room is unused and the bed is made, but there's a suitcase."

"That's true, but there's a more obvious discrepancy. It's a cold year, as you said. I've yet to see a single mosquito. Except for that one up there." The lone mosquito was still on the ceiling, next to the lightbulb.

She tested the bed with her hand: It would take her weight. Then she climbed up on it and inspected the insect. It didn't move. One flick and it fell to the floor, bouncing into a corner of the room.

Charles retrieved it. "It's a toy, a model. Made of wire. Do you think that's significant?"

But she was already busy pulling the sheets from the bed. There was no mattress, just a hard metal framework covered in canvas. "Give me a hand with this."

They applied pressure to the bar at the top of the bed and were able to lift it up; the bed was covered with a kind of metal lid. Inside, it was hollow. A fine mesh was stretched across the opening, with a large rent in the middle, and through this they could see the missing tenth body. Charles went to her side. "The doctor?"

She nodded.

"He's Unwin, then?"

She shook her head. "No one would do this to himself. I've seen this kind of mesh used for cheap camping equipment. You can sit or lie on it and it will take your weight, but try to stand on it and with the pressure you'll fall straight through. The lid must have been open, disguised as part of the wall. So when he stood on the bed, he would have stood on this mesh." She tore the rest of the netting away from the edges. "The base is covered in spikes, barbed so that he became hooked on them. And this lever would have released that catch once he put his weight on it, which made the lid spring shut. Then he bled to death in the dark." A half inch of blood filled the base of the hollowed bed.

"And the mosquito?"

"Just a trick to get him to stand on the bed."

Charles slammed his hand against the wall. "Such diabolical trickery. Maybe Unwin wasn't one of the guests, then. Has it occurred to you that he could have come here weeks ago and set these traps in place? He didn't need to be here to watch them play out."

"That doesn't quite work. The traps wouldn't be enough by themselves. Think of the man garroted outside, for example."

"But all ten of them are dead."

She put her hand to her forehead. "I know, but one of them must be guilty. It's just a case of working out which one."

"Well, if we've reached an impasse, then I say that at this point we let the police take over. The tide still looks high enough."

She rolled her eyes. "No, Charles. Come with me."

They went back downstairs, to the lounge covered in ash and fragments of wood. "The chronology is fairly easy to establish. But let's be explicit about it, and the rest should fall into place. The first day is for arrivals. Then there are all the accusations over dinner and the first death, the woman who swallowed her fork. I imagine they retire early, too shaken to spend an evening talking to strangers. And the servants presumably too busy cleaning up the body to clear away after dinner. That could be taken care of at dawn. Meanwhile, two of the guests are poisoning themselves with candles. The other five wake up the next morning and make their way down here. But the servants have been dispensed with already, and breakfast is not forthcoming. Perhaps they assume that both of the Stubbses have gone to the mainland, but eventually suspicion sets in. Two of the guests are sleeping implausibly late. They search the rooms and find the bodies, and it's clear that something sinister is under way. I would suggest that at this point they search the island for any intruders and find the bodies of Stubbs and his wife. That's when things must have broken down; there had been five murders and there are five left alive. They find nobody else as they search the island, so they know that one of the five of them must be up to something. There's an urgent conference in the lounge, complete with exploding logs. Rather than trying to find safety in numbers, they gather supplies and lock themselves in their rooms. There's even a fight for the best room. Do you follow me so far?"

Charles nodded eagerly.

Sarah continued: "That may have taken them through to the second evening or the following morning, but at some point the two ladies leave their room and move their stash of supplies to the study next door. Why? Because the bedrooms aren't safe. One man is boiled in the bathtub, another is slowly bleeding to death inside his bed. Between the two of them their screams would fill the whole top floor of the house. And both of them are behind locked doors. The older man, the one on the grass outside, is the only other guest left alive at this point. The two ladies knew each other before they came here, so their suspicion lands on him. Whether justified or not, they run to the study and push the desk against the door."

"But then how did they die?"

"Oh, that's easy." She walked to the mantel and pushed in a loose brick. "When this is pulled out, it creates a gap at the back of the chimney, and smoke will pour into the room next door, through a hole in the wall. The door to that room has no lock, but it locks whenever the window is open. You opened the window and I saw the bolt slide out from the doorframe; I could hear the pulleys running through the walls."

"And the window was too small to climb through. So they are being asphyxiated, and the only way they can save themselves is by closing the window—the one thing they will never try. Unwin has a putrid sense of humor. So the older man outside presumably lit the fire that killed them? But you don't think he is Unwin?"

"Let me consider that for a moment."

She sat down in one of the plush armchairs and began that habit again of applying pressure to her forehead to induce concentration, this time with the base of her palm. It didn't matter now that Charles could see her doing it; he wouldn't interrupt. He just watched, openmouthed. He couldn't hear her breathing and began to grow concerned, then she lurched upright as if waking from a nightmare. Her speech, however, was entirely calm.

"No, he wasn't Unwin. Though it's true that his death is the hardest to explain. All along there has been another presence here, though I couldn't quite connect it with anything. The schoolteacher, Mrs. Richards, choked on a tine of her fork. Or so I told you, but I looked in her mouth and felt along her throat and there was no obstruction. Either I was wrong or somebody removed it later. We found two burnt candles next to two dead bodies, but we didn't find any matches. The body in the bed was covered by a lid, itself covered with sheets to look like a bed. The lid was set to spring into place at a great deal of speed, and yet when we found it, the sheets on top of it were perfectly neat. And that was inside a locked room, but we found no trace of the key. Then the two women that died in the smoke-filled room were locked in by the mechanism of the window being opened, but when we found it the window was closed. And the desk was neatly placed against the wall."

"Well, the last man left could have done these things. The man lying in the grass outside. And if he was Unwin, he'd have had a key to all the rooms."

"Yes, but his death looks too much like murder. It was the hardest to work out, because there is so little of the mechanism left. But Unwin wouldn't have attacked him outright, even with a garrote: Too much could go wrong. There had to be a trick to it. And, of course, it's obvious when you step back and think about it. We found his body by the place where the boats are usually tied up: He had no reason to be there, unless he was about to take one. And how do you induce a man about to take a trip by boat to put a wire around his own neck?" Charles had no answer for her. "By handing him a life jacket. Or something made up to look like one, with a wire in the lining. All it would take is some cardboard and cheap fabric. It goes over the head, then the wire is around the man's neck and the weight is released. And that brings us to the other thing puzzling me: why none of them tried to take a boat on the second day, when half of their company was found to be dead. The sea was stormy that day; they wouldn't have made it. But I would have expected one of them to try it anyway; it's a more palatable death than any of these. Unless there was someone there to talk them out of it, to persuade them to wait another day, someone whose authority on the matter had recently been shown to them."

"You mean?"

"Stubbs."

He gasped.

"It was clear all along. I won't forgive myself for missing it. He was the only one that knew the route here through the rocks. When the storms were raging on the second day, he convinced them all to stay on the island. He had their trust because his wife had died; they thought of him as one of the victims. The deaths in the bed and the bath must have happened either that night or early the next morning, then the two women were killed by the morning fire. At high tide Stubbs announces it's safe to leave and they find there are only two of them left. The trick with the life jacket takes care of that, then Stubbs cuts the boat loose and goes to join his wife. He has a full set of keys so he can tidy the place up first. It should have been obvious; his death is the only one that looks remotely like suicide."

"But I don't understand, what was his motive?"

"I think he was dying. There was coughing at night. And we found a handkerchief in his pocket, spotted with blood. What if he decided to take some others with him? People guilty of unpunished crimes. Only a servant would know so many secrets. And he was a devout man; remember the Bible we found in his bedroom. Whether he saw his mission as justice or revenge, I don't know."

Charles was almost too shocked to speak. "My God, the man was a devil. I can't comprehend it."

Sarah gave him a look of sympathy.

He paused and took her hand. "Sarah, I am very proud of you, you really do have a mind for this kind of thing." She nodded shyly. "But let's not be too forthcoming with the police. We wouldn't want to give them the impression that we've been snooping around here. I'm sure they'll work it all out for themselves."

• • •

The sun had just set when the two of them got into their boat; the tide was coming in again, after a long and tedious afternoon, and the worst of the rocks were covered.

Sarah spoke. "Charles, it has just occurred to me: Should we attach a note to the front door, saying that we've gone for the police? In case anyone else comes here before we get back?"

He grunted. "It's a noble idea, but I don't have a pen or any paper. It's not very likely that anyone would come here at this time."

"But in the morning they might. And we don't know when we'll be back. There was a desk in the library, next to the kitchen. The top drawer had both a pen and some paper; I checked in there earlier."

"Well, then. You wait here and try to keep warm." He stood up; the boat rocked. "I shall be back soon."

He strolled up the slight incline and through the front door of the house.

The window of the library looked out onto the short wooden landing where Sarah sat in the boat. It was dark inside; the generator had switched itself off long ago. But she saw the rough shape of Charles enter the room, saw the dark smudge as he walked past the window, then she heard him swear as he tugged at the stuck drawer, heard the metallic thump and the yelp of a hinge as the trap she'd seen there earlier clicked into place, heard the brief cry as his head was severed from his body. It was a quick death.

"Charles," she said, "I told you it wouldn't work out." She took up the oars. "Forgive me, Henrietta." And she glanced in the direction of their house, wondering if the girl was still watching through the telescope. It was almost certainly too dark to see anything.

As she navigated through the rocks, along the route she'd memorized that morning, she found herself at several points rowing directly away from the meager beach with its two dead bodies. And with the play of moonlight on the water, there were a few moments when it seemed as if Stubbs was winking at her.

10

THE FIFTH
CONVERSATION

J ulia Hart finished reading the fifth story: *"And with the play of moonlight on the water, there were a few moments when it seemed as if Stubbs was winking at her."*

She lowered the manuscript.

The rain was gone and the sky was a flat, moderate blue, with a few clouds of different shapes and sizes, like a range of hats in a shop window. Grant and Julia were sitting in a quiet churchyard at the top of a slight hill, about a mile along the coast from his cottage; they'd walked up there after lunch. The ground was already dry.

"That was a bleak story," said Julia.

"Yes, it was." Grant lifted his hat and wiped his forehead with a handkerchief. "Ten dead bodies discovered on an island. It's an homage to my favorite crime novel."

"I thought as much."

"That ending was particularly nasty, when Sarah killed Charles for no reason."

"I suppose it wasn't entirely unjustified," said Julia, "given the context."

Grant shook his head in disagreement. "It's another depiction of the detective as a malevolent figure, an arrogant character who sees themselves as superior to the law."

"And it's another one set by the sea." Julia took out her notebook. "Is the sea an obsession of yours?"

"No, I wouldn't say that. It reminds me of my childhood, that's all."

Julia spoke hesitantly, remembering his outburst the previous night. "Did you grow up by the sea, then?"

Grant looked momentarily lost, watching her pen move back and forth. "We had holidays there, that's all."

She waited for him to say more, but he didn't. "I think that one's my favorite," she said. "In spite of how bleak it is."

He pulled his hat down over his eyes. "I am glad to hear that."

Julia was watching a pile of rocks a few yards away from them. She thought she'd seen a snake slithering among them a few minutes earlier. Just a small one. But it could have been a trick of the light.

Grant got to his feet and pushed the hat back up to his hairline. "Let's do some mathematics. I think it's time I went through the actual definition, don't you? It's simple, really."

Julia looked up. "I would like to hear it."

"Good." Grant found a broken olive branch, lying in the dirt by the rocks. He sat back down and started to draw in the sandy ground between them. "This is straight from my research paper, 'The Permutations of Detective Fiction.' Section one, subsection one."

He drew four circles on the dusty earth and labeled them S, V, D, and K.

"Do you know what this is?" he asked.

She squinted at the shapes, unsure of how to interpret his question.

"It's called a Venn diagram," he went on. "This is one in its embryonic form. Each circle represents a set, or a collection of objects." He drew a large oval around the four smaller circles, covering all of them, and scratched a *C* in the corner nearest her. "The sets are all made up of members of the cast. The cast is just the collective name we give to the characters in the book. Even the incidental ones. So the sets are collections of characters."

"Go on," she said.

"The circles represent the four ingredients that we've already discussed: a set of characters called the suspects, another called the victims, the detectives, and then the killers. To this we add four requirements. The number of suspects must be two or more, otherwise there is no mystery, and the number of killers and victims must be at least one each, otherwise there is no murder. We express those mathematically by talking about the cardinality, or size, of the sets: The cardinality of *S* is at least two, and the cardinalities of *K* and *V* are both at least one."

"Yes," she said. "That's straightforward."

"Then the final requirement is the most important: The killers must be drawn from the set of suspects. *K* must be a subset of *S*."

To illustrate this last point, he rubbed out the circle labeled *K* and drew it again, smaller, inside the circle labeled *S*. "That is how we show subsets in a Venn diagram."

"And so far that's just a summary of what we've said yesterday and this morning, I think?"

"Correct. But it's been stated formally now. And that defines a simple mathematical structure that we're going to call a *murder*. The next line is very important. I put a lot of thought into the phrasing of it."

She waited, her pen ready to write it down. "Go ahead."

"We say that a story qualifies as a *murder mystery* if the reader can sort its characters into these four sets and—crucially—the set of killers is identified in the text after the other three sets have been completed. That sentence is what joins the world of mathematics to the imprecise world of literature."

"And that's the entirety of the definition?"

"Yes, that is all of it. Any further stipulations you might want to make—rules on when the suspects must be introduced, when the murder must take place, and so on—would just open you up to a number of exceptions and counterexamples."

She looked puzzled. "I suppose its simplicity is what makes it hard to understand. It's not the structure itself that confuses me but why it should be considered significant."

He shrugged. "Mathematics often begins like that."

"There's nothing about clues, for instance, which are a staple of the genre."

"Yes, precisely." Grant leaned forward. "That is exactly why it's significant. With the definition in place, we can now make the argument that clues are not an essential part of a murder mystery. Go through any murder mystery and delete all the clues; you'll still have a murder mystery. As long as it fits this structure. So the definition is liberating, to some extent. Do you understand?"

"I think so."

"Let's take another example: the case of supernatural crimes. They're often considered forbidden in murder mysteries, but there's no reason the murder shouldn't be done by a ghost walking through walls as long as the ghost is introduced as one of the suspects before being exposed as the murderer. The definition tells us it will still be a valid murder mystery."

"Then what about the stories in this collection, *The White Murders*?"

"Ah." He clapped his hands together. "That's the other thing we can do with the definition: We can calculate with it. The standard murder mystery has a detective, a victim, and some suspects, with no overlap between any of them, and a single killer taken from the group of suspects. Well, now we can look at what we might call the *aberrant cases*, where either the group sizes are irregular or two or more of the groups overlap. There are only four components to a murder mystery, so the number of permutations is relatively small. We can calculate and list every single one of them. Every possible structure. That's what these stories were meant to explore."

Julia turned to a specific page in her notes. "So we've had a murder mystery with two suspects, one where the victims and suspects overlap, another where the detectives and killers overlap, and one where the killers and suspects are the same?"

"That's right," said Grant. "And the defining feature of the story we've just read is that the victims and the suspects are the same. In other words, there are no suspects other than the victims and no victims other than the suspects. We know that one or more of the victims killed all the others. The diagram for that would look like this."

He rubbed out the circle labeled V and wrote a new V next to the S.

Julia copied it down. "I've thought of something, though." Grant motioned for her to proceed, swirling the olive branch as a substitute for his hand. "How do you deal with the case where there are different crimes within a single story, each with different killers and victims?"

Grant sat back and pulled his hat down. He frowned. "That is a good question. We have to treat them as separate murder mysteries that happen to be bundled together in a single book. There's no other way to do it. It's cheating, really."

Julia was still making notes. "I see," she said, and closed her notebook. "That's very helpful. Should we walk back to your cottage while there is still some cloud cover?"

He didn't respond to her suggestion. "I am enjoying these discussions, you know. I've had so little stimulating conversation in recent years." The frostiness that was between them that morning had thawed out with the coming of the sun.

"I'm glad," said Julia.

Grant placed a warm hand on her shoulder. He was still holding the olive branch and she could feel it scratching the back of her neck.

It hurt a little. "Before we go," he said, "you must have something to share with me?"

Julia laughed. "Yes, I'd forgotten." She opened her notes again. Their routine was more like a ritual now. "Well, I did find another inconsistency. Or unexplained detail, or whatever you'd like to call it. There was a dog on Blue Pearl Island. What happened to it?"

Grant smiled. "That is the puzzle for this afternoon?"

"Yes," said Julia. "It seems to be. When Sarah meets Mr. and Mrs. Stubbs in the lane by her house, there's a dog walking behind them with the fisherman. We're led to assume it belongs to the fisherman, but its presence is never explained. The only sensible conclusion is that it belongs to Mr. and Mrs. Stubbs. And that it stays with them on the island."

"Why do you say that?"

"Charles and Sarah find several signs of it as they explore the house. What else could explain the chewed meat in the kitchen corridor, the smell of excrement by the jetty outside, the animal hairs on the rug in the lounge, and the animal tracks in the hallway? The rest of the island is barren, with only a few seabirds living on it."

Grant scratched at the ground with his branch. "I suppose you're right. It's unlikely that anything bigger could survive there."

"But the dog has vanished by the time Sarah and Charles arrive. So what happened to it?"

"It was another victim, I assume."

"Perhaps. But would Stubbs kill his own dog? And what happened to its body?" Julia smiled. "I'd like to think it swam back to the mainland."

Grant nodded. "It's a possibility, at least. We can think it over as we walk back. Shall we go now?"

Julia got to her feet. "You go on," she said. Something had just occurred to her. "I want to stay here for a moment and make some more notes."

"Well," said Grant. "Then I shall see you back at the cottage."

She leaned against the low stone wall of the churchyard and waited until he was almost out of sight. Then she walked around to the distant side of the church, where a number of gravestones rose from the dust. The sun was behind the clouds, so not one of them was casting a shadow. But the names written on them were just about legible. She walked steadily along each of the rows, looking to her right and left. Eventually she came to a stop at the side of the churchyard nearest the sea. Before her was a modest butter-colored headstone.

Julia closed her eyes. She'd suspected since their first conversation that Grant had been hiding something about his past. Now she knew what it was.

II

THE CURSED VILLAGE

Dr. Lamb had a view of the twilight in two rectangles. That's the last beautiful thing I'll ever see, he thought, as he looked through the window. His companion, a man called Alfred, was standing in front of it, blocking the light.

"Well, how bad is it?" Dr. Lamb pushed himself up to a sitting position.

Alfred turned toward the bed. There were tears in his eyes. "If I give you the mirror, you can diagnose yourself."

"As bad as that?" The doctor's voice was hoarse.

"It's plain to see," said Alfred. "The small of your back is bright yellow."

Dr. Lamb swore, and his composure dissolved into a string of weak coughs. They were autumn leaves crunched under footsteps; everything reminded him of his body's inevitable decay. "What will you do now?" he asked.

Alfred put a hand on the doctor's forehead, the index finger overlapping his hairline. "I have to take my things and leave. I can't risk the scandal of being found here. You understand, don't you?"

The doctor grunted. "We had a good run, didn't we?"

"Yes," the other man sighed. "It's a shame it has to end like this."

Dr. Lamb watched him pack for a few minutes and then drifted off to sleep. He woke up to the sound of the door closing. He gathered the blankets around him and went to the window. Alfred was walking away down the street. His last lover, abandoning him.

He turned back to the bed. "Well, then, there it is. My literal death-bed."

The rest of the room was bare. There was just the desk in the corner, with a rectangle of white paper on top of it that he'd placed there the day before.

If his illness had entered its last stages, he knew what that meant; there was a vial of morphine and a clean syringe waiting for him in the bathroom. But there was one other thing he wanted to do first.

He shuffled over to the desk and sat down in the chair. The blankets spilled over the sides and brushed against the floor. He slid the sheet of paper toward him, took up a pen, and wrote Lily Mortimer's name at the top of it.

• • •

Five years before that, she'd come to see him. She'd taken the underground train out to his neighborhood, climbed up out of the earth, and stepped out onto the cold street.

A man tried to sell her a newspaper. She shook her head and walked purposefully along the pavement, looking at the road signs. She'd caught the train at Piccadilly Circus, where the huge streets, lined with shops, had seemed easy to navigate, but out here there were only houses and offices, and everything seemed squashed together. They were tall, pale buildings with imposing black doors, lined up along the frozen street like gravestones in the snow.

It was her first time in London—in fact her first time leaving the village alone. She was only seventeen years old. When she'd told Matthew she intended to come here, he'd just sighed and lifted the dog onto his lap, as if that expressed his feelings on the matter.

One of the narrow residential streets had a name she recognized, and a few minutes later she was outside the building she wanted. She rang the doorbell. A young woman opened it. "Hello. I'm here to see Dr. Lamb."

"And your name is?"

"Lily Mortimer."

Dr. Lamb greeted her at the door of his office and sat her down in a chair, asking the receptionist to bring them some tea.

"Lily." He took her coat. "It's been many, many years, but you haven't changed. I think you must be the most dependable patient I've ever had. When you were a child, your poor sister would bring you to see me whenever you scraped a knee. I think she was a little overwhelmed by the responsibility. But I suppose you don't remember any of that."

Lily smiled. "For me, life began with that broken arm. I think I was five. I fell out of a tree."

The doctor put his head back and laughed kindly. "I'd forgotten. That one almost killed her with worry. How is she, your sister?"

"Oh, Violet's all right. She married Ben, of course. A few years ago. They live in Cambridge."

Dr. Lamb grinned, picturing the pale, melted girl he'd known wearing a white veil. "And the rest of the village? Your uncle Matthew?"

"The same as ever. Matthew has a dog now. And the village hasn't changed. You'd still recognize it, if you ever deigned to come back."

"Good, good." The doctor adjusted a pen on his desk and moved some papers around, to signify the end of pleasantries. "And how can I help you?" The awkward silence spread like spilled ink. "Something about Agnes's death, I understand?"

The mention of that name seemed to bring the cold in from outside.

"I wanted to see you . . ." Lily began, knowing it was her turn to ask questions. But her questions were darker and more direct than his, and she wondered how to approach them. "I wanted to ask why you left the village so quickly after it happened."

He breathed in sharply. "That's a little personal, isn't it? Do you really think it's relevant?"

"I think so. Do you mind me asking?"

"Perhaps not. But tell me what you're really getting at."

"As I said when I wrote to you, I'm trying to understand the circumstances of my grandmother's murder. You lived and worked in the village for twenty years, then left within a year of it happening. Leaving your patients behind rather abruptly. So it must have affected you?"

"In fact, the two things were unrelated. I wanted a different kind of life, that's all. Perhaps the murder hurried me along. People looked at me differently afterward. You can blame your aunt for that."

"My grand-aunt," Lily corrected him.

"No one would even have considered me a suspect if she hadn't insisted on it. But everybody wants to believe that a doctor can also be a killer—it's so macabre, so topsy-turvy. There were whispers everywhere I went. It was like walking through tall grass."

Lily nodded. "But that would have passed, in time. What exactly is different about your life here?" She was thinking about his surgery in the village: a large room just like this one. "From the outside it seems remarkably similar."

He stood up, slightly insulted by the statement, and went to the window. At that moment the receptionist brought in their tea. Dr. Lamb watched her pretty hands arranging things on his desk and her fine figure as she walked away.

"I have a receptionist here, for one thing." He sat back down. "Someday you'll understand just how small that village is."

Lily returned his patronizing smile. "Oh, I'm aware of that, Dr. Lamb. And I'm sure I'll make my own way in the world soon enough.

But I'd like to know the truth about my grandmother's murder first. It's a chapter of my life that I'd like to finish."

"Then you're imprisoned there, for a crime you didn't commit. Can't you leave the past in the past?"

"But it's still the present for me. It changed the course of my life in a way that nothing else ever has. I've thought about it every day since it happened. Perhaps you wouldn't understand that."

The doctor looked at her with sadness. "I'm very sorry, it must have been awful for you." He drained his teacup down to the black dots at the bottom and placed it back on the saucer. "Unfortunately, I can't tell you anything about it that isn't already public knowledge."

• • •

But of course he'd been lying. And now here he was, five years later, riddled with cancer and on the edge of death himself, with no one left to protect and no career left to lose. After Lily had departed that day, he'd found himself wishing that he'd given her some kind of hint or clue, something that might have helped her make progress in her search and revived the exhilaration of the first few weeks after the murder, when the world had seemed split into devils and saints. He hadn't done so then, but there was nothing stopping him now.

It was five years since her visit and more than ten years since the murder itself. He no longer knew her address, of course, but if he sent a letter to Lily Mortimer, care of the Grange, it was bound to reach her.

So Dr. Lamb took up his pen and began to write.

• • •

"Unfortunately, I can't tell you anything about it that isn't already public knowledge."

Lily sipped her tea slowly, as if to show him he couldn't end their conversation so easily. "You might not know who killed her, but any recollection of the details would be helpful. I was so young when it happened, it's hard to separate memory from imagination. And Uncle Matthew won't talk to me about it; he says it's too painful. I'd hoped you might do so instead."

The doctor smiled. "I'll fill in the details, if I can remember them myself. But chronologically the story begins with you, doesn't it? You and William. Shouldn't we start with how you found the body?"

"Yes." Lily nodded. "I can go first."

• • •

The murder had happened six years earlier.

The gardens at the Grange were full of secrets, and Lily and William—eleven and nine years old, respectively—were not particularly surprised by the boat they found floating in the small pond under the willow tree, though they'd never seen it there before. It could have been an alien artifact, dropped from a spaceship during the night. But to them it was primarily an oversized toy, almost the size of the pond itself, and they didn't hesitate before planning their morning around it. There were things in the garden they were often told not to play with, they reasoned, but never anything made of wood.

Lily climbed into the unsteady vessel and sat on the low seat that ran across the back of it, her shoulders very straight, as if she were practicing her posture. It bobbed gently with her weight. William stayed on the bank and reached across to take hold of the stern.

"I'm on the ocean," said Lily.

"Whereabouts?" William asked suspiciously.

"The Arctic."

He began to rock her from side to side. "It's a storm," he said. "An ice storm."

Gracefully, she kept her balance. "That feels more like a whirlpool. We're being taken down to the abyss. The captain has drowned."

He began to hammer his fists on the side. "It's a shark swimming by."

"It's a whale," she corrected him. "A sinker of ships."

An apple flew past William's head and hit the side of the boat, bouncing into the water. Lily opened her eyes; she and William both turned around, knowing who would be there.

"Some very large hailstones," said a man in his early thirties, with scruffy brown hair and a mustache floating over his satisfied grin.

"That's mean, Uncle Matthew," said Lily. "You could have knocked me right into the water."

"I'm playing by your rules, aren't I?" He towered over them, his hands on his hips. "Besides, Lily, I wasn't aiming at you."

William stayed silent and watched his own reflection.

"What are you doing here anyway, Uncle Matthew?" Lily asked him. "You're always causing trouble."

The man shook his head in disbelief. "Trouble? You silly thing. I'm off to meet Aunt Dot at the station. I came over with Lauren. She's looking after Mummy, giving your sister the morning off. We'll be joining you for lunch."

William glanced back at the white house. From this side, only the attic window was visible; the lower half of the house was strangled by trees. He swore under his breath.

Matthew leaned toward the two of them. "Would you like an apple?"

"Yes, please," said Lily. He passed one to her.

William hadn't answered, but Matthew knelt down by him anyway.

"I think yours went in the water. You might try to catch it next time."

• • •

"I hate him. I hate him. I hate him."

They were both in the boat now, on the back seat. Matthew had left them ten minutes earlier, content with his little act of cruelty.

The family that lived at the Grange was an incomplete, twisted thing, born of tragedy and circumstance. Lily and William, the two children, were cousins to each other, and Matthew was uncle to both of them. Their grandmother Agnes Mortimer had had three children; Lily's father had been her son and William's mother her daughter, but both had died—the son in the war and the daughter during childbirth—leaving Matthew as her only living child. Lily's mother had died a few years after her husband, from the Spanish flu, and Lily and her sister, Violet, had moved to the Grange to live with Agnes. William had arrived the following year, after his father had vanished one afternoon. So now the three orphans lived with their grandmother, a widow herself, in this tall white house at the edge of the village.

Agnes was too old and unwell to look after them properly, but Violet was mature enough to help out, and Matthew, who had married Lauren and moved to a smaller house in the village, gave them assistance when they needed it. The only point of friction in the arrangement was between William and his uncle Matthew, who saw the young boy as a miniature version of the brute who'd taken his sister away. The two of them hated each other.

"Well," said Lily, "one day you'll be as big as him, then he won't be able to bully you anymore."

William laid a handful of leaves and twigs and bits of grass on the seat in front of him, to make an illustration of his tormenter. He arranged the leaves into a mustache over a mouth made of twigs. One eye was a stone and one a large crumb of dirt.

"Why don't we take all these leaves," said William, "and put them through his letterbox?"

Lily shook her head. "But what about poor Aunt Lauren?"

William went quiet; his mind was not quite made up about Lauren.

"We could put them in his pockets, then, when he comes back. Leaves and slugs and droppings."

"It wouldn't work," said Lily. "He would know it was you."

"Then we could follow him through the fields and throw stones at him. He wouldn't see us, if we hid."

Lily frowned and adopted her most adult tone of voice. "That's exceedingly dangerous, William. You might kill him."

William hit the plank with his fist; leaves flew into the air. "I want to kill him. I want him dead."

Lily said nothing. It scared her when he was like this. The boat rocked gently.

"I can't abide you in this mood." She was trying hard to talk like an adult again. "I'll leave you alone and you can sit here until your anger goes away. The ocean is very calming."

William looked at her, his chin in his hands. "Can I have a bite of your apple?"

She considered the question, then shook her head. "I'm afraid there's very little left. It wouldn't be practical."

• • •

"So," the older Lily said to Dr. Lamb, six years later, "William and I were not actually together at the time it happened. We were separated for about an hour. I went into the house and found Violet in a somber mood, sitting with Agnes's breakfast tray balanced on her knees and staying very still, like it was some kind of penance. My sister was like that sometimes. I said something to her and she didn't reply, so I took a book outside with me and read under a tree."

"And William?"

"I don't know. I didn't see him again until he came outside and found me. I'd been reading for forty minutes or so. He had calmed down by that time. In fact, he seemed excited."

• • •

William and Lily had spent the last few minutes playing in one of the many unused rooms upstairs. The Grange had always been too big for its few inhabitants and nothing had ever needed to be thrown away, so fifty years' worth of memories were pushed into forgotten corners or in some cases separate rooms full of curiosities. Agnes had lived in the house for decades, so long that it felt like one of the family. Haughty and withdrawn on the outside, but full of character and clutter within, there to comfort and chide them. To the two children it was a source of never-ending wonder.

Lily looked at the assortment of chairs that were scattered across the floor and selected one made of delicate dark wood, shiny with varnish, and handed it to William. He positioned it carefully on top of a large, flat desk. Then they placed two small tables to the left and right of it, as makeshift armrests, and found an ornament to go on top of each. A brass lion doorstop and a porcelain dog. They were trying to build a throne.

"Let me go first," said William, climbing onto the desk.

As William sat down, one of the chair legs slid off the desk and he tilted back toward the wall. His legs swung sideways into one of the tables and knocked it to the floor, the brass lion landing with a thump.

William climbed down to retrieve the lion. Lily took his hand. "Don't," she said. "I'm bored of that game."

"What should we do instead?"

"We could draw pictures."

The idea didn't inspire him. She was better at it than he was, and he knew that was why she'd suggested it. Then the taste of childish cruelty lit up his face. "I know. I can show you something."

"What is it?"

"Follow me." He took her elbow and turned her toward the door.

The house had two staircases, so it was easy to sneak around without being noticed. They went up one floor and stopped on the landing, where the two staircases merged into one. Slim and rickety, this final staircase led up to what they called the attic bedroom, where Agnes slept.

William pushed Lily toward it.

"But what if she's angry?" Lily whispered.

"She's asleep." William crept up the stairs to the tall wooden door and turned the handle. "It's all right."

The door swung open. The room was almost empty, with only a window and the white bed in front of it. There was nothing on the bed except for a pile of old blankets and pillows. Lily wondered if her grandmother—not quite herself since the incident several weeks ago—had spent the morning building a fort with these sheets, as she stepped tentatively around the pile. William walked behind her.

Lily reached the window and stopped. Her grandmother's old, twisted feet were sticking out from the bottom of the bundle of bedding. They were gray and yellowish and not moving at all. William walked into the back of Lily. She turned around to face him, her eyes flattened with fright. Together they took hold of the blankets and pulled. The whole lot of them fell to the floor.

Lily screamed at the sight of her grandmother, lying on the sheets like something washed up from the sea. William stared with disbelief at her dead, distorted face and started to cry. This wasn't what he'd imagined at all.

· · ·

The local doctor, Dr. Lamb, was sent for and arrived at the house fifteen minutes later. He had been there many times in the last two months, since that afternoon when Agnes had collapsed and been carried up to bed. She'd had a minor stroke, and he had come to check on her several times a week since then.

Lily's sister, Violet, accompanied him to the top of the house, hoping to find some comfort in his presence. She waited on the landing at the bottom of the single staircase, while he went in to examine the body. He opened the door and knew at once what had happened. "Suffocated, in her own bed."

Her mouth was open shapelessly, like a loop of string draped across a table. The rest of her face was subsumed by that cavity. Her long, fragile neck was covered in bruises. He shuddered, looking at it. Somebody had leaned their entire weight on that mouth. Had they actually pushed the jaw out of its socket, or was that just the vacant expression of death?

He left the room, slightly shaken. He sat down on the top step of the narrow, wood-lined staircase that led up to it and lit his pipe. Violet stood at the bottom, her body pressed flat against the wall for support and her face turned to look at him. He stared down at her like a king sitting on a throne. "There's nothing for me to do here." He smoked. "We shall wait for the police, that's all."

"The police?" Violet whispered.

"Your grandmother died of asphyxiation." That was Dr. Lamb's verdict. "Smothering. It seems that someone covered her in all those blankets and pillows while she slept, then put their weight on top of them. She never woke up."

The young woman started to cry.

• • •

"And is that still your opinion, six years later?"

Dr. Lamb had offered Lily a drink, getting up and pouring himself a whiskey. She'd never had whiskey before, but it was a day of new experiences.

To underline the question, she took a sip of her drink, unprepared for how much it would hurt. Her throat flushed red. The doctor smiled.

"That she was smothered? Yes, there's no doubt about that. There were no other marks on her—she hadn't been hit or scratched. Just smothered under those blankets."

Lily held her glass very tightly as she spoke. "Would that have been painful?"

"Yes," said Dr. Lamb, glancing down at the floor. "I'm afraid it would have been terrible. Like a cat being drowned in a bag. But in her own bed."

"And although someone did that to her—an innocent old lady—no one was ever caught; her killer just carried on with their life."

"I know, it seems rather unreal when you put it like that. We thought your grand-aunt Dorothea might solve the crime, at first. She certainly tried. But if she succeeded, she kept it to herself."

"That's the thing I remember least clearly, those few days following the crime, when Dorothea was around. I was so afraid, I couldn't pay attention to any of what she was saying. To me, it was just a lot of adults talking."

The doctor tried to lighten the mood. "I've read some detective novels you could describe the same way."

Lily didn't respond. She was concentrating very hard on each sip of whiskey, worried that if she didn't she might be sick from the pain of it. "Please," she said, "tell me what you remember."

• • •

Dorothea Dickson, the victim's sister, approached the front door of the Grange, her shoes crunching rhythmically on the gravel. She was about to ring the doorbell when she noticed Lauren pacing among the flower beds. A willowy thing, almost a flower herself, Lauren was Matthew's wife and Agnes's daughter-in-law. Her long blond hair was as smooth as glass.

"You'll make honey if you keep that up. Or spin yourself a web."

Lauren turned to her with two startled blue eyes. "Oh, Dot," she said. "We were expecting you, of course. But I'd forgotten you were coming."

The two women went to each other, and the older took the younger's hands. "What is the matter, darling? It must be my sister," she said, knowing that Lauren would never come to this house or garden to indulge any other kind of grief.

"Yes, I'm afraid so. How can I say this? Oh, Dorothea." The blond head bobbed. "She's dead. Agnes is dead. I'm so sorry to be the one to tell you."

The older woman kept her composure. "There, now. It's what we've all been preparing for. Since she had that fall."

Lauren put a handkerchief up to her eyes; it turned muddy with her tears. "No, I'm afraid you don't understand. It wasn't that at all. She was murdered this morning."

"Murdered?" Dorothea let go of the other woman's hands and took a step backward. She looked up at the house, as tall and thin as a spike. A policeman looked down at her from a second-story window.

"At least the doctor thinks so. He said she was—oh, I can hardly say the word." Dorothea took her hand again and gave it a squeeze. "Smothered," said Lauren, without too much difficulty.

"Where is Matthew?"

"He's inside, with the police. Here, I'll take you to him."

Lauren guided her around the flower bed, to the two French doors that opened out from one of the lounges. As they turned the corner, Dorothea noticed Raymond—the gardener at the Grange—walking with Violet through the rows of apple trees in one of the neighboring fields. He was comforting her, with an arm across her shoulder; Dorothea wondered if there was something romantic between them.

She entered the house and found Matthew leaning hopelessly in the corner of the lounge, requiring the support of both walls at once. His leafy mustache was wet with tears. Dorothea pried him from his position and gave him a hug. "Poor Mummy," he mumbled into her shoulder, trembling. "Auntie Dot, I'm so sorry."

"Now, now." She patted him gently, then held him out before her. "Matthew, you look like a bottle of milk. Do you know who did this?"

"No." He shook his head, competitiveness rising inside him. "I've given the police my theories, but, no, not for certain."

"When did it happen?"

"Lauren was the last one to see her alive, I think." The last to admit to seeing her alive, thought Dorothea. She turned around, but Lauren was no longer there; she'd delivered Dorothea to her husband and then drifted away. "She's been coming here to help Violet, since Mummy's stroke the other month. She took up her breakfast and found her alive and well. That was at ten this morning. We think it must have happened around eleven."

"Where are the children?"

"They're both with the doctor."

"And where is Agnes now?"

"In her bed." Dorothea looked toward the staircase. "There are police up there, Auntie. They won't let you see her."

"Well, there's no use in not trying."

Fifteen minutes later, Dorothea had said a tearful goodbye to her dead sister's body and was coming back down the stairs. She found Dr. Lamb in the library, occupying Lily and William with the gory details of human frailty.

"There's something called oxygen. It's like food for your blood. And the air is full of it. So when you breathe, it's like your blood is eating. That's why if you hold your breath you feel something a bit like hunger. And you drown if you don't get enough of it. That's like starving."

William looked horrified. "What about strangling?" he asked in a whisper.

"Yes, that's a very similar thing, only then it's because someone is blocking the blood flow to your head. So your brain doesn't get any food." He put a warm hand on the child's neck. "You see?"

Lily, standing silently to one side, watched Dorothea come into the room. She gave a little wave. Dorothea bent down and kissed her.

"Dr. Lamb," said Dorothea, "may I have a word with you?" He looked up and nodded solemnly, then guided the children out through the door.

The doctor had been living in the village almost as long as Agnes herself, and he was still as good-looking as ever, though his hair was now entirely gray. But his mouth was boyish and there was a wisdom to his eyes that suited him. "Miss Dickson, isn't it?" He smiled sympathetically. "I'm so sorry for your loss."

· · ·

"I don't remember that," said Lily, seventeen again, the empty whiskey glass on the table beside her.

"There's no reason you should," said Dr. Lamb, loosening his collar. "It's hot in here, isn't it? Should I open a window?"

"I'm cold," said Lily, slightly embarrassed.

He parted his hands in a gesture of resignation. "Well, anyway, your grand-aunt, as you call her, wanted to know everything I could tell her about the crime. She was a very inquisitive old lady."

"That's what I remember most about her. She always wanted to know what I was learning in school, details and everything."

"A natural detective." Dr. Lamb nodded. "Well, she asked me if I would attend a family meeting later that day. After sunset, she said, making it sound rather dramatic. She'd questioned the police already and thought the family had a better chance of working it out among themselves." Dr. Lamb looked out of the window, with a shadow of amusement on his face. "Of course, I believed I was being invited there as an expert witness. Not as a suspect."

· · ·

The relatives of Agnes Mortimer stood along one side of the lounge, with their two guests as bookends. Her son, Matthew, and his wife, Lauren, stood in the center, with Violet and Dr. Lamb to their left and the two children—Lily and William—and Raymond, the gardener, on their right. Dorothea faced them and began to pace back and forth.

"Agnes was an opinionated old woman," said Dorothea, "and a secretive one. And at times she was as tough as digging in winter. But I know she was loved by everyone here."

Raymond looked around the room to see if anyone would object to that. Loved like a rainy day, he thought. But nobody spoke. Only Lauren turned to look at him, and he dropped his eyes as if caught doing something shameful.

"Nonetheless," Dorothea continued, "she was murdered earlier today, cruelly and coldly, in her bed upstairs. My younger sister."

The police had taken the body away with them, in the back of a miserable little car. They had spent the afternoon questioning the household—lingering longest on Raymond, the outsider—but they'd made no arrests and had abandoned the house before sunset, like a swarm of insects moving as one. "The police believe she was killed by someone she knew." Dorothea looked at each of them in turn. "The motive is not yet clear, though I have my own suspicions." She held her hand up, a finger raised in the air, and shook it at the gathering in an undirected gesture of accusation; her solid bracelets clattered against one another, making her arm a musical instrument. "I have gathered in this room everyone that was in the vicinity of the house at the time she was killed, have I not?"

Raymond cleared his throat. "Not quite, ma'am. Ben Crake has been hanging around the house today; I've seen him."

Matthew stepped forward; the sense of someone being under suspicion stirred him to action, like a hopeful wolf sensing its prey. "Ben Crake, that's right. I saw him too. Did anybody tell the police about him?"

Dorothea looked confused and a little annoyed at the interruption. "Who is Ben Crake?"

Violet took a handkerchief from her pocket and twirled it compulsively around her fingers.

"A young man," said Matthew, "who lives in the village. He was at school with Violet. He's often here on some pretext or another."

"He's my friend," said Violet softly.

"The wrong kind of friend."

"You know, he's actually rather pleasant," said Lauren, dismissing her husband's hopeful tone. "Not the type to commit murder at all."

"Impressions can be deceptive," said Dorothea. She turned to her nephew. "Where did you see him?"

• • •

Matthew had been walking through the fields on his way to the station, when a figure in a brown coat seemed to leap out at him. Though he knew the landscape well and knew that it was just a trick of perspective, it still gave him a shock. "You made me jump," he said to the apparition.

Ben didn't answer.

"Oh," said Matthew. "It's you. What are you doing here?"

Ben stroked his jaw. "It's Matthew, isn't it? You're Violet's uncle. I'm watching for birds." And he raised his binoculars, as if in a toast.

"I see." Matthew nodded. "You gave me a terrible fright."

"I was keeping very still, trying not to frighten the sparrows."

Matthew, who had spent his whole life in the countryside but still considered it an inconvenience, stared at him uncomprehendingly. "Well, I must be on my way."

Ben put the binoculars up to his eyes and looked at a tree. A few shapes flew from it, an autumnal Morse code. "Say hello to Violet for me."

When Matthew was out of sight, he turned back to the house and raised his binoculars again. The side facing him had a single window, right at the top.

• • •

"Was he watching the house?" asked Dorothea.

"Sort of," said Matthew.

Violet touched the handkerchief to her eyes.

"He seemed to be," said Raymond.

"That is most intriguing."

Dr. Lamb interrupted them. He had the breathy, exhausted tone of somebody sapped by impatience. "Listen, Ben is perfectly fine. He's just a young man, smitten with a young woman." Violet's heart was hammering; she almost fainted. "I've known his family for years; his father owns an antiques shop in town. They're very pleasant people, binoculars or not."

"And yet if he was watching the house, he must have seen something. Why didn't he speak to the police?" The sky outside was tepid and growing dark, but when Dorothea spoke, she gave the impression that a storm was raging, that a crack of thunder or flash of lightning was about to follow each one of her pronouncements. "Did anyone else see anything suspicious?"

Nobody answered.

"Then we should take it in turns to say where we were at the time of the murder and whether we noticed anything of interest."

"Do you suspect one of us?" Violet asked nervously. "Do you suspect Ben?"

Dorothea approached her. "It's too early to say." And she stroked the young woman's hair. She was now part of the semicircle, leaving the middle of the room empty, as if they were sitting around a campfire, about to tell stories. "Who wants to go first?" The question was met with silence. "Well, who was the last one to see her alive?"

Lauren turned to face Dorothea. "I suppose that would be me, then."

• • •

Every day since her stroke, Agnes had woken up to an overwhelming feeling of dizziness and disorientation. She lay very still, fighting the urge to be sick, and imagined that her wooden room was built in the prow of a ship or hung from a hot-air balloon, swinging from side to side.

The light coming through the window was so bright, so smothering, that anything around the edges of the room was apt to blend into
the walls, taking shape at the oddest moments. "It's irresponsible to be
keeping secrets at this time."

A face loomed at her out of the wood; Lauren had entered the room
without her noticing.

"If you feel worse, you must tell us." Lauren was a blond floaty
thing, married to her son, Matthew; Agnes could see the attraction, but
she'd never liked the woman herself. "Let's have a little fresh air, shall
we?" Lauren opened the window and stood looking out at the view.
"There's Raymond, sweeping the paths. You don't know how lucky you
are to be free to sit and watch him all morning. A fine figure of a man,
all sweat and muscles." She turned and winked at her mother-in-law.
"Don't tell Matthew I said that, of course." Agnes thought Lauren insufferable but found it was usually best to stay silent until she grew bored
of talking. Now she was nibbling on some toast that she'd brought up
on a tray. "That doctor too. He's always up here, isn't he? The two of
you alone together."

She gave Agnes a brief look of disdain. "Why aren't you talking to
me?"

Agnes put one hand to her throat and reached out toward the tray
with her other. She made the sound of creaking floorboards, as if her
lungs were a haunted house.

Lauren looked at the glass of milk at the edge of the tray and then
up at the old lady. "You can get it yourself. Do you think I'm your
maid?"

Lauren smiled. For a moment she pictured herself throwing the
food out of the window—two pieces of toast like two palm prints in
the soil and then the impact of the milk, like a retch into a flower
bed—but resisted the impulse. "Do try to sort yourself out in time for
lunch." She stepped toward the door. "And don't forget, your sister is
coming today."

There was a squeaking and a slamming of wood, then the blond apparition was gone.

• • •

Dorothea bowed her head. "The last friendly face she ever saw."

Lauren nodded. "Yes. I left Agnes and came downstairs. Violet was asleep on the couch, so I had nothing to do and went home. I thought I might do an hour of housework before coming back to join you for lunch. When I returned, she was dead."

"Thank you." Dorothea squeezed Violet's hand. "Perhaps you could go next, dear."

Violet shivered. "Yes, all right." But she could barely speak, suddenly overcome with fear and guilt.

• • •

She'd been dreaming about Ben.

How strange to think that two months ago he was just an image from her childhood and now he was in her thoughts all the time. As if her lust for Raymond wasn't shameful enough.

There were three dreary lounges on the ground floor of the Grange, connected to one another like the chambers of a digestive system. Matthew found Violet asleep on a low couch in the darkest of the three, the blinds drawn down and inaccessible behind an unbroken line of desks and tables.

Matthew approached his niece. He was bored. Pretending concern, he put a hand on her forehead as if checking for a fever. The touch woke her up and she opened her mouth to scream, then saw in the dim light that it was only her uncle and instead the scream became a hot rush of breath, like a stifled sneeze. It was a more appropriate response to his presence.

"You poor child," he said. "You must be exhausted."

There was something putrid about his touch after her sultry dreams of Ben. She looked shamefully into the darkest corner of the room. "Uncle Matthew, forgive me. I woke up early to prepare for lunch, but I got so little sleep last night. I just planned to sit down for a moment."

"There's nothing to forgive, Violet. Your efforts in this house are heroic. Only sixteen, and effectively the head of the household." Seventeen, but she didn't correct him. "Lauren has taken Mummy's breakfast up. We thought it best not to wake you."

Violet got up and walked through to the kitchen. Matthew followed her, still talking. "In some ways it will be a blessing for all of us when this is over. Then we can make sure you're taken care of."

Violet smiled weakly. She felt a pang of sadness about her grandmother's failing health. "Not too soon, let's hope."

"Dot will be arriving in an hour. I thought I might go to the station to meet her."

Violet frowned, facing away from him. Her grand-aunt's visit meant more work for her. "Yes," she said. "That would be nice of you."

"I think I might set off soon, then."

Violet looked out of the window. "Here," she said, as he went to the door. "The children are playing by the pond. Take them an apple each, will you?"

He nodded, and she handed him two apples from the bowl that were as large and bright as tennis balls.

• • •

Violet looked at each face in turn.

"After that I went back to sleep, until I heard my sister scream about an hour later."

"Thank you," said Dorothea. She looked sympathetically at Lily, who was standing half hidden behind Matthew. "Then the children found the body. That would perhaps be a logical point for you to take over the narrative, Raymond?"

He seemed surprised to have been mentioned at all. He stood up straight, proud to play his part. "That's right. I heard the scream. I was outside in the garden, picking up leaves."

...

Agnes had been unbearable lately. Confined to her room, with only a view of the garden for entertainment, she had taken to watching and commenting on everything Raymond did. He had spent some of his time, over the last few days, repairing a boat he'd found in the garage; yesterday he'd made the mistake of starting work on it—turning it upside down on the driveway so he could paint it—directly under her window. He'd made it through most of the day, but in the late afternoon he heard her calling weakly to him. It hurt her to shout, so instead she opened her window and rattled her stick against the top and bottom of the frame.

He looked up at the window: an eyeball with a needle stuck in it. She's unhinged, he thought.

"I don't pay you to play with that wooden toy," she said to him, after he'd walked up the three flights of stairs to her room. She only spoke to him, or about him, in terms of money.

Instead, she'd asked him to pick up all the fallen leaves in the garden, to tidy it up for her sister's visit. "Of course, ma'am." Then he'd walked back down the three sets of stairs, picturing her broken body bouncing down each step and landing with a broken neck at the bottom.

He was up early on the day Agnes died, hoping to finish the boat. But tiredness had proved too much for him and he'd kicked the wood in frustration, leaving a footprint in the fresh white paint. Then he'd dragged it over to the pond and dropped it in. He wanted to check that it would float. The white paint swirled into the water.

He took a shovel and wheelbarrow and began collecting leaves. He was stooped down at the side of a hedgerow when Lauren and Matthew arrived, neither of them noticing him. And the wheelbarrow was almost full by the time he spotted Ben standing one field over, hiding behind a tree and holding his binoculars up to his eyes. When the wheelbarrow wouldn't take any more without spilling, he pushed it over to a compost heap at the corner of two fences and tilted it forward, then stood back to admire the amount he'd gathered. Some were starting to turn brown, but most were a poisonous green, and the heap looked like a plate of vegetables. Then he noticed an indentation at the side of the pile: a small hole where something heavy had been thrown at it.

He put his hand in and pulled out a dead squirrel. Its body lay heavily across his gloved hand, rigid except for where the head hung down from the edge of his palm, as if it were dangling from a string. He felt around the neck with his thumb. There was nothing there, just soft skin like worn fabric with some wiry tendons inside. The creature had been strangled, to begin with, then all the bones in its neck had been snapped.

He tossed the body back into the compost and muttered under his breath, "Why do you do it, William?"

An hour later, the job was finished and he was putting the shovel back in the shed, when he heard a scream come from the house and saw Violet run out of the front door, followed by the two children.

He was with her in a matter of seconds. "Violet." He gripped her wrists tenderly. "What's wrong?"

"Agnes—she's been hurt."

Raymond tried to push past her, into the house, but she halted him with a warm palm on his chest. "No, go for Dr. Lamb." He didn't hesitate; he just turned and ran.

The doctor's house was over a mile away, at the other end of the village, and although Raymond was in a rush, he was already pacing himself so he could run the whole way there. So when he emerged from the lane that connected the Grange to the main road and found

Dr. Lamb sitting on the low wall that surrounded the war memorial, smoking a pipe, he thought at first that he must be dreaming.

• • •

"Thank you, Raymond," said Dorothea. "That is most intriguing. Perhaps, Dr. Lamb, you could take your turn next. What were you doing at the time Agnes was killed?"

Dr. Lamb looked confused. "I'm sorry?"

"What were you doing at the time she died, please?"

The doctor was astonished; the rest of them stared at him blankly. "I thought I was here as a witness, not a suspect. Why on earth would you think it matters what I was doing?"

"Perhaps it doesn't, but you were in the vicinity of the house at the time it happened. And that fact is currently unexplained."

"What I did with my day is none of your business. Talking to you about it could violate the confidentiality of my patients." No one seemed impressed by this line of argument, and they continued to look at him expectantly. "If you must know what brought me to the war memorial, it's simply that I was taking a walk around the village. It's a habit of mine late in the morning. I only stopped for a minute to sit and light my pipe. Raymond found me there, I sent him on to the police, and made my way down the lane. Of course, by that time she was already dead. Thirty minutes dead, by the look of her."

"Well, then," said Dorothea, slightly intimidated by his raised voice. "Thank you for clarifying."

• • •

Lily was listening to that same voice, six years later. "She didn't dare accuse me again after that, not to my face."

"And did you really think it so unreasonable that she considered you a suspect, or were you just being petty?"

Dr. Lamb laughed at this unabridged insult. "I'm not sure I

remember. I really was just taking a walk, though. The whole thing was quite ridiculous."

"I suppose it was."

"But let me continue. This is the part you'll be most interested in."

• • •

The doctor paced around the center of the semicircle. "Your line of thinking, Dorothea, is flawed. Anyone could sneak up on this house from any angle. The garden is a mess of hedges and trees, and the house itself is more doors than walls. If you want to know who did this, you'd be better off looking for a motive."

"And nobody here has a motive," said Matthew. "Then it must have been an outsider?"

"Exactly," said Dr. Lamb.

"The motive was money." Dorothea spoke quietly, but everybody stopped to listen to her.

"Money?" said Matthew. "What do you mean?"

"Agnes wrote to me a little over a week ago. She thought that somebody was trying to poison her. She'd woken up one morning last week feeling close to death, convinced that something had been put in her drink."

• • •

This was different from her usual dizziness. It felt as if there were something feathery living inside her—a restless swan crouching in her guts, with its neck extending up through her throat. She gritted her teeth in agony and drew the obvious conclusion: Someone had tried to poison her but had underestimated the dosage required. Any one of them could have done it; the jug of water was left by her bed throughout the day, and who knows where it had been before that?

• • •

The doctor sounded outraged. "Did you mention this to the police?"

"I had hoped that wouldn't be necessary." Dorothea stared at him calmly. "She also had the impression that her room had been searched. A few little things were out of place."

"But," said Matthew, "Mummy had nothing to steal."

"That's not entirely true," said Dorothea. "Your father, when he was alive, when the fields were overflowing, used to buy her jewelry. A piece every year for their anniversary."

"Yes, I've heard the story," said Matthew. "But she sold them all. When times became hard."

"No," said Dorothea. "She lied to you. She sold everything else, but she couldn't bear to part with her diamonds."

"How ghastly," said Lauren, quite excited. "And have they been stolen?"

"I don't know," said Dorothea. "I don't know where she kept them. They were hidden somewhere, at first because she felt ashamed that she'd lied about them, then later for their safety."

"Did anybody else know about this?" Matthew looked around the room.

"I knew she'd kept a few small pieces," said Violet. "But not the diamonds. I've even cleaned that room, every inch of it. There's nowhere they could be."

• • •

The last of the day drained from the sky and there she still was: Agnes, sitting by the open window in a room now dark, listening for footsteps on the stairs.

She leaned forward and pulled an old, cracked slat of wood from the frame, against which the window would sit when closed. Behind that was a thin slit extending into the wall itself, a hiding place chiseled into the bricks. Out of it she pulled a tatty cloth pouch, and then she carefully poured its contents onto the table beside her chair. A stream of jewels tapped onto a silver tray. Rubies, emeralds, and diamonds, all half black in the moonlight. It wasn't safe to look at them during the daytime, only when the creaking staircase that led to her room had held its breath for the night. There were thirty of them, forming a shallow pile; it looked like a treasure trove from a children's adventure book.

This is what they were all after, this shallow, heavy fortune.

• • •

Dr. Lamb poured them both another drink. "You can't still be cold?"

Lily ran her hands along her arms. "I think it's the topic of conversation that is chilling my blood."

"I'm sorry," he said. "We can stop."

"No, no. I'm fine, really."

"I think we've reached the end, anyway. I left your aunt Dorothea to her childish games."

"My grand-aunt, Dr. Lamb. It's important to get the details right."

"Very well, I left your grand-aunt to her speculation and walked out, so that's where my story must end. She persisted in playing detective for a few more weeks, even questioning the rest of the village. Of course, that only convinced them we were all suspects. And that's when I started thinking about moving. I understand she died a number of years ago?"

"That's right, a year after Agnes. Entirely natural causes, in her case."

"I'm sorry."

"She never questioned me, of course."

"I did notice that omission. Do you remember anything of that day, apart from finding the body?"

"Oh yes," said Lily. "I remember it all quite clearly."

• • •

After Dorothea's gathering dissolved, William and Lily found themselves in one of the cramped storage spaces on the second floor. It was a rare treat for them to be up so late. They should have been sent to bed, but everyone was distracted and nobody wanted to acknowledge the end of such a momentous day. Now the two of them were alone together.

Lily was picking at a loose strip of wallpaper. "Dottie's playing detectives. Do you think she'll solve the crime?"

William didn't respond. He was standing by a forgotten windowsill, lined with Christmas cards from several years ago, and watching the indistinct movements outside. She approached behind him.

"William, when we went to her room, you already knew her body would be there."

He shook his head. "I didn't."

"You said you wanted to show me something."

"I didn't know it would be like that." The boy was sobbing.

She crept up to him slowly, then put a comforting, probing hand on his shoulder. He turned around. He was crying openly now, with tears dripping from his chin. She looked at him. He held out a chubby closed fist. It hung in the air like a moon. With her other hand she touched it and it opened; she looked down into the cupped flesh, red with indentations. Centered in his palm was a glistening diamond ring.

• • •

"And that was that," said the older Lily. "I'd solved the crime. My young cousin, William, had murdered her. To my eleven-year-old mind, I was the greatest detective in Europe."

"Well," said Dr. Lamb. "You certainly kept that to yourself."

"Of course. I was appalled by the crime, but I still wanted to keep him out of trouble. I would always have taken his side. And I thought for a long time that he really had killed her. He'd shown me proof, after all."

"But now you're not so sure?"

"When you put away childish fancies, it doesn't quite hang together.

Does it? He hadn't confessed; he'd only shown me one of the missing diamonds. It's much more likely that he found the body by himself—before we found it together—and that the ring was on the floor, by the bed."

"Or somebody could have given it to him. But you never asked him about this?"

Lily looked sad. "I would have asked him for more details, once the initial shock had passed. But nothing could have prepared me for how quickly we lost each other. It can't have been more than a couple of weeks later. Matthew inherited the house and didn't want William living there. He'd always hated him, on account of who his father was."

"That's right—he went to live with the gardener?"

"With Raymond, who had always felt sorry for William. They got on well, and Raymond and his wife had no children of their own. So it seemed a fortuitous arrangement. But the three of them moved away almost immediately. Raymond didn't want to work at the Grange after what had taken place, and he'd heard of another job. So they left, and I haven't seen my cousin since. William wanted nothing to do with any of us after that, after we rejected him."

"Then that's the only lead we have?" The doctor raised an eyebrow. "One suspect, who was probably too young to have killed her anyway."

"There is more," said Lily, lining her mouth with another sip of whiskey. She was quite used to it now and wondered if she should ask for a cigar. "First there was Dorothea's funeral, just over a year later. That was followed closely by Violet's wedding."

"To Ben Crake?"

"That's right, to Ben Crake, who had been hanging around the house on the day of my grandmother's murder. He didn't go away after Agnes's death. I think Violet felt freed by the tragedy and started to talk to him quite openly. They were soon engaged."

"Your uncle must have been delighted."

"Oh, Matthew didn't like it at all. But he didn't make too much fuss. He'd been kind in letting Violet and me go on living at the Grange, even if he was beastly to William, but still we felt like a burden, and I'm sure he was relieved to get rid of her. And Violet herself was desperate to escape. The marriage was inevitable."

"How romantic," said Dr. Lamb.

"Anyway, none of us really suspected Ben of being a murderer. The notion seemed ridiculous—he knew almost nothing about our family. He certainly wouldn't have known about any diamonds. It was only Uncle Matthew that insisted we treat him as a suspect."

"But at some point you began to agree with him?"

. . .

The small family—Lauren, Matthew, and Lily—sat around the kitchen table, eating a late lunch. There was a knock at the door. It was Violet.

"Uncle Matthew. Lauren, Lily." She stepped into the kitchen. "How are you all?" She sat down. "I just had to show you the ring that Ben has bought for me." They'd been married for six months by this point. "He's been saving up. You'll understand why when you see it."

She held her hand out over the crowded table, showing a large diamond set in a simple silver band. "Isn't it beautiful?"

Lauren and Matthew looked at each other. "Yes, it's very beautiful," said Lauren.

"Very," said Matthew.

Lily said nothing, though she noted how similar it looked to the ring William had shown her eighteen months before. Could Ben have been involved in her grandmother's death? Was that really possible?

If only Dorothea was still with us, she thought.

. . .

"But you've made far more progress with this case than Dorothea ever did," said Dr. Lamb.

"Have I? Ben, William, the rest of them. These are all strands that can't be reconciled."

"But you have real suspects. She only had suspicion."

Lily felt that there was something missing from her understanding. "Even you may have heard about what happened next. It was quite sensational."

Dr. Lamb nodded. "The incident with the gardener, Raymond."

. . .

On the evening of Lily's fifteenth birthday—Lauren had bought her a dress and was watching her parade around the lounge in it—Matthew came home from work in a frightful state. "I got the gossip from the stationmaster. You won't believe it." Forgetting all about Lily's special day, he poured himself a sherry and sat down. "It's the strangest thing."

His hair was disheveled, where he'd combed his fingers through it repeatedly; his fingernails glistened with grease. "It's Raymond," he said.

Lily sat down next to Lauren. The name of their old gardener, whom none of them had seen since the month after the murder, put them both on edge. They knew that whatever Matthew said next would lead them back to Agnes's killing.

"He's dead." Neither of them moved, not wanting to reveal themselves. "Killed, in London. It seems to have been a robbery. Apparently, he was going around town trying to sell some diamonds. In the slums, trying to avoid anywhere legitimate. The bloody fool got himself robbed and killed. They stabbed him."

Lily had a vision of Raymond struggling to breathe, his throat constricted, as he held a hand loosely over a hole in his stomach.

Matthew looked from her to her aunt. "Do you know what that means?"

They both knew exactly what it meant. Lauren put it into words:

"Where did he get hold of these diamonds, unless he was the one that murdered your mother?"

"Precisely," said Matthew. "I always thought he was suspicious."

• • •

"That was almost three years ago," said Lily. "I tried writing to William to check he was all right, but my letter never reached him. It was returned, unopened. Apparently, Raymond's widow had moved again and taken him with her."

"An unlucky child."

Lily sighed. "The poor boy. He'd be fifteen now. And that brings us to the present day."

"Did you ever confront your sister?"

Lily, a little drunk now, narrowed her eyes at him. "What do you mean?"

"I won't suggest that she was involved in the murder, but she clearly lied about her movements that morning."

Lily downed her drink. "You're not such a bad detective yourself, Doctor. *Doctor, detective*—the two words are quite similar now that I say them out loud."

"Take it slowly." He took the glass from her hand.

"Yes, it's true. When I saw Violet on the morning of the murder she was in a terrible state, shaken and distracted. I have asked her about it since. She'd gone up to collect Agnes's breakfast tray, after Lauren left, and Agnes had screamed at her and accused her of wanting her dead. Well, that wasn't so unusual, but Violet was haunted by it. She never told the police."

"Then Violet was the last to see her alive?"

"The last to admit to it."

"Of course." The doctor looked thoughtful.

"I have one more question for you," said Lily, emboldened by the alcohol. "A memory, in fact, that I'd like to ask you about."

The doctor nodded.

"After I left William in the boat and before I settled down with my book, I walked around the garden several times. I was looking for somewhere to sit. At one point I put my head around a hedge and saw you and Lauren in each other's arms, at the distant end of the lane. You were kissing her."

The doctor spun his chair slightly toward the wall, as if to deflect the accusation. "That's right, your aunt and me. Does that bother you?"

"That depends on what the two of you did together."

He sighed and checked his watch—either in search of some excuse to end the conversation or as an aid to recalling the past, she couldn't be sure. "We lied to the police, obviously. We adjusted our accounts of the day to avoid mentioning that little encounter. But the truth is we'd been seeing each other for months by that point and we were together when the murder happened, at your uncle's old house in the village."

"How sordid," said Lily dreamily.

The doctor grunted. He took a pen from his desk and leaned forward. "Perhaps you are too young to understand the impulse." She looked, with a sting of shame, at the whiskey glass in his hand. "Lately I've come to think that the human reproductive system"—he circled the air with his pen, pointing it vaguely at her womb—"is more an engine of destruction than of life."

She drew her knees up into her stomach and perched her feet on the edge of her chair. "Then you have no regrets?"

"What I have is an alibi, if you're really concerned with solving the murder."

She shrugged off this rebuke. "Well, can anyone confirm this alibi? If not, it's not much good."

"Have you asked your aunt Lauren about it?"

Lily's mouth straightened, her skin stretched a little tighter. "I'm sorry. I thought you knew. She died, last year." She thought back to

Lauren's body in its casket, the eyes bloodshot and the neck swollen. "It was a viral infection, a freak thing."

The doctor paled. "I didn't know."

He became thoughtful and silent. For all his shock at the image of Lauren's body convulsing on the cold floor, he couldn't help but feel a sense of triumph. She was one of his sins and he'd outlived her. Maybe, in fact, he would outlive them all. "I am sorry to hear it," he said. "God knows, your family has been through enough."

She wondered if there was meant to be something diminishing in that remark and looked down at the floor. "Well," she said, as a final formality, "is there anything else you can tell me about that day?"

He got to his feet. "In fact, there is." He filled his glass again. "After you leave this room, it might occur to you to wonder how Lauren and I knew such a rendezvous would be safe, at Matthew's own house on a day when he wasn't working. It's because he was going to the train station to meet Dorothea, or so he said. That's a twenty-five-minute walk in each direction. But he never did meet her, did he? She arrived by herself. Which makes you wonder, where did he really go?"

• • •

Leaving Dr. Lamb suspended between his office and his deathbed, let us take a step back.

Here it is my duty, as the author of this story, to assure my readers that they have now been presented with enough evidence to solve this mystery for themselves. The more ambitious of my readership may wish to pause for a moment and attempt to do so.

• • •

And now it was five years later.

Dr. Lamb had a view of the twilight in two rectangles. He was looking out of the window, through his glasses. He'd written her name and nothing else. *Dearest Lily.*

Then a sadness had consumed him. His sins seemed impossible to justify now that he'd reached the end of his life and seen how little difference they'd made to it; for the same reason, they were impossible to regret.

Five years ago you came to me with questions about your grandmother's murder. I did not tell you everything I knew at that time, for reasons that will become clear. In fact, I did the opposite, and my last hint to you was a piece of misdirection; your uncle did walk to the station, but he'd got the train times wrong. Perhaps you suspected this and were too polite to say so? You were an impressive young woman, and I hope the intervening years have served you well. Dorothea would have been proud.

He sighed deeply; he was delaying the moment of confession and he knew it. *At that meeting you got me to confess to one of my sins, my affair with your aunt Lauren. But not to the other, to the part I played in Agnes's murder. It all began with Ben Crake.*

• • •

"Excuse me." The doctor was walking past the war memorial one late summer's day, when the young man called out to him.

"Hello, Ben. How are you?"

Ben got to his feet. "Have you just come from the Grange, Doctor? Do you mind if I walk with you?"

"Yes, I have, and no, I don't mind. Come along. Do you want to know about Violet?"

"Not today," said Ben. "Today I want to ask you about diamonds."

• • •

It was the first I'd heard of them, wrote Dr. Lamb. *But Ben was insistent. Agnes had asked his father to help her sell them, when she'd briefly considered it—he knew a lot about that kind of thing, being in the antiques business—and when she pulled out of the sale, she'd sworn him to secrecy. But, of course, he'd told his son all about it. Ben knew I was in her bedroom often and asked me if I'd seen them. I had not, but I asked Lauren about it. She told me the story, that when Agnes's husband was alive and their future was bright, he'd bought her a diamond every year for their anniversary. Before the war. But she thought the old woman had sold them years ago.*

The light was growing dim. He squinted at the page.

I told her that Ben had assured me otherwise, and together we concocted a plan. This was after Agnes's fortuitously timed illness, and I was spending a lot of time at the house; I promised to find some way to sedate her on one of my visits, then Lauren would go in and search her room. We didn't intend to take all of the diamonds, just enough to split handsomely between the three of us—giving Ben his cut too—but Lauren was unable to find them. She spent an hour searching; they were nowhere. We didn't know that Agnes had woken up still feeling the effects of the sedative and had grown suspicious, so a few days later we planned our second attempt. This time I would come with her and help with the search.

· · ·

Ben scanned the nooks and partitions of the gardens with his binoculars, finally spotting the two of them, Lauren and Dr. Lamb, through a gap in the trees. "They ought to be more careful," he said to himself.

He intercepted them at the top of the lane, after circling widely around the gardener, busy collecting leaves at the other side of the house, and Violet's younger sister, who was reading under a tree; he'd already seen Matthew leaving the house for the station. "I'm coming with you."

Lauren looked at him suspiciously. "Why? Don't you trust us?"

"We want to maximize our chances of finding them, don't we?"

The doctor shook his head. "But if you're seen, how will we explain your presence?"

"It shouldn't come to that," said Lauren. "Violet is asleep in the lounge. If we use the other staircase, she won't hear us."

"Fine." The doctor parted his hands, then turned to Lauren. "Did you give her the sedative?"

Lauren nodded. "It's in her milk."

"Then let's make sure we find them this time."

"I've been watching her," said Ben, lifting his binoculars, "but I haven't seen where she keeps them."

"You won't find them." A small voice trickled out of the trees. "She doesn't take them out in the daytime." There was a rustling of leaves, and a shape climbed out from one of the nearby elderberries. It was William, his hands black with crushed fruit. "I know where they are. They're very well hidden."

"Where are they?" asked Ben.

Lauren knelt down in front of the child. "William, how do you know where they're hidden?"

"She was out of the room once. I crawled under her bed. I was going to surprise her, but when she came back in, she slammed the door, so I was too scared. I stayed there all night. She takes them out at night."

The doctor struggled to suppress a smile. "Then won't you tell us where they are?"

The boy shook his head. "I'll show you," he said, with an air of importance.

Lauren looked up at Dr. Lamb, then glanced briefly at Ben. She turned back to the child. "William, can you keep a secret?"

• • •

Dr. Lamb massaged his hand; he'd covered two pages already. The light was failing, and he wanted to get it all down before dark. He picked up the pen again.

Well, there you have it. The four of us went up to her bedroom together, sneaking past you and Raymond and Violet without too much difficulty. William showed us the loose piece of wood in the window frame and behind it just the edge of a canvas pouch emerging. It came out like a worm pulled from an apple, with a little resistance. Then we emptied it onto a table. There were more than we had imagined, and they were dazzling. It felt fantastic. And young William was the most excited of all of us.

• • •

"You!"

They turned around. Agnes was sitting up in bed. Where her head had left the pillow, there was a dark, wet stain. She had felt too weak to make it to the window after breakfast, so she'd poured the glass of milk very carefully into her own pillow, to give Lauren the impression she'd drunk it. Then she'd lain back and covered it with her hair.

"I knew somebody was up to no good. But all four of you!"

Ben stepped forward without hesitating. He took some spare blankets from a dresser beside the bed and threw them over the old woman. Briefly, she looked like a ghost. Then he nudged them all forward. "Come on, there's no going back now."

She had seen too much and they knew what they had to do. There were no objections, even from William, who seemed to think it was all a game. They threw every piece of bedding they could find over her and then climbed on top. The four of them, all equally committed to her murder. She was barely able to struggle beneath their combined weight, but they could still feel movement, and they sat there holding on to one another until it had stopped. Then they stayed in place for another few minutes, to be sure. But not one of them was willing to lift the blankets and look at her dead body.

• • •

We changed the pillow, of course. Nobody noticed that the mattress was slightly damp. And we sealed up the hiding place. But we left everything else as it was. At worst you can call me an unwilling accomplice.

He sighed, wondering if that was accurate. Even now it was a struggle to speak honestly.

Lauren and I sold our share through Ben's father, who asked no questions. But William had already moved away by that point. We'd given him a share, of course, and hoped that it would keep him quiet. And it did, for a few years. But he must have told Raymond all about the diamonds at some point, and the fool evidently took them to London and advertised them too widely and wound up getting stabbed in an alleyway. Dr. Lamb smiled. *It's not much, but that's the only thing resembling justice that I can offer you.*

He was growing impatient, and his hand hurt.

Lauren seemed to lose interest in me after the murder. I think the guilt was too much for her. So I left her with Matthew and I came here, to London, where there was no one to notice the sudden change in my fortunes. And I lived comfortably, that's all. I think that's the most that any of us got out of the murder, just a bit of comfort. I wish I could say it was worthwhile, but I'm not sure that would be the truth. I hope you can find it in yourself to forgive us. Yours, Dr. Godwin Lamb.

He put the pen down and stared sadly at the darkness outside. Then he began to cough. He coughed for several minutes. Then he went to the bathroom, leaving a dot of bright-red blood by his signature.

12

THE SIXTH CONVERSATION

Julia Hart ran her finger along the final paragraph. "*He coughed for several minutes. Then he went to the bathroom, leaving a dot of bright-red blood by his signature.*"

It was late, and her eyes had started to feel heavy halfway through that last page. "Forgive me," she yawned.

Grant filled the silence. "Another sordid tale. We've discussed the definition of a murder mystery already, so perhaps the most helpful thing I can do now is to describe how this story derives from it."

"Yes," said Julia, picking up her pen. "I would be interested to hear that."

They were sitting in a wooden hut, a few hundred yards along the beach from Grant's cottage. Inside it was a rack where a single small boat was stored, with space for another. They'd opened the wide doors that faced the sea and were sitting just inside, on two wooden folding chairs. Before them the perfectly smooth sand ran down to the water, as neat as a carpet.

"We've looked at several stories now where just one of the suspects turned out to be the killer. And this morning we looked at a story where all of the suspects turned out to be killers. Well, it's immediately clear from the definition that there's also a halfway point. We can have exactly half of the suspects turn out to be killers, or any other proportion."

"And here we have Ben, Lauren, William, and Dr. Lamb," said Julia. "The shadowy stranger, the young boy, the doctor, and his mistress. Four killers. And I counted nine suspects, in total."

Grant nodded. "The point is that any subset of the suspects could turn out to be guilty. It could be a quarter of them, a half, or even all but one of them. All of these solutions are equally valid, according to the definition. This story simply illustrates the point." He leaned forward in his chair. "I told you the definition was liberating, and this is why. It almost creates a new genre: Now, instead of guessing who the killer is, the reader must guess for each individual suspect whether or not they were involved in the crime. The number of possible endings increases exponentially."

Julia looked thoughtful. "Don't you worry that it's almost too much freedom? If a whole group of the suspects were guilty, then it would be next to impossible for the reader to guess the solution exactly, which might make it feel arbitrary."

"It's a challenge for the author to make an ending like that feel satisfying, that's true. But in itself it's no more arbitrary than any other ending. Remember that I've rejected the view of detective stories as logical puzzles, where the clues define a unique solution and the process of deriving it is almost mathematical. It's not, and they never do. That's all just sleight of hand."

She was writing down everything he said. "It's certainly an interesting way of looking at it."

"We mustn't forget," Grant continued, "that the central purpose of a murder mystery is to give its readers a handful of suspects and the promise that in about a hundred pages one or more of them will be revealed as the murderers. That's the beauty of the genre." His eyes drifted to the sea, as if it would have been impolite to say the word *beauty* while looking at her. "It presents the reader with a small, finite number of options, and then at the end it just circles back and commits to one of them. It's really a miracle that the human brain could ever be surprised by such a solution, when you think about it. And the definition doesn't change that, it just clarifies the possibilities."

Julia nodded. "Yes, I've never thought about it like that. The craft, then, is in the misdirection: in picking the solution that in some ways seems the most unsuitable to the story you've written but in other ways fits perfectly."

"Yes," said Grant. "And that's what differentiates a murder mystery from any other story with a surprise at the end. The possibilities are presented to the reader up front. The ending just comes back and points to one of them."

An antique lamp was hanging from the ceiling behind them. The sun had set while Julia was reading, and now the hut was a box of sour yellow light buried in the astral blue of the evening, like a gemstone in a cave. Julia felt that it was her turn to speak.

"Just like the other stories," she said, "this one has a small detail out of place. It took me a few readings to notice it."

Grant was nodding. "I would like to hear it."

Julia turned the pages of her notebook. "The first things that struck me were the many references to strangulation, though Agnes was killed by being smothered. First the squirrel was found strangled. Then we see the doctor explaining strangulation to William. The house itself is even described as being strangled by trees. It's as if these details were put there to foreshadow something that never comes to pass."

"Yes," said Grant. "That's interesting. I didn't notice that."

"And then on a second reading I realized that every single death that occurs in the story is described with at least one symptom of strangulation, even when it makes no sense. The doctor at the start is presumably dying of cancer of the liver or pancreas, but his voice is hoarse. Agnes has bruises along her neck, but there's no explanation for them. And when Raymond is stabbed, Lily imagines him with his throat constricted, unable to breathe. Even Lauren's corpse had bloodshot eyes and a swollen neck, and she died of a virus."

"Yes," said Grant, "that is very puzzling. It's more subtle than the others, perhaps."

The lamp was flickering behind them. Grant reached up and lifted it down from the ceiling. It was running low on oil. He extinguished it, leaving only the moonlight.

"Have you always lived alone out here?"

"Yes, I have," said Grant. He pushed himself up in his chair and turned toward her. "Earlier you asked me if I was obsessed with the sea. I have an answer for you."

"I'd be interested to hear it."

"To me, the sea is like having a pet dog asleep on the hearth. When I'm near it, even inside my cottage, it's like I can feel it breathing. It's a companion of sorts. It's less lonely to live alone by the sea."

Julia shook her head. "I'm afraid that I can't relate to that." The faint smell of rotten flesh came back to her on the breeze, and she looked at the sea and couldn't help but imagine herself drowning in it. "To me the sea has always been mildly terrifying. It moves like a set of jaws, chewing on everything inside it. Doesn't it remind you of death sometimes?"

Grant's response was enigmatic. "You'd think it would, but it doesn't."

Julia said nothing.

• • •

Thirty minutes later, Julia Hart returned to her hotel room, making her way up the stairs in the dark. She turned on the electric light and sat down at the desk by the window. The bright reflection blocked her view of the stars, except the few she could see where the room was in shadow.

She rubbed her eyes and opened the window, so that the cool night air would keep her awake. Then she picked up her pen.

On the desk in front of her was a small book, bound in green leather. It was an original copy of *The White Murders*. She slid it toward her and opened it near the end, weighing it down with a pebble. She picked up her notebook and turned to a blank page. She tore two squares from the edge of the page and wrote out a question on each of them, then she leaned forward and pinned them to the windowsill. One read, *Who was Francis Gardner?* The other, *Did he have anything to do with the White Murder?* She thought for a moment and then added a third, this one a reminder for the morning: *Talk to the hotel manager.*

She turned to a fresh page and checked the time. There was so much that she still had to do. She inhaled and held her breath for a moment, trying to focus her thoughts; the buzzing of the electric light made it sound like the walls were full of insects.

Then she breathed out and started to write.

13

THE SHADOW
ON THE STAIRCASE

t was a Monday morning: the first opportunity for anything interesting to happen after the stifling quiet of Sunday. Before midday,
the great detective Lionel Moon received two deliveries that made
no sense to him.

He found the first as he was leaving for work. A box of chocolates and a card. He stepped into the corridor outside his apartment and
saw the shallow rectangular box sitting in the middle of his doormat.
It looked like a model of a farmhouse in a field of wheat, with the card
as a kind of roof. As he picked it up, he felt the chocolates rattle inside
and had an image of bones bouncing around in a coffin. The card was
signed with an *X,* in two swoops of dark-blue ink. "Is this a gift," he
asked himself, "or some kind of warning?"

Lionel Moon had very few friends and none that he could imagine
buying him chocolates. He stepped back into his apartment and placed
the box on a small table next to the door. Then he locked his apartment
and left the building.

He found the second delivery that evening, as he was arriving home from work. An envelope was taped to his door, with his name written on it in large, wandering handwriting. He opened it, still standing in the corridor; inside was a photograph of a photograph of himself, leaving the building. It had been taken from the street outside or perhaps from the shop across the road. He knew it was a photograph of a photograph because the image within the image was slightly distorted, as if it had been laid on a table and tilted back away from the camera. It had a thick white border that wasn't quite straight. There was a vague shadow covering both the border and the image inside it. "A picture of a picture," he said to himself. "What on earth does that mean?"

If he'd given it any thought he might have assumed that these two deliveries, the chocolates and the photograph, were in some way related. But in fact the effect of the photograph—of seeing himself both in profile and in miniature, striding purposefully across the palm of his own hand as he held it out in front of him—was that he forgot about the chocolates altogether and didn't even notice them as he entered his apartment.

"A message. But what is it trying to tell me?"

He took the envelope and its contents through to the kitchen, then sat down to study them while waiting for a pan of soup to warm on the hob. The pan was a knotty metal thing, and the soup inside it was yellow. Though he was considered one of the best detectives in Europe, Lionel Moon lived a very simple life. He rented a few rooms—a kitchen, lounge, and bedroom—in a tall apartment building on a handsome street that led off from a London square. At the end of the hall was a shared bathroom. His landlady—Mrs. Hashemi, a widow—lived alone on the top floor.

He heard the soup bubbling and took the saucepan off the flame, then poured its contents into a chipped white bowl. He ate his dinner while examining the envelope, careful not to spill anything on what might later become evidence. There were no unusual markings on it and nothing to say where it had come from. He put it down and picked up the photograph. Not so different from an envelope itself, he thought, with one image contained neatly inside another. Only there was no way to open it and examine the contents.

"It seems vaguely threatening."

If someone had sent him an ordinary photograph of himself, he would have assumed that it was meant as a warning: a message that someone was watching him, delivered in pictorial form. But a photograph of a photograph felt much more ambiguous. He looked closely at it and realized that it was a picture of a page in a magazine. There had been a few magazine profiles of him over the years, when his name had come up in celebrated cases. There were some black marks along the bottom that must have been the top of a line of text. Someone had opened the magazine on a table and photographed the page.

"But why?"

He had grown tired of the detective's life, but the mystery still managed to captivate him; he forced himself not to think about it. He rinsed the bowl and saucepan in cold water and put them away in a cupboard, then put the photograph back in its envelope and placed it on a shelf in his lounge. Then, because he'd come home from work rather late, he turned out the lights in the kitchen and went straight to bed.

• • •

Like all of the most effective nightmares, this began with an absence of meaning where meaning should have been present: The photograph of the photograph was still a mystery to Lionel Moon when two days later he returned home and found a third delivery waiting for him. Fate seemed to have become a cat, leaving these curious, mangled items at his door. This time it was a dead body.

He had passed through the door to his apartment without noticing anything unusual; it was only when he'd reached the kitchen that he realized something was amiss. The door to his bedroom was standing open, though he knew he'd carefully closed it that morning. He always did, to keep in the heat; the rooms were cavernous and the building was often cold. But now there was half a foot of empty space between the door and the doorframe, a dark rectangle as tall and thin as a lamppost. Lionel took his gun from inside his jacket and held it in his right hand, then peered through the gap in the doorway.

A dead body lay on his bed. It was the body of a man, fully clothed in a dark-brown suit: middle-aged, unshaven, and tough-looking. Lionel noticed with distaste that the dead man was still wearing his shoes and that the sheets of the bed were bunched into wrinkles beneath their weight. His face was swollen beyond recognition, and his skin was a velvet purple. He'd been poisoned, most likely, or had possibly fallen ill with some disease. There were no obvious signs of a struggle; the man could have been put there before or after he died, it was hard to tell.

One side of his face was extensively scarred with what seemed to be burnt skin: those unmistakable patterns of blistered and buckled flesh, though they were old and only slightly visible. The scarring extended to his hairline, which was covered by a hat. Inspector Goode, who had been Lionel's partner for many years, had a saying: "If you enter heaven, you're allowed to forget the pains of your life, but in hell you must remember them." Lionel thought of that every time he saw the tortured face of a freshly dead body. Were those contortions the effects of painful memories being lived through all over again or just the effects of death? He reached across and closed the corpse's eyes, sealing the truth behind them.

"Where do you think he is, then, heaven or hell?" The words came from behind him. Lionel turned and saw Inspector Goode standing in the doorway. Lionel's breathing faltered, as it always did, because the inspector had been dead for almost a year. There'd been a gas leak in the building where he lived; Lionel had found the corpse himself and a few days later had helped carry his coffin to a slot under the eaves of a small church. It was as if the dead man had chosen to huddle there out of the rain and smoke a cigarette for all eternity.

But that hadn't stopped the inspector from coming back to continue their partnership, just as if he'd never died. It had started straight after the funeral. Lionel thought he'd seen the dead man standing in the crowd, smiling at him. Now it would happen during the most innocent domestic moments; whenever Lionel was alone, the inspector was likely to appear. He had long ago given up wondering whether he was losing his mind and had now just come to accept it. "Afternoon, Goode." He turned back to the corpse. "What do you make of it?"

"He swallowed something that didn't agree with him. Check his pockets, will you?"

Lionel did as his dead partner asked. There were no further clues, either to the man's identity or to where or how he'd been killed.

"Why do you think the body was brought here to me?"

"I can think of three possibilities." Inspector Goode held up three fingers, and Lionel noticed that they cast no shadow on the wall behind him. Just a figment of my imagination, he thought. "It could be a warning," the inspector said. "Or a partial confession, by the killer."

"Or an attempt to frame me for murder?"

"Yes, that's the third option. But be stoic about it, why don't you? It's hard to frame someone for murder. And besides, you have the upper hand. There's a clue you haven't noticed yet."

Lionel spoke defensively. "I've barely had time." He left the bedroom and examined the door to his apartment. It was untouched; the lock was still working and there were no marks upon it. Then he checked the windows, even though he lived on the second floor. A ladder or a length of rope could have been used to climb up to them; it wasn't impossible. But they were all latched shut and none of them were damaged.

Inspector Goode watched him from the doorway; he was whistling impatiently.

As Lionel was checking the farthest window in the corner of his bedroom, he noticed movement in the building opposite. The woman that lived there was standing at her kitchen window, looking vaguely in his direction as she prepared a stew. He stepped to one side, hoping that she hadn't seen him, and watched her through a gap in the curtains.

The building that she lived in was less distinguished than his own, and the walls facing him were more brick than window, but through years of observation he had created a convincing picture of the family that lived there. There were three of them. The father worked long hours and came home late; his wife spent her days on domestic chores and in caring for their child, a young boy, who was perpetually in bed with some illness or another.

They seemed to be an unhappy family, but the boy's bedroom was opposite the bathroom at the end of the hall, and in the summer, with the frosted-glass window propped open, Lionel would amuse himself by making faces at the child—his wet head becoming a procession of rain-soaked gargoyles—and the boy would always laugh.

"Can she see the body from there?"

He turned, expecting Goode to reply, but his former partner had vanished as soon as Lionel had noticed the woman.

He looked at the bed. It was blanketed in shadow, and the angles convinced him she probably couldn't. He sighed with relief. It was crucial that nobody should call the police before he had taken the time to investigate. If the body was going to be used to frame him, there must be a reason the police hadn't been contacted yet. Perhaps the murderer would return later to plant more evidence or was busy establishing an alibi of their own. He couldn't act, or allow anyone to intervene, until he understood more of the situation.

The woman appeared to lose interest and turned away from the window. He watched her put a bowl of stew on a tray and leave the kitchen, then he emerged from his hiding place.

He had one advantage over the murderer, it occurred to him: He was home much earlier than usual. It was the middle of the afternoon on a Wednesday, a time when he would normally have been at his office. It gave him the chance to catch them off guard.

He walked back into the lounge. Inspector Goode was sitting in an armchair. Lionel sat down opposite him. "Where did you go?"

The inspector smiled. In life, he had always acted as if he knew the answer to everything; at times Lionel had found him insufferable. "I stepped outside for a moment. Did you find the clue?"

"The lock on the door hasn't been forced. The murderer must have had a key to my apartment." There was no other way they could have got in, since the windows were latched shut. And that meant that some-one he knew must have been involved. Paradoxically, he found the thought comforting: It introduced limits into a situation that had pre-viously seemed infinite in its possibilities.

"Good. Then you don't need me to tell you the suspects."

"The first is Mrs. Hashemi." His landlady, who lived on the top floor. She was the only person who had a key to his apartment other than himself. "But she's not a murderer, not like this."

Those last three words seemed to amuse the inspector. "She's more of the oil-on-the-staircase type, you think?"

Lionel frowned. "This is serious, Eustace. Someone is out to ruin me."

The humbled apparition shrugged its shoulders. "Well, what about the young girl?"

"The second—Hanna." Lionel leaned forward in his chair. Hanna was the young woman that came to clean the building and the apart-ments several times a week. She took their keys from the landlady's rooms. "She could have given the key to someone."

Lionel felt sure that neither Hanna nor his landlady wanted him framed or would be capable of committing murder. But they could still have been involved, providing the key to his apartment in exchange for money. Or maybe they'd been threatened?

"Should I question Mrs. Hashemi?"

"You would lose the advantage of being home ahead of time. And what if she warns her associates?"

Lionel closed his eyes. Was there anyone else it might have been?

There was his neighbor, Mr. Bell, a photographer and fellow night owl. A friend, almost; but Lionel couldn't trust anyone in the circumstances. And Mr. Pine, his neighbor downstairs—a quiet, bookish man who worked at one of the universities—but Lionel hardly knew him and hadn't seen him for weeks. "And not one of them has any motive."

...

Lionel Moon knew the criminal mind. He knew it to the point of exhaustion. It would take a professional to plot something like this, he was sure of that. So he put the question of the key to one side and asked himself: "Who would want to frame me?"

The first man that came to mind was a Hungarian counterfeiter called Keller.

Keller had been leading a counterfeiting ring in London for many years when one of his associates had tried to take more than his fair share of the profits. Keller had bound the man's hands and feet and run him alive through an industrial meat grinder, then had taken his blood and used it as a replacement for ink, printing a hundred fake pound notes with the victim's innards. He'd given one of these to each of the men in his gang, to remind them of the price of betrayal. Inevitably, one of them had got drunk and tried to spend it.

And that's how it had come to the police. From the shopkeeper's description and the broad set of smudges and prints that had covered the note, Lionel was able to piece together the main habits of the gang and then one by one deduce their identities. It was a masterpiece of analytical detective work, like a circle spiraling inward. As usual, there was little to incriminate the leader of the gang, so Keller had been convicted on some petty charge.

That had happened four years ago. Keller had been released the previous month and Lionel had been restless ever since. He was too old to defend himself now, and for all he knew, Keller was eager for revenge. After all, Lionel had destroyed his whole livelihood and his reputation.

"And isn't Hanna Hungarian also?" Lionel wondered if that was just a coincidence.

• • •

There were others that held grudges, of course. Too many for him to remember.

Just three weeks earlier he'd been discussing these past cases with his new partner, Inspector Erick Laurent. Some of them had been legendary. There was the case of the prolific art thief Otto Mannering, in which Lionel had deduced the culprit's profession, education, and age from the paintings he had chosen to steal. Then there was the case of the young boy found cut in half in a reservoir north of London: Lionel had established that not only were the two halves parts of two separate bodies but that the top half was in fact a young girl made up to look like a boy.

"And was there an original?" Laurent had asked him. "A first case that inspired you to take up detection?"

"Yes, there was." And Lionel had told the tale he'd told a hundred times before.

He was an orphan, he said. St. Bartholomew's orphanage was a cruel place, and one afternoon he ran away. He was ten years old. He walked about eight miles and came to the edge of a plowed field, where he noticed a small hillock of dirt at the side of a ditch. It seemed to be a recent addition to the landscape. On top of it was a rose and a child's toy. He brushed away some of the dirt and found the face of a dead young girl staring out through the scattered mud. It was his first encounter with death, and he ran to the nearest road and didn't stop running for several miles. He was picked up about an hour later and returned to the orphanage.

Since he'd already been in enough trouble, he never told anyone about finding the body. Only when he was seventeen years old and had left St. Bartholomew's for London did he find himself, on a rainy Sunday, suddenly struck by a desire to solve the case. There was no record of a missing girl in the area at that time; he took a day trip out to the orphanage, stopping briefly to revisit the rooms he'd lived in as a child, but he wasn't able to find the field again and had returned to London disappointed. He knew, of course, that the girl's family or custodians must have killed her and not reported her death—it was the only possibility that made sense—but he never discovered who she was or why she'd been buried in such secrecy.

Erick Laurent had stroked his beard. "That is most intriguing," he'd said.

And the two men had agreed: Once tasted, detection was like a drug. The best mysteries—the ones that kept them both awake at night—were the ones where there was an absence not of the perpetrator or of their method but of its meaning. Like the one before him now: The dead body on his bed could mean so many things, and he wouldn't be able to rest until he knew the truth.

Only as he was thinking this did he remember the photograph that he'd received two days before.

. . .

He found the envelope and laid its contents on the kitchen table. A photograph of a photograph of himself, almost unrecognizable in his youth, leaving his building and turning left. What could it mean? And was it related to the body on his bed?

"Let us go through this logically," he said to himself. If the purpose of a photograph is to depict the brief, restricted episode of reality during which it happened to be taken, then does a photograph of a photograph depict the same moment of reality, the same section of time? Or is it in some way a comment upon the original depiction, intended to be inherently satirical or critical? Is its intention to draw focus toward the fact of the photograph as an actual physical object—a glitter of silver dots nestled in a smear of gelatin—as if someone was saying, *Look what I found*? Or had it been taken by someone who didn't know of any other way to make a copy?

Lionel closed his eyes; the questions were tiring to him now. Both the body and the photograph seemed unreadable; there weren't enough clues to make sense of either. He wanted badly to smoke his pipe, though he'd given that up years ago.

Somebody slapped the table in front of him, and he opened his eyes to see Inspector Goode leaning over him. "Wake up, Moon. You're not finished yet. You've identified two suspects to begin with, so begin with them."

Lionel said nothing. At that moment he heard the familiar thud of somebody climbing the stairs. It was Mrs. Hashemi: He recognized her way of walking; he could picture it from his kitchen table. Her exuberant, ever-smiling mouth, which hung open whenever she was not in conversation with someone, would be bobbing up and down as she took each step. She would stop on the first landing and light a cigarette, and sure enough there was the absence of sound as she stopped to prove him right. It occurred to him then that he surely knew her well enough that if she was somehow involved in this crime, her reaction on seeing him home at such an unexpected hour would make it clear, whether it was excitement or fear or nervousness. "I'll surprise her."

Goode clapped his hands together. "That's the spirit!"

Lionel crept to the door and waited. When Mrs. Hashemi was nearing the top of the steps, about to pass by, he put his head through the door and looked around. He tried to act as if he was expecting someone; when he saw that it was her, he smiled politely and wished her a good day. She frowned and spoke in a near whisper: "These stairs. These bloody stairs." No anxiety at all, just her usual good humor.

Lionel made no reply; he nodded and stepped back inside his apartment.

So that settled it. His landlady was not involved. The revelation hardly surprised him. "Well done, Moon," said Inspector Goode. "Now go and get the other one."

. . .

Lionel wanted to watch Hanna going about her work, just for a moment. She was a timid girl, and he felt sure that if she'd passed the key to his apartment to somebody else, she wouldn't be able to hide the fact; he imagined her checking the time constantly or looking over her shoulder at every sound.

But the risk of him being seen was too great. So he put on a disguise: a simple wig of bright-orange curls to cover his balding head, and a long black jacket that he dug from the layers at the bottom of his closet. It would be enough to disguise him in the dim light of the corridor, which was all he could hope for. There was nothing more ridiculous, he'd often thought, than a detective in an elaborate costume. He was embarrassed just at the thought of it.

He crept softly out of his apartment and stood at the top of the stairs. A sticky scraping sound came from below.

He stepped carefully down the staircase, making as little noise as possible. When he was halfway down, he stopped and lowered his head: From there he could see her, at the end of the ground-floor corridor. She was holding a mop and humming to herself, moving it mechanically back and forth. "She doesn't seem nervous or tense." But it was hard to tell from this distance.

He hurried down the stairs and out onto the street, as if he was in a rush to get somewhere, glancing at her as he passed. But his impression didn't change. She seemed relaxed; she didn't even turn her head at the sound of his footsteps.

He almost ran into Inspector Goode, who was standing by a post box on the pavement outside. "It's not her either," said Lionel.

Goode put his arms out behind him and lifted himself up onto the top of the post box, where he sat with his shoes dangling four feet from the ground. It was the kind of agility only a dead man could achieve. He looked down at Lionel. "Then you must ask yourself whether there are any other suspects."

● ● ●

Lionel Moon returned to his apartment and paced around the lounge. "Who else could have done this, then?"

Mrs. Hashemi had a friend, the man who owned the florist's shop at the end of the street. Lionel often passed him climbing the stairs to her room, a bunch of flowers in his hands. His arms were covered in tattoos, remnants of a different life, but Lionel had always found him to be friendly and thought he was probably harmless.

He stopped pacing; he could hear the echoing sound of piano notes coming from somewhere nearby. He stood in silence for a moment. They seemed to be coming from one of the rooms next door. It must be Mr. Bell. He tiptoed to the connecting wall and flattened his head against it. He could hear the swell of floorboards moving ever so slightly up and down, and he realized that a piano was not being played at all; a gramophone was being listened to.

The movements ceased and Lionel had the absurd image of his neighbor pressed, like him, against the other side of the wall. Suddenly there was a thundering knock at his own front door. He had been concentrating so carefully on the music that he'd not noticed the footsteps approaching up the staircase.

The visitor knocked again, louder this time. Lionel stayed flat against the wall and tried not to breathe. Then he heard the sound of retreating steps, though they were hurried and he couldn't tell if they were heading upstairs or down.

He walked over to the kitchen table and laid his gun upon it, pointed away from him. Then he sat down. He waited; he had a hunch that the visitor would return. From this position he could see the whole of the lounge, and the gun was readily to hand. He was mildly disappointed that the case was already entering what must be its final act, before he'd had the chance to solve it. But that disappointment had become a common occurrence lately, as his retirement had approached and his thoughts had slowed down.

The next minute lasted for a long time. Inspector Goode did not appear.

Then the footsteps returned, joined now to those of his landlady. He recognized hers immediately. There was another set of loud knocks, then a pause. Silence. Nothingness. He heard the sobbing panic of Mrs. Hashemi as she fumbled to unlock the door; he heard the slow creak as it swung open; then a man walked through the doorway. It was his new partner, Inspector Erick Laurent.

Lionel was so surprised that his hand instinctively went to the gun. But the movement was subtle enough that it wasn't noticed, and both Laurent and the landlady hurried past him to the bedroom. Neither had seen him sitting there.

"He's dead," he heard Laurent say, followed by a cry of shock from his landlady. The two of them emerged from the room in hurried conversation, and neither looked his way. "Please, phone for a doctor," Laurent was saying. "It looks like murder. Here, Dr. Purvis is a friend of mine." Laurent scribbled a telephone number on a scrap of paper and handed it to Mrs. Hashemi. "Tell him that Lionel Moon is dead."

She ran from the room.

A moment of cold, stalled comprehension passed over Lionel, then his partner's words sank in. He stood up, weighed down by the gun. "Laurent," he said; the man didn't turn around. Lionel walked to where his partner was standing and waved his hand in front of him. But Laurent didn't seem to see him; he just walked through to the bedroom and looked down at the bed. In a state of desperation, Lionel followed him.

The corpse had seemed familiar, but only now did he recognize it as himself. The swelling hid too much of his face, and the scars had thrown him; he'd forgotten about the fire in the orphanage, when he was only a child. The whole building had burned to the ground. He was shocked also by how much older he looked here than in the photograph.

"If you enter heaven, you're allowed to forget the pains of your life, but in hell you must remember them." Lionel took it as a good omen that he'd forgotten about the fire.

Something else came back to him, and he returned to the lounge. Laurent seemed to follow him. That damn box of chocolates he'd been sent on Monday morning was sitting on the kitchen table, unnoticed until now. Last night he'd come home from work late and a little drunk—Laurent and he had shared some whiskey, to celebrate the end of a case—and he'd forgotten himself and eaten one. Or was it more than one? He looked inside the opened box: There were several missing. Foolish, he thought. A foolish, unforgivable thing to do.

But who would send him poisoned chocolates? And a card signed with a kiss? As one mystery ended, another began. He thought through the possible suspects, searching for someone with motive and opportunity, someone who knew his habits, someone who even knew of his weakness for chocolates. And this time it clicked.

He walked over to the window. The woman in the flat opposite was hiding behind her curtains, peering discreetly at his building. She knew what was happening and was watching the situation develop. He thought of the sickly child, and his skin went tight. For months—maybe even years, he wasn't sure—this woman had been poisoning her own son. And Lionel Moon had witnessed the whole thing without even realizing it. What was she stirring into his stew? Rat poison or weed killer; he knew of such cases. She must have hated Lionel watching her all the time and so she'd finally decided to do away with him. For her own safety, he assumed. Had she put some of the same stuff—a stronger dose, of course—into the chocolates and sent them to him? "There is no other explanation."

Behind him, somebody cleared their throat. He turned around. It was Inspector Goode, his deceased friend and former partner. He came over and reached up to the top of Lionel's head, taking the orange wig that he'd forgotten he was wearing. "It's important to have dignity where you're going," said Goode. "Follow me." The two of them left the apartment, leaving Detective Laurent alone in a room full of clues and red herrings, with a mystery to solve.

Lionel Moon's great regret, as he passed through his front door for that final time, was that he still didn't know why someone had sent him a photograph of a photograph two days earlier or what it was supposed to mean.

14

THE SEVENTH CONVERSATION

L ionel Moon's great regret," read Julia Hart, "*as he passed through his front door for that final time, was that he still didn't know why someone had sent him a photograph of a photograph two days earlier or what it was supposed to mean.*"

She lowered the manuscript. Grant McAllister looked up at her. "Well," he said. "That's the end, then?"

"Yes," said Julia. "The book ends with an unresolved mystery."

"He solved his own murder, at least."

"That's true. This story has a slightly different feel to it than the others. Don't you think?"

"Perhaps." Grant considered it. "There are supernatural elements, if nothing else. I've already mentioned that the definition doesn't forbid them."

"But they do make it rather unfair on the reader." She made it sound like an accusation.

"Maybe." Grant shrugged. "But this story represents the case where victim and detective overlap. We've looked at the overlap between suspects and detectives and suspects and victims, so this next step was inevitable. But even though the definition allows for it, it's hard to pull off in practice."

"And that's why you resorted to the supernatural?"

"Yes." Grant scratched his nose.

They were taking coffee in the rose garden, on the grounds of Julia's hotel. Grant had offered to meet her there to save her walking to his cottage. It was her third morning on the island and already set to be another blisteringly hot day.

He'd turned up soon after breakfast in his loose white suit and hat, his trouser cuffs stained orange from the walk. And he'd promptly spilled coffee on the sleeve of his shirt.

"This is a very elegant hotel," he said. "Your employer puts you up in style."

"It was the only hotel we could find on the island," said Julia. "Is there another?"

"That's a good question," Grant laughed. "I've never needed one. Now that I come to think of it, there probably isn't."

He was gazing distractedly around the garden, whistling to himself.

Julia interrupted his thoughts. "Is there anything you can tell me about this story? You said it was a difficult structure to pull off. Why is that?"

"Only because the detective is optional in our definition. So if you obfuscate their role too much by making them also the victim, the reader might not realize there was a detective at all. Having the victim come back as a ghost was a way around that. It was worth a shot, at least."

He was looking at a bird that was sitting on a statue—a woman holding a vessel of water—carved from a smooth white stone that looked as solid as chocolate. Julia was watching him. She felt nervous, now that everything was moving toward its conclusion.

"I think you succeeded," she said. "And I like that it's different from the other stories." She took a folder from her bag and opened it on her lap. She didn't want him to suspect anything, not yet. "I had a go at reading your research paper again last night." She looked like she hadn't slept; her eyes were red. "It was more comprehensible now you've explained some of the main points to me, but there was still a lot I couldn't follow."

"There's a lot we haven't discussed."

"I was particularly interested in the list you give in section two, subsection three."

Grant gave her his full attention. "Go on," he said.

"May I read it to you?"

Grant nodded. "Of course."

She looked down at the folder. "*Armed with this definition,*" she read, "*we can now set out mathematically the fundamental variations on the classic murder mystery.*"

"Yes," said Grant, closing his eyes. "The permutations of detective fiction."

"*The cases are as follows,*" Julia continued, taking a deep breath. "*That where the number of suspects is equal to two. That where there are three or more suspects. The aberrant case with infinitely many suspects, which we allow but don't consider worthy of comment. That where the set of killers has a size of one, a solitary actor. That where the set of killers has a size of two, partners in crime. That where the set of killers is equal to the entire, or almost the entire, set of suspects. That where a large share of the suspects, three or more but not all, are killers. That where there is a single victim; that where there are multiple victims. Any case formed by replacing A and B with any combination of suspects, detectives, victims, or killers— except that of suspects and killers, which has already been accounted for—in the following: the cases where A and B are disjoint, where A contains B as a strict subset, where A and B are equal, where A and B overlap but neither is contained in the other. Notably that includes the cases where all detectives are killers, all suspects are victims, all detectives are victims. That* where the suspects entirely consist of detectives and victims, and likewise for the killers. That where the killers are only those detectives that are not also victims. That where the killers are only those victims that are not also detectives. That where every suspect is both victim and killer. That where every suspect is both detective and killer. That where every suspect is victim, detective, and killer all in one. Finally, the case where all four sets are identical: suspects, killers, victims, and detectives. And any consistent combination of the above."

Grant's eyes were glowing with satisfaction. "That makes me nostalgic for my days of doing research," he said.

"It's an exhaustive, exhausting list. Was it ever your intention to write a story for each one of those permutations?"

Grant was watching an ant crawl to the tip of a sundial, a few yards away from them. "There would be far too many. Especially when you take that last sentence into account. It was an aspiration, perhaps. But never an intention."

"And yet you stopped at just seven stories. Why was that?"

It took him some time to answer. "Nobody was interested in murder mysteries after the war. They became outdated very quickly, next to all that real death."

"Some of the conventions are out of date, perhaps. But the structure itself is alive and well."

He looked doubtful. "Do you really believe that?"

"What I mean is that if you read a crime novel now, it's impossible not to wonder how it will end. That emphasis is borrowed from the murder mystery. You might not be wondering specifically which character committed the murder—maybe that's been clear all along—but you'll still be wondering which of a small, finite set of possible endings the author will commit to. So the structure is still there."

Grant was smiling. He sat in silence for a moment. "Yes, I think you make a good point. I've never looked at it like that before. But it doesn't disprove my claim that the conventional murder mystery is out of date. I felt that very tangibly toward the middle of the forties, and that's why I stopped writing them."

"It's a shame," said Julia, and she picked up her coffee cup.

"Did you notice any inconsistencies in this story?" He took his own coffee cup and drank the last mouthful of bitter liquid. It was lukewarm.

"Yes. An easy one this time." Julia shrugged. "The whole orphanage burned down when he was a child, but as a teenager he visits the rooms where he'd lived when he was young. So did it burn down or not?"

"I see," said Grant. "Yes, I should have spotted that one."

Julia put her empty cup down and pointed behind him. "Have you ever been up there?"

She was pointing to a section of the coast just outside the town, where the land rose to a considerable height and a sheer cliff looked down suspiciously at the sea. "Yes," he said quietly. "I know it well."

Julia couldn't take her eyes off it. "It looks very dramatic. I have a draft of the introduction in my bag. Perhaps we could walk up there to read it? To make an occasion of it."

Grant raised an eyebrow. "I'm impressed," he said. "When did you find the time to write that?"

"Last night, mostly. After I left you."

He whistled in admiration. "Then yes, if you like. I haven't been up there in a very long time. But I'm keen to hear what you've written. And the island is worth seeing in its entirety."

"Good," she said, and packed up her things.

15

THE FINAL CONVERSATION

Julia Hart looked back as she struggled up the loose hillside; Grant had fallen behind, and for the first time the difference in their ages was apparent, though his excitement was undiminished. She waited for him to catch up, standing slightly off the path. "I'm sorry," she said. "This didn't look so steep from below."

Grant stopped to wipe his forehead with a handkerchief. "It's not that bad," he said, "only the heat makes it so much harder." The corners of his white clothes were circled with sweat.

Julia turned back to the path. The hill in front of them led up to the dramatic precipice that they'd seen from the rose garden of her hotel. The top half of it was scattered with small patches of yellowing woodland. "Those trees will give us some shelter," she said. "We can take a break when we reach them."

"The last time I did this, I found it easy." Grant was squinting at her outline. "Growing old is a graceless thing, I'm afraid."

They started moving again.

It didn't take them long to reach the line of slender, questioning trees that marked the start of the brief woodland; the path they were following led them straight through the middle of it. After thirty yards or so they came to a clearing ringed with swollen rock formations. The light inside was a gaudy yellow and green from the sun shining through the leaves.

"A natural amphitheater," said Grant, stroking one of the rocks. "It's a few years since I last came here."

"This island seems to have everything."

Grant had regained his energy now that they'd come to a stop. He lifted himself onto a rock and turned to face Julia, his legs dangling over the side. "I fell in love with it the moment I arrived."

Julia looked around. She wished they'd brought some water with them, or some wine. "I've never been anywhere like it."

He took off his hat and fanned himself with it. "I must admit, I was apprehensive of your visit at first. I've lived a simple life for the last few years. But I've found it stimulating." He wiped his forehead again and let the damp handkerchief fall heavily to the ground.

"I don't think we should go any farther," said Julia. "It might be easier to talk here, out of the wind."

Grant nodded. "And you have a draft of the introduction for me to hear?"

"Yes." She tapped her bag. "But before we discuss that, I think we should make a decision about the title of the book."

"*The White Murders*. Do you think we should change it?"

"I won't be the only one to notice the similarity between the White Murder and *The White Murders*. We should at least decide what we'll say if the question arises."

"Then I think we should change it." He tossed his hat from one hand to the other. "How about *The Blue Murders*?"

"It sounds rather seedy."

Grant chuckled. "Then do you have a suggestion?"

"Perhaps." She took a deep breath. "But I'd still like to know why you called it *The White Murders*."

Grant picked up a twig and started to peel the bark with his finger-nails. "I told you, I found it evocative. If it sounds similar to something else, that's just a coincidence."

"There are quite a few of those coincidences throughout the book. The White Murder certainly caught your imagination."

Grant tore off a leaf and placed it on the rock beside him—a defensive move in a game of chess. "I'm not sure what you mean."

"Do you remember the details of the White Murder?"

A long period of silence passed; Grant looked like a lizard on his rock, barely moving at all. "Only what you told me the other day."

"Then listen." Julia was standing in front of him like a teacher at a blackboard, with a wall of trees at her back. "The White Murder took place on the twenty-fourth of August, 1940. Miss Elizabeth White was murdered on Hampstead Heath. She'd been taking her dog for a walk, just before sunset. When she reached the Spaniards Inn—a well-known public house that stands on the edge of the heath at the north end—a man stopped to speak to her. She was seen by several witnesses talking to a man in a blue suit. The two of them continued onward together. An hour or so later she was found in the road outside the Spaniards Inn. She had been strangled. That was at half past nine at night. Her dog had gone missing and was never seen again. They never found her killer."

Grant shook his head. "That's all very interesting. But why are you telling me this?"

Julia continued: "It might not seem relevant at first glance. But here we have your stories, seven of them, each one containing at least one detail that doesn't quite make sense. The first one has a Spanish villa with an impossible layout and an impossible chronology. The second has a scene that ought to take place during the day but turns out to be set at night, at nine-thirty exactly. The third has a duplicate man wearing a blue suit whose presence is never explained. The fourth highlights the word *white* by replacing it everywhere with its opposite. The fifth has a dog that seemingly vanishes; the sixth is filled with descriptions of strangulation though no one in the story is actually strangled. And the seventh has a resurrected orphanage named for St. Bartholomew, whose feast day happens to be the twenty-fourth of August. And all of these stories are brought together under a title, *The White Murders*. That's quite a lot of coincidences."

Grant swallowed audibly. "Yes, that is quite a lot."

"Then do you still deny it?"

He spent a long time considering the question, seeming to calculate. "I don't think that would do me much good. You've got me. Those are all references to the White Murder." There was a pained look on his face. "I don't remember doing that. Putting those in, I mean."

"It seems unlikely that you would forget. It must have been quite a careful, deliberate act, to work in that many of them."

"Yes, perhaps."

"It must have taken a long time."

"I don't remember."

Julia stared straight through him. "Grant, it's becoming increasingly hard to believe what you're telling me."

He tapped his heels against the rock. "What can I say?"

A flurry of wind filled the clearing then, and a cloud of dust and leaves seemed to rise from the ground, swirling in circles; the island was suddenly loud. Julia let the noise die down before answering him. "I don't expect you to say anything. I don't expect anything at all, because I don't believe that you are the author of these stories."

The clearing became quiet again.

An amphitheater with a single person sitting in it is nothing more than an elaborate throne, so Grant sat there in that grand chair, unable to move, as if he were a king caught in checkmate. "What a strange thing to say." His voice cracked and he began to cough. "Why would you say a thing like that?"

"It's true, isn't it? You're not the author of these stories. You're not Grant McAllister. You're somebody else entirely."

The blood drained from his face. "Of course it's not true, not at all. Why on earth would you think such a thing?"

"Yes, I'm sure you'd like to know." Julia took a step toward him. "Well, I'll tell you: I've been suspicious of this situation from the start. I've seen authors embarrassed by their early work, others stubbornly proud of it. But I've never met one so frankly uninvested in it." She started to pace from side to side with one hand held aloft, a finger pointed at the sky. "You've explained the mathematics to me at great length. But you've told me almost nothing about the stories themselves. How they came to be written, why you made the decisions you did."

"I wrote them a long time ago."

"There's also the fact that Grant was born and raised in Scotland, but you don't have a Scottish accent. And Grant would be about ten years older than you appear to be."

"I grew up close to the border. I look young for my age."

Julia stopped in the center of the clearing. "And you fell into my trap."

At her use of this word, Grant looked around, as if worried that his life might now be in danger. But the moment of panic passed and he relaxed again; Julia was watching him, and under her stubborn gaze he seemed to sink into a kind of stoic resignation.

"What did you do?" he asked.

"It started with that first story. I made a mistake, that's all. When I was reading it out. My head was spinning from the heat; my vision was blurry. I'd ringed the last few lines of the text in red pen, to suggest a change of wording. But in fact I missed them entirely. So I only read out half of the ending. And you didn't even notice."

"A few lines, that's nothing."

"A few lines," said Julia. "But they changed everything. The story had Megan and Henry arguing over which of them killed their friend Bunny, do you remember? He's lying on a bed upstairs with a knife in his back. They're trapped in his house on a very hot day, trying to decide what to do next. They know that one of them is the murderer, but neither will admit to it."

"Yes, I remember."

"Time passes and they make no progress, so they decide to have a drink. Megan takes the glass that Henry gives her, holds on to it for a minute, and then gives it back. Henry drinks from it. A few minutes later he collapses. It's clear that he's been poisoned, and Megan effectively admits to doing it. You assumed that she was also guilty of murdering Bunny."

"Yes," said Grant. "What is your point?"

"The next few lines contradict that idea. Do you remember what she says to him after he collapses?"

Grant shook his head.

. . .

"That's the thing about lying, Henry." She stood up and towered over him. "Once you start, you can't stop. You have to follow it where it takes you." Megan finished off her drink. "Well, I can't listen to any more. I know you killed Bunny, and you know that I know. I'll be damned if I'll let you kill me too."

. . .

Grant's eyes widened. "So she killed Henry in self-defense?"

"Yes," said Julia, "because Henry murdered Bunny. I only realized later that I'd missed those lines, which changed the whole ending. And yet you didn't pick up on it. Could you really have forgotten something so deliberate?"

His voice rose. "After twenty long years, of course I could."

"Yes," said Julia, "I thought so too. So I reserved my judgment; I decided to test you. I'm afraid to say, you didn't pass."

He closed his eyes. "What do you mean?"

"My mistake with that first story gave me an idea. We read the second story that afternoon. It was set in a town by the sea, called Evescombe."

Grant nodded. "Go on."

"A man called Gordon Foyle is accused of pushing Vanessa Allen from the cliffs. But he claims that it was an accident. All we know for sure is that they passed each other by, walking in opposite directions. The detective is a sobering character called Mr. Brown."

"A bulky man in black, I recall."

"He finds a lady's scarf coiled in the bushes at the top of the cliffs. It has a boot print on it—the heel of a slim Wellington shoe."

"And he concludes that she must have been dragged backward toward her death."

Julia nodded. "But that's the only bit I changed. That and the ending."

Grant stared at her, his face full of questions. "You changed the ending?"

"And a few of the details leading up to it. I did it intentionally this time, when you went for a walk. I sat down with the story and tweaked it slightly. As I said, it was just a test. To see if you'd notice. I was expecting confusion; I was prepared for anger. I thought I could talk my way out of it and that would have been the end of the matter. But in fact you didn't notice."

"You tricked me?" Grant threw his hat down in protest. "And I've been helping you. I've been kind to you."

"You've been lying to me."

"I'm old, I forget things. Can you really hold that against me?"

"You're not that old," said Julia, picking up the hat and handing it back to him.

Grant sighed; he sounded both intrigued and nervous. "Then how did it end, originally?"

• • •

"So anyway," said Inspector Wild, "let me enlighten you."

He struck a match and was about to light another cigarette, when Mr. Brown leaned across and flicked the match from his fingers. It smoldered on the red carpet, leaving a black mark that looked like a drop of spilled ink. "Wait just one moment," said Mr. Brown. "I don't want to give you the satisfaction, when I already know what happened."

Inspector Wild lifted his eyebrows. "You can't possibly know. We agreed there was no evidence."

"Well, I found some," said Mr. Brown. "Enough to give me a good idea, at least."

His friend looked at him suspiciously. "Let's have it, then."

The ruddy old man sat back in his chair. "I present to you the victim's scarf." And here Mr. Brown took the folded square of white, stained material from his jacket pocket and handed it to the inspector, who spread it open on the table.

"Where did you find this?"

"It was caught in a heather bush. Your colleagues must have missed it."

"And what is it supposed to tell us, exactly?"

"Here, you'll see, is a footprint from a Wellington boot. Wide, in a man's size. I checked it against the prints on a half page of newspaper in the victim's cottage, and it wasn't hers. You'll be able to tell me, no doubt, that Mr. Foyle was wearing Wellington boots that morning?"

Inspector Wild nodded. "He still had them on when we arrested him."

"Very good," said Mr. Brown. "Then answer me this: How can a man step on a woman's scarf while each is walking past the other? On a windy day the ends of it would be up in the air, not that it's really long enough to trail along the ground anyway."

Inspector Wild was intrigued. "Go on."

"The question put a certain image in my mind. Picture Gordon

Foyle standing above Mrs. Allen, his foot level with her head as she dangles from the cliff, with his boot inadvertently placed on her scarf."

"Then you think he's guilty?"

"No." Mr. Brown touched his fingertips together. "I think he's innocent. If he'd pushed her from the cliffs, she certainly wouldn't have ended up in that position. She'd have gone headfirst. But if she'd lost her footing and slipped, she might have caught hold of the edge of the cliff—leaving her scarf trailing over the lip of it, there for him to tread on. Well, what else do we have to explain? The place where the heather was disturbed? Let's assume he's being honest about that. He saw her fall, a few yards ahead of him, and pushed through the heather to the edge of the cliff. From there he could see her hanging on, so he ran back to the path and around to the spot where she'd fallen. Does that fit with everything we know so far?"

Inspector Wild looked slightly bemused. "I suppose so."

"He looks over the edge and sees her there. His first instinct is to help her, of course. But then he thinks again. He doesn't really want her to survive, all things considered. So he stands there and watches her struggle for a few minutes, until her bloody hands become slippery and twisted and she has to let go, landing fatally a few moments later. The scarf unravels as she falls and blows into a bush. He probably doesn't even notice it." Mr. Brown took up his drink. "Well, Inspector, now you can enlighten me."

Inspector Wild gave his friend a wry smile. "What can I say? It seems like you got a lot of that from guesswork, but you're exactly right. The wife of the man with the boat saw just what you described. Gordon Foyle is innocent, in the most unpleasant sense of the word."

"I can't disagree with that. Well, then, he'll walk free?"

The inspector nodded. "Most likely. Though I doubt the daughter will want him back."

Mr. Brown shook his head in sympathy, and it was as if his tired, wavering face were a marionette, suspended on strings from his skull.

"The poor girl—first her mother dies, and now she finds out that the man she loves watched it happen and didn't try to help." He thought of her words: *I don't know what I'd do if they hanged him.* And he smiled at the irony; the more difficult question was, what would she do when they didn't?

"Death is always messy," said Inspector Wild. "But our duty is to the law and nothing else." And the two men lifted their glasses in a half-hearted toast, then faded back into their armchairs.

• • •

Grant snorted. "That's very clever. But it proves nothing. Most of the story was left unchanged. Are you surprised I didn't notice the difference?"

"I'd only just met you," said Julia. "I wasn't looking for proof that you were lying; I was hoping to be proved wrong."

"Then you admit it's not conclusive?"

"No, of course it's not. But I didn't stop there."

Grant snapped his twig in half. "Then there's more?"

Julia nodded. "That first test was too subtle to prove anything. But it didn't dispel my doubts either. I knew that I had to test you again, using the next story."

Grant moaned. But he couldn't disguise his interest. "That was the ugly one, with the two detectives and the body in the bathtub?"

"That's right, the one you found distasteful. I apologize for that. I sat down that afternoon and rewrote it substantially."

"What did you do?"

"Remember, the story is set in a square called Colchester Gardens, in a tall white terraced house where Alice Cavendish lives with her family, the cook, and their maid. A man in a blue suit is seen outside the house one morning, talking to her sister. Alice takes a bath that afternoon and somebody steps in and drowns her."

"Then those two detectives turn up to investigate."

"Laurie and Bulmer, with their brutal methods. They question the maid, the mother, and the father, then a young man called Richard Parker, and finally the man in blue. They all have alibis, except for the unfortunate soul in the blue suit. Bulmer tortures him until he confesses, then he hangs himself."

"A happy ending, all around."

"And that's when we learn that Inspector Laurie is himself the murderer. The poor man in blue has been framed."

"And that was all down to you?"

Julia bent forward in a very slight bow. "Yes, that's right."

"Then what is the real ending?"

• • •

Sergeant Bulmer smoked a cigarette and then stepped back inside the cell. This time he carried a razor blade. Michael Percy Christopher was lying on the floor in the shape of a puddle, breathing through his mouth. His slight mustache was matted with blood. Bulmer towered above him.

At that moment the lights in the room went out.

Bulmer froze, his thumb pressed against the flat cold back of the razor blade. "Power's out again," he muttered, speaking to his partner, who was standing outside; that part of the building was always having problems. He waited for over a minute, but the lights didn't return.

Bulmer felt all alone in the darkness; the shadow at his feet had already ceased to exist. Then its thin voice spoke to him: "Please, I'm ready to talk."

"You're ready to confess?"

The sound of a head being shaken. "It wasn't me. I didn't kill her. I'm a detective, like you."

Bulmer sighed. He had no desire to listen, but what else could he do to pass the time? "You're not with the police."

"No, a private investigator."

"Your card said theatrical agent."

"That's my cover. My clients like me to be discreet."

Bulmer grunted. "Well, what's your story?"

He heard the man lift himself onto his knees. "I'm known for set-tling blackmail cases. There's a lot of it in the theater. Ask around in the right circles, my name will come up. Two men came to see me one day. Their names were Richard Parker and Andrew Sullivan. Alice Cav-endish was blackmailing both of them."

The love interest and the childhood sweetheart. "Why?" asked Bul-mer. He spoke without looking down. If the lights had been on, he'd have had this man against the wall. "With what?"

"She wanted Parker to marry her. They'd met once. He'd been drunk and had told her too much about his time in the war. He'd gone out to France with a cousin of his; he'd seen to it that only one of them came back. Well, Alice was the kind of young girl that could get a man to open his mouth, once he'd had a drink or two. So he confessed every-thing and the next day she demanded they get married. It was a good match for her, but not so much for him."

"And Sullivan?"

"They used to be close. She caught him in a compromising situ-ation once. He's a man of unnatural tastes, let's say. With him it was purely for money."

"I don't believe you."

"She was that kind of girl. Entitled, emancipated. You see that a lot when you work in the theater."

"So how do Sullivan and Parker know each other? The two of them are friends?" Bulmer wondered why Inspector Laurie wasn't interven-ing. He must have been listening, somewhere in the darkness.

"Not quite. Alice got sloppy. They'd leave their messages to her in the park outside her house, in one of the trees there." The spot where Bulmer had found the old letter from Richard Parker. "But she used the same place for both of them. One day they ran into each other there and started talking. That's how the whole plot began."

"What did they do?"

"They came to me for help. The way to settle a blackmail case is to turn it back onto the blackmailer, that's what I told them. If you can find out where they're vulnerable, that's usually enough. So I looked around; I asked some questions. It turned out there were other victims. The maid, for one."

"Elise?"

Bulmer couldn't see the man nodding but assumed he was doing so. "She'd stolen jewelry from Alice's mother. Alice found out and threatened to have her dismissed. In that case she didn't even ask for anything, she just enjoyed the power. The father too."

"Alice's father?"

"Stepfather, in fact. Elise told me all about it. Alice had threatened to tell her mother that he'd made advances at her, if he didn't do what she said."

"Stepfather?" Bulmer sighed. "And then what?"

"I took all four of them on as clients. And I set up the meeting in Alice's house. She didn't know it was going to happen, of course. But she was just a spoiled young girl with a strong sense of entitlement. I thought if they confronted her together, she would back down. I brought the two men to the square, sent Andrew Sullivan to get her stepfather from his office, and waited for the cook to leave. Then I knocked on the door. Elise answered it. She had her fiancé with her, the man who owns the greengrocer's shop. She told me Alice was bathing. That was a stroke of luck, I thought. It would make her more vulnerable. So I sent them all inside. All five of them. They went up the stairs to confront her." His voice turned quiet. "I don't know what happened after that."

The lights flashed on, just for a second; Bulmer saw Laurie standing outside the cell, his hands around the bars, that half smile on his face again. Bulmer didn't bother to look down at the man in blue before the darkness came back. "So you're an accomplice?"

"I didn't know they were going to kill her. I told them to talk to her."

Bulmer thought back through their alibis; it seemed like he was seeing them from another angle now and each one was false, like a wooden stage set. For Elise, her alibi had been her fiancé. But he'd been involved in the murder as well. With Mr. Cavendish and Richard Parker, it had seemed from the state of their hands that they couldn't have committed the crime. But with three other pairs of hands it would have been no trouble at all. And why hadn't her mother told them that Mr. Cavendish was only the girl's stepfather? Andrew Sullivan had appeared to be out of the country, but they hadn't checked; he would only need to hide out in a London hotel for a few weeks with his mother. "They held her underwater, then? All of them."

Something came to him out of the darkness. He spoke again. "If you'd known they were going to kill her, you would never have left your card at the scene." Deduction, the detective's art form; Bulmer had got it at last.

He grinned in the pitch black.

"Yes, yes." The voice came from directly below, and he felt a pair of hands wrap around his shoes. A warm, pleading cheek pressed against his left calf; it felt as if someone were trying to iron his trousers. "Please believe me."

The lights came back on, brighter than before. They seemed to impose a silence on the room. Laurie had managed to enter the cell without being heard. He was standing a few steps from Bulmer now, looking disdainfully at the supplicant on the floor. Bulmer kicked the man loose and turned to his partner. "Did you hear all that?"

Laurie nodded. "It makes a certain amount of sense."

"What do we do, then?" asked Bulmer. "Arrest the five of them?"

"We have no evidence," said Laurie. "This man's testimony won't hold up in court. Not against five."

"Then what?"

"We have plenty of evidence against Mr. Christopher here. It's best for all concerned if the case is closed as soon as possible. Do you understand me?"

"Yes," said Bulmer. He sighed and lifted Michael Christopher up by the armpits.

"Good," said Laurie. "Make sure it looks like suicide."

The man in blue started to howl. Bulmer hooked a gloved finger through one of his nostrils and held the man's jaw shut with his thumb. "Quiet," he said.

Laurie turned to leave. He placed a final hand on his partner's shoulder. "He's not innocent, you know. He arranged the whole thing."

Bulmer grunted, then tore off Mr. Christopher's blue suit jacket and tied one arm of it around the man's long neck. "And the damn fool confessed to it too."

• • •

Grant had his excuses ready. "I think I blocked that one from my memory."

Julia didn't answer him directly. "The case where all of the suspects turn out to be killers."

"I see that," said Grant. "Then it's the same as the fourth story?"

"Yes," she said. "The one with the fire and the party full of actors. Of course, that one was originally something quite different."

Grant looked defeated. "You changed that one as well?"

"I had to be careful. I'd worked out this plan of changing the endings, but I was still bound by certain constraints. After all, the stories derive from the mathematical work. I could only change them in ways that were consistent with that. Otherwise, the whole thing would have fallen apart."

"You had to stick to the rules, so that I would incriminate myself."

"I had to keep you talking. So inventing a whole new ending was never an option. Instead, I simply switched the endings to the third and fourth stories."

Grant couldn't help but smile. "That is very clever. Then the fourth story?"

"It originally had the ending I gave to the third. It starts with a party in a restaurant. A nearby department store is on fire. Helen Garrick is asked to look after the crime scene until the police arrive. She examines the body: The host has been beaten to death with a hammer."

"In a toilet, locked from the inside."

"The other guests at the party are all actors. Each tells Helen their own tall story, until the whole scene is mired in chaos and confusion. Time passes and the police don't show up. The suspects grow restless."

"And the perceptive reader will have noticed that if Helen was downstairs when the murder was happening, she should also be considered a suspect?"

"And that's the ending that I gave to the previous story: The detective did it."

• • •

Helen interrupted proceedings by toppling the bottle of red wine onto the floor. It landed with a concussive smash, leaving a stain not unlike the one in the toilet, all thin blood and fragments of glass. "I'm sorry," she said. "But I've sat and listened to your theories all evening. I don't want to hear any more."

If there was any doubt that she'd knocked the wine to the floor on purpose, she dispelled it by nudging a wineglass over the edge with her fingertips.

She sat in an island of smashed glass.

"I don't believe we've met." James approached her and offered his hand. "I'm James."

"My name is Helen. I'm supposed to be in charge here."

"Ignore her," said Griff. "She's drunk. A friend of the restaurant manager, I think."

"Well, why not?" asked Helen. "The world is ending outside. Who wouldn't want a drink, under the circumstances?"

"Finally," said Scarlett, taking her coat from behind the door. "I think we have permission to leave."

"I wouldn't if I were you." Helen kicked some of the smashed glass toward the door, like a child playing in a puddle. "You'll miss all the fun."

Andrew Carter stepped in front of his sister, Vanessa. "What are you up to? Have you gone mad?"

Griff peered at Helen's pupils. "You're gone," he said. "You ought to lie down."

"But don't you want to hear my confession?" Helen got to her feet, then climbed on top of her chair. "You've been trapped in this room with me for several hours now, and not one of you has thought to ask me why I was at this restaurant by myself, when I live over twenty miles away. Nobody has asked me why I volunteered to keep watch on this crime scene, when my last train home leaves in a few hours. Didn't that strike you as a little suspicious?" The six faces looked blankly at one another. "Did it not occur to any of you that it might have been me that killed him? You could at least have shown a little bit of gratitude."

A gasp filled the room. Somebody at the back of the circle dropped a glass in shock. With the sun in decline and the windows almost black with smoke, she was speaking to an audience of blurred silhouettes. "I've spent the last hour or so searching for a way to explain this crime. Something I could give to the restaurant manager, to divert attention from myself." She'd thought of demon dogs, figures crouched on rooftops, vast conspiracies; none of them seemed any good. "So I've patiently listened to everything you've had to say. It's been like an afternoon in school. Stories of Harry's womanizing, of being paid to pose as his bride. Well, I can't take it anymore."

"You're the one who murdered him," said Vanessa. "But why? Who are you?"

Helen sat down and put her head in her hands. Why didn't she save this for a cozy conversation with a police detective, over a cup of tea? But she was too drunk to stop. "Oh, just Helen. Helen Rhonda Garrick. One of Harry's women, like the rest of you. I'd heard he was having a party. He didn't want me to come, of course. So I booked a table downstairs. I came up here between courses and saw you all looking out of the window. That was a stroke of luck. Harry wasn't with you. Then I heard a flush and he emerged from the lavatory. The men's, of course, in the corridor outside. He wasn't pleased to see me, but I followed him into the room and ushered him into the women's toilet, without any of you turning around. I told him I wanted to speak to him in private. Well, you can imagine what happened next."

"Do tell us," said James, who hadn't seen the state of the body and was captivated by Helen's performance.

She blushed. "I dropped my bag on the floor. Harry, always the gentleman, bent down to pick it up. I pulled the hammer from my sleeve and struck him on the back of the head. Just once, and he fell like an ice cube out of a tray. It was incredibly satisfying, that first hit. After six or seven more, his head was a bloody mess."

Vanessa fainted into her brother's arms. Scarlett turned to Griff and raised her eyebrows. Wendy stepped forward. "I knew it was you. The woman that Harry wanted to get rid of. You're the reason he asked me here."

"Yes, quite probably. It didn't work, though, did it? The noise of the fire and the commotion outside covered the sound of the killing. Then I smashed the window and moved the pieces of glass inside. I climbed out through the frame, scratching my thigh on a shard of glass, then went across the roof and down the fire escape, leaving the toilet door locked behind me. Then I went back into the restaurant and sat down, just in time for my second course."

Scarlett sounded unimpressed. "Why are you telling us all this?"

Helen put her head in her hands. "Because I want to confess. I thought I could do this, but I can't. The guilt, it's too much." She closed her eyes and saw the sisters standing around her in a circle, the same disapproving glare on each of their faces. "Not about Harry, you understand. I feel no guilt about that. He deserved to die, for the way he treated me."

"Don't be absurd," said Griff. Andrew shook his head.

But the women of the group simply looked at one another.

Wendy spoke for all of them: "Then what is it you feel guilty about?"

Helen sobbed; she could feel the machinery of judgment that she'd grown up with finally taking hold of her. "I needed a diversion. Something to keep everyone occupied while I killed him." She took a deep breath. "I started the fire in the department store."

At that moment there was a loud thump on the door. It creaked open. The restaurant manager's head appeared, with a grin on his impish face. "I am sorry to disturb you, but we have been told we must evacuate the building immediately."

He disappeared down the stairs; Helen turned back to face her confessors. They stared at her, too shocked to speak. James broke the silence: "Well, what a strange day this has been." He picked up his hat and coat. "You're insane."

Vanessa was in tears, propped up by her brother. Griff and Scarlett looked appalled. None of them spoke to Helen as they filed out of the room.

"He really was an awful man," she said to Wendy, the last of them to leave. "My intentions were good, at least."

Wendy departed and Helen was alone.

Her hands were shaking with alcohol and adrenaline. She picked herself up, put on her coat, and left. The restaurant was eerily empty as she passed down the stairs and out of the door. She helped herself to a half-finished glass of wine. Courage, she thought. Then she walked along the street and stepped into the burning building.

She felt the heat wash her clean.

• • •

"That fourth story took a lot of work. On the first afternoon, while you were sleeping, I was writing as feverishly as I could manage. And again that evening after our meal."

Grant narrowed his eyes. "Is there more, then?"

"I gave you yet another chance to prove your innocence with the fifth story. I rewrote the ending to that one yesterday before lunch, working in the bright sun until the backs of my hands burned."

"What did you change this time?"

"The story has a man and his wife exploring an island, finding all of its occupants dead."

"Charles and Sarah. I remember."

"There were ten people on the island, including two servants. They were all invited there for different reasons, by a mysterious man named Unwin. But when they arrived, Unwin was nowhere to be found. The point of the story was that all of the suspects were victims, so it was easy to switch the killer from one victim to another. That's how I ended up with Stubbs as the culprit."

Grant closed his eyes. "But originally it was someone else?"

• • •

They went back downstairs, to the lounge covered in ash and fragments of wood.

"The chronology is fairly easy to establish," said Sarah. "But let's be explicit about it, and the rest should fall into place. The first day is for arrivals; then there are all the accusations over dinner and the first death, the woman who swallowed her fork. I imagine they retired early, too shaken to spend an evening talking to strangers."

"Shock can be exhausting," said Charles.

"Meanwhile, two of the guests are poisoning themselves with candles. The remaining five wake up the next morning and make their way down here. The servants are missing and so are the two guests. They search the rooms and then the island, finding the four bodies. That's when things must have broken down. Half of the inhabitants had been found dead already. But they discover no one else on the island, so they know that one of the five of them must be up to something. Rather than try to find safety in numbers, they gather supplies and lock themselves in their rooms. Do you follow me so far?"

Charles nodded eagerly.

"At some point the two ladies leave their rooms and move their stash of supplies to the study next door. But why? That's not exactly clear to me yet. At the same time, one man is being boiled in his bath, another is slowly bleeding to death inside his bed. Both are behind locked doors. The man on the grass outside is the only other person alive at this point."

"Then how did the two ladies die?"

Sarah walked to the mantel and pulled out a loose brick. "When this is pushed in, it opens a hatch at the back of the chimney, and smoke pours through a hole into the room next door. The door to that room has no lock, but it locks whenever the window is open."

"And the window is too small to climb through. So if anyone is being asphyxiated by the smoke, the only way they can save themselves is by closing the window. It's sickening." Charles shook his head. "Then the man lying outside was the killer? He's the only one left."

"Let me think about that for a moment."

Sarah sat down in one of the plush armchairs and began applying pressure to her forehead to induce concentration, this time with the base of her palm. Charles stared at her, slightly repulsed.

"No," she said, "he wasn't the killer. His death is the hardest to explain. But that's because there is so little of the mechanism left. We found his body by the place where the boats are usually tied up. How do you induce a man about to take a trip by boat to put a wire around his own neck?" Charles had no answer for her. "By handing him a life jacket, with a wire in the lining. All it would take is some cardboard and cheap fabric. It goes over the head, then the wire is around the man's neck and the weight is released."

"Then if he wasn't the murderer, who was?"

"If one of the ten was the killer, they must have killed themselves afterward. Whose death looks the most like suicide?"

Charles shrugged. "Stubbs, I suppose."

"And surely the complexity of these crimes means they would have required two people working together. Who might have had an accomplice?"

Charles gasped. "Stubbs and his wife, you mean?"

"Almost, but not quite. Stubbs would make perfect sense as the culprit, except he would never have had the money to pull off something like this."

"Then who?"

"Who else? When the motive for a crime is to pass judgment, look for the most judgmental. That old lady in there, Mrs. Tranter. She killed the lot of them, with the help of her companion, Sophia."

Charles shook his head. "But how?"

"I won't forgive myself for missing it," said Sarah. "The one thing that seemed to have no explanation: Why did they leave the security of their locked bedrooms for that meager study next door?"

"I don't know."

"No, it makes no sense. Unless they knew that they would be safe walking around the house. And then later, much later, they went to that room to die."

"But smoke inhalation is no way to kill yourself."

"It's not. And that's not how they died. They must have taken something, when all the killing was done with. Arsenic or something similar.

They lit the fire and lay down in that room so that the smoke would mask the smell, burying their secret alongside them."

"But what was their motive?"

Sarah thought about it. "I think Mrs. Tranter was dying. There was coughing at night. And we found a napkin under her handbag, on the dining table. It was spotted with blood. What if she decided to take some others along with her? People guilty of unpunished crimes. She must have persuaded her companion to help or coerced her in some other way; but only someone steeped in gossip would know so many secrets. She was a devout, austere woman. Remember the Bible we found by their bodies? There was a bottle of pills beside it. Whether she saw her mission as justice or revenge, I can't say."

Charles was almost too shocked to speak. "I don't believe it. Could a woman really be so evil?"

Sarah gave him a look of sympathy. "That's a lesson you'll have to learn one day, Charles."

• • •

"Then I did the same with the sixth story," said Julia. "That was the one we read last night, where the matriarch of a country house was smothered in her bed for the sake of some diamonds. The main structural feature of that story was that roughly half the suspects turned out to be killers."

"Yes," said Grant. "I can see where this is going."

"That's the same structure it had originally, only I switched the halves."

Grant's laughter was full of despair. "That's very fine work indeed. I told you the ending was effectively arbitrary. And you put my words into practice."

"In that story, a young woman called Lily Mortimer visits Dr. Lamb. She is hoping to solve her grandmother's murder, which happened six years earlier. The two of them discuss their memories of the incident.

There are nine suspects, each with their own alibi. Lily, who was a child at the time, was playing with her cousin, William. Her sister, Violet, was asleep on the sofa. Her uncle Matthew was walking to the train station to meet the victim's sister, Dorothea. The other suspects are Dr. Lamb; Matthew's wife, Lauren; the gardener, Raymond; and a local man with a romantic interest in Violet, called Ben."

"And the doctor, his mistress, William, and Ben turned out to be the killers. But the real ending was the opposite?"

• • •

Dr. Lamb had a view of the twilight in two rectangles. He was looking out of the window, through his glasses. He'd written her name and nothing else.

Dearest Lily.

Then a sadness had consumed him. He felt like he would be destroying something inside her by writing this letter. But the truth had to be told.

Five years ago you came to me with questions about your grandmother's murder. I did not tell you everything I knew at that time, for reasons that will become clear. You were an impressive young woman, and I hope the intervening years have served you well. He was delaying the moment of revelation and he knew it. *At that meeting you led me to confess to one of my biggest sins, my affair with your aunt Lauren. But I must tell you about a time, five years before that, when I myself played the role of confessor.*

He'd been walking past the war memorial one autumn day when Violet Mortimer had called out to him. "Dr. Lamb, do you have a moment?"

He'd stopped and turned toward her. "Violet, what's the matter? You look like you haven't slept."

The young woman burst into tears. "It's Agnes," she said. "I need to tell someone. I need to tell someone everything. Oh, Dr. Lamb, I need to confess."

So you see, wrote the doctor, *Violet told me the whole truth of the matter. And that's what makes this letter so painful to write, Lily. It was your own family that murdered your grandmother. Your own family that smothered her. Squashed her almost, like an insect in her bed.*

It had started with Dorothea and Matthew.

The first time Dorothea had visited her sister after the stroke, she'd taken her nephew to one side and told him about the diamonds. "I've always known she still had them, but she won't tell me where they are. What if she dies and takes the secret with her to the grave?"

Matthew was appalled at the idea of so much wealth going to waste. "Don't worry, Auntie. We'll persuade her. They're my rightful inheritance." He looked up and swore at the ceiling. "This house isn't human, after all. She's no right to bequeath them to it."

But his confidence was misplaced. When Agnes was visited that afternoon by her sister and her son, the dinner tray balanced awkwardly between them, she was feeling weak and dizzy, and their talk of diamonds made her angry. "You're no better than thieves," she whispered, spitting her glass of milk over the pillow in protest. "I'm not dead yet, you know. And all you care about is my money."

Matthew took Dorothea to one side later that day. "Help me get those diamonds, Auntie Dot. Before she goes. I'll share them with you, half and half. But I must have them."

Dorothea smiled. "The only thing I ask is that you take care of me in my old age."

"Of course." Matthew took her wrist. It was close enough to shaking hands on the deal.

They made their second attempt at acquiring the diamonds a few weeks later. Dorothea came to the village and pressed a sedative into Matthew's hand. "When you get to my age, the doctor will prescribe you anything."

He'd slipped it into Agnes's tea and spent the evening searching her room, but to no avail. "I'm sorry, Auntie. I've let you down."

"Next time," said Dorothea. "They have to be somewhere."

Soon after that they made their third attempt. Matthew went to meet his aunt at the station. Dorothea took his hand as she lowered herself from the train. "This time we'll succeed," she said, a knowing smile splitting her wide face. She told him her plan as they walked through the fields. "Violet was always Agnes's favorite. She will tell Violet where they are."

Matthew nodded. "It might work."

When they got to the house, they found Violet asleep on a couch. Dorothea woke her and told her about the diamonds and what she must do. "Otherwise, they'll be lost forever. A small fortune, taken from this family and given to nobody."

Matthew's attempts to look earnest hardly helped, as he nodded along, with a glint in his eye. But Violet saw the sense in what they were saying. "But why do I have to do it?"

"You're the only one she trusts."

All the more reason for it not to be me, thought Violet. "I want to talk it over with Raymond."

"What on earth for?" Matthew was aghast; his niece and the gardener were too close as it was. Raymond was married. A scandal in the family would be no good for any of them. "It has nothing to do with him. He's just the gardener."

Violet was insistent. "He's my friend."

But, as it happened, Raymond advised her to do as her uncle suggested. "It's your inheritance too," he said. "You have a right to it." So the four of them—Matthew, Dorothea, Violet, and Raymond—met outside Agnes's room, late that morning; Violet looked up at the three faces, each expecting so much of her.

She was terrified.

She stepped into the room alone. Agnes was awake. The old woman smiled sweetly. "Violet, dear, what a nice surprise."

"I've come to collect your breakfast things." She sat down on the edge of the bed and picked up the tray. "And I wanted to ask you some-thing. About the diamonds Grandpa gave you."

As soon as Violet said the word, Agnes sprang forward and grabbed hold of her granddaughter's wrist. The breakfast tray fell to the floor. "You too!" The old woman was hysterical. "It was you that tried to kill me. You that put something in my drink. You and Matthew and my sister." Violet screamed. Raymond ran into the room, followed by the other two. He pulled Agnes away from her.

Agnes glared at the four of them. "All of you. Thieves, nothing more. I shall have you taken out of my will, and you," she said to Ray-mond, "can find employment elsewhere, immediately."

The gardener shrugged. He picked up a knife from the floor, where it had fallen from the breakfast tray, then leaned across the bed and held it to Agnes's eye. "Where are the diamonds, you old witch? I'm fed up with the way you treat me."

Agnes whimpered. She waited for the others to step forward and help her, but none of them did. Then she raised a fragile finger and pointed at the window. "In the frame, on the left."

Matthew checked the place she'd indicated. "They're here," he said.

"Good," said Raymond, stepping away from the bed.

Agnes turned to her granddaughter and sister, who were standing quietly at the side of the room. "You'll burn in hell for this, both of you."

Raymond took a pile of blankets from the nearby dresser and threw them over the bedridden woman. "Come on," he said, "we can't leave her alive."

Agnes screamed when she heard this; Violet gasped in shock. Her grandmother's fragile shape wriggled frantically under the blankets. Raymond climbed on top of the squirming pile and put his weight on her shoulders. "Come on," he said. "All of you."

"We must," said Matthew. "There's no choice now." He ushered the two women toward the bed, taking their hands. The three of them fell onto the pile of blankets and closed their eyes, holding firm until eventually the movement beneath them stopped and there was no further sound.

Violet spoke softly. "Do you think she's all right?" But nobody answered her.

"Look," said Matthew. He opened the canvas pouch he'd taken from the window and poured the contents into his hand. Diamonds fell through his fingers. "It's a fortune."

And so, wrote Dr. Lamb, as the light in his room grew dim, *it didn't feel like they were committing murder at all, or so Violet told me. They split the diamonds four ways. They hadn't planned to include Raymond, but the circumstances had changed. Dorothea crept out of the house and returned an hour later, making sure she was seen by Lauren. Matthew hung around downstairs, and Violet went back to her couch. Raymond returned to his leaves. And that was that. Dorothea was sure someone else must have known about the diamonds, so she raised them herself to deflect suspicion. The rest was just a pantomime. Of course, Violet couldn't keep her composure for long after that, and soon she was racked with guilt. She could no longer look at Raymond, let alone be friends with him. So she came and confessed everything to me. I believe she married Ben as a kind of penance. He was obsessed with her, always watching her through his binoculars. Raymond took it terribly and moved away. Later, he tried to sell his share of the jewels in some ghastly slum; he was stabbed and killed in the process. Dorothea died before she saw any of her fortune. Matthew was content with inheriting the house and went back to his quiet life. I don't know what he did with his diamonds. It's true, then, that crime doesn't pay. There's a lesson for us all.*

Dr. Lamb massaged his hand; he'd covered four pages already. He wanted to get it all down before dark. He picked up the pen again.

Lily, it pains me to tell you this horrid truth. He sighed, wondering if he really cared. So close to death himself, he still found it a struggle to speak honestly. *I've been protecting you for a long time now. We've all been protecting you. Lauren knew too, of course. I told her about it. And*

Violet confessed everything to Ben. But we all decided it would hurt you too much if you knew. That's why we kept it from the police. Even young William worked it out, when he found that diamond ring in one of Matthew's pockets; maybe he would have told you the truth, if Raymond hadn't taken him away. Well, you're old enough now to make your own decisions. You must do what you feel is right.

He'd wanted to end the letter on something hopeful. That would have to suffice.

Yours, Dr. Godwin Lamb.

He put the pen down and stared sadly at the darkness outside. Then he began to cough. He coughed for several minutes. Then he went to the bathroom, leaving a dot of bright-red blood by his signature.

• • •

"So there you have it," said Julia. "Once again, you failed to notice that the ending had changed."

Grant avoided her eyes. "My memory is much worse than I've made out."

"And that takes us up to last night." Julia was talking to the side of his head. "I went back to my hotel, sure that my hunch was correct. We'd read six stories, all of them with their endings changed, some of them substantially. And you hadn't noticed a single one. Twenty years is a long time, but you should have remembered one of them. At least one, I was sure of that. You must have had a favorite. Still, I decided to give you the benefit of the doubt. We only had one story left. I would try one final test."

Grant turned back to her. "What did you do?"

"It didn't seem like enough just to change the ending again. So instead I threw out the original story altogether and wrote an entirely new one to replace it. I went through your research paper, 'The Permutations of Detective Fiction,' and picked out one of the structures described there. Then I wrote it up as a story of my own. I was awake almost all of the night working on it. By this morning I had a completely new story. And yet you still claimed it as your own."

"The one we read an hour or two ago?"

Julia nodded. "Lionel Moon, the dead detective. I wrote that story myself."

"Then what was the story it replaced?"

"It was a short one," said Julia. "It had two detectives. Both men, both well-known amateurs. They are investigating strange goings-on in a supposedly haunted building, an abandoned orphanage called St. Bartholomew's."

"What are their names?"

"Eustace Aaron and Lionel Benedict. They cannot agree on the existence of the supernatural, so they make a pact to spend the night in the attic. That should settle the matter. They set up their camp beds and wait for the sun to set, drinking cocoa made on a portable stove. The building is derelict. After a while they both begin to smell smoke. They realize that there is a crack in the wall leading through to the chimney and someone has lit a fire downstairs. The room is gradually filling with smoke. They try to leave but discover that the door is locked and the key has vanished. They stay calm and assume that the fire will burn itself out. They smash the window. They shout for help, but the orphanage is deep in the countryside."

"Then how does it end?"

• • •

Lionel Benedict stood at the window. He could feel the cloud of smoke building behind him. "It's not enough," he said, looking at the hole in the glass. It was about the size of a fist. The window's diagonal was about the length of his forearm. He punched out the rest of the glass, cutting his knuckles. "It's still not enough."

He turned to his companion. "Aren't you interested? We might die here."

Eustace Aaron was looking in the mirror of a splendid blue vanity table, the only piece of furniture in the smoky room besides the camp beds that they'd brought with them. It was either old and impractical or built for a child, and he had to lean down to see his face in it. "I'm ahead of you, Lionel. We are going to die here, it's inevitable now. The smoke is building up. I'm trying to come to terms with it."

Lionel watched as his younger counterpart studied his own features, his fearsome eyes and sharp teeth, as if they somehow summarized the life he had lived.

He turned to the crack in the wall. It reached from the floor to the ceiling, with numerous branches. A tree in winter. Smoke was seeping from every inch of it, and there was no way they could block or cover the whole thing. Lionel closed his eyes; the thought of his death terrified him.

"There's a locked drawer here," Eustace said over his shoulder. "A locked drawer in an abandoned house. That'll be our last mystery. Will you help me to solve it?"

Lionel walked over to his companion, and together they kicked at the dresser until it leaned awkwardly to one side and the drawer could be maneuvered out of it. Inside was a dark-blue cardboard box. "Maybe it's a key," said Lionel.

Eustace shook his head, feeling the contents rattle softly as he picked it up. "Chocolates," he said, and he lifted the lid to confirm his hypothesis. They had paled with the passing of time, but each one was in the shape of a fruit, and the fact that they hadn't shrunk or dried out seemed to make them look obscenely, lusciously turgid in their individual compartments. "Would you like one?"

"They must be twenty years old." Lionel's face showed his repulsion and Eustace put the box down on the dresser, picking out one for himself. "I shouldn't," said Lionel. "It might make you ill."

Eustace laughed as if Lionel had made a joke. He bit the chocolate in half. Lionel watched him eat, expecting some kind of comment.

When none came, he spoke wearily, as if to fill the silence: "Eustace, I have to tell you. It was me that lit the fire downstairs. I was hoping to force us out, so we couldn't finish our investigation. I thought it would add to the mystery. Someone must have seen me do it and taken the opportunity to lock us inside. Someone who wanted us dead."

"I know who tried to kill us," said Eustace, swallowing the last of the chocolate. "I've already worked it out."

Even though he was about to die, Lionel Benedict couldn't help but feel a pang of jealousy. He turned away from his friend and examined the chocolates, wondering if there was a clue on the box. Even at arm's length, its color was dulled by the smoke. He found nothing. Then, reluctantly, he took one of the chocolates and bit into it. The inside tasted of sour cherries.

"You still don't believe in ghosts?" he asked. Lionel was trying to distract his friend, to give himself time to solve the case.

"No, I don't. Do you, Lionel? Even after this?" Eustace gave him an ironic smile. "You're not convinced now that life is meaningless and cruel?"

Lionel walked over to the window and spat the chocolate out through the stream of smoke. He watched the gray clouds that were taking shape outside the window. "Now more than ever."

"Of course." Eustace shrugged. "You're hoping to come back as one."

Lionel shook his head. He searched his pockets and found a publicity photograph of himself; he kept it there in case he was ever asked for one. He closed his eyes and let it drop from the window, an attempt to preserve a small fragment of himself. The fresh air widened his lungs, and when he next inhaled he took a mouthful of smoke deep into his chest. He started to cough. He stumbled to Eustace's side. "My head is light, I can't think. Tell me who it was. Who locked us in here to die?"

"It was me," the other man admitted. "I wanted to make sure we stayed here the whole night, to settle the case forever. So I locked the door and got rid of the key. We'll be rescued in the morning."

"We'll be dead by then."

"Yes, from smoke inhalation. I didn't know that you'd lit the fire downstairs when I locked us in. That was unfortunate."

"What happened to the key?" Lionel took the other man by the lapels.

"It's gone," said Eustace. "I kicked it under the gap in the door. It's no more than four yards away from us, but we can't get at it." He smiled, as if this was funny.

Lionel went over to the door and put his head against the ground. He could see the key, resting on the second of several steps that led down from the attic. Eustace was right, it was out of reach. He shook the door once again but found it as huge and immovable as before. It was made of both metal and wood.

"You fool," said Lionel, getting to his feet. "You did this to us."

Eustace reached back and touched the slanted mirror of the dresser, then angled it so that Lionel could see himself in it. "And so did you," he said, as he started to cough.

The two of them died a few hours later. By that point the room was thick with smoke and they'd both begun to cough up black phlegm. There was no moon and the night was dark. They were found the next morning, with their fists bloody from beating on the door.

• • •

"I see," said Grant, coming to life. "Then Aaron and Benedict are the suspects, killers, victims, and detectives, all in one. It's another limiting case. Here the Venn diagram is a simple circle."

"Yes," said Julia. "And it's nothing at all like the story I wrote, which we read together this morning. You were lying then and you've been lying to me for the last two days. Are you still going to deny it, even after this?"

Grant slid down from the rock; he stood in front of her with his hands in his pockets. "Does it make any difference if I do? You seem convinced."

"I'd say the evidence is overwhelming."

He shook his head. "Then what happens now?"

"I want you to tell me the truth. Then I will go back home. Publication of the book is canceled, of course."

"Canceled?"

Julia nodded. "What did you expect? Our agreement was with Grant McAllister, not with you."

"Will you go to the police?"

She shook her head. "I wouldn't know where to start with an accusation like this. Besides, I don't speak the language."

"Then no," Grant sighed, "there's no point in me denying it now. I'm not Grant McAllister, and I didn't write these stories. I expect you'll want to know who I am?"

The sun passed behind a cloud, and the darkened clearing came alive with the sound of birds.

"I know who you are," said Julia. "Your name is Francis Gardner."

The man across from her fell back against the rock. "How can you possibly know that?"

"This island has a memory, even if you don't. And the old man who owns the hotel I'm staying at was only too happy to talk to me this morning. I heard all about the two foreigners that used to live together in a cottage by the sea, just off the path that leads to the church. How they were inseparable, indistinguishable even, until one day one of them died. He couldn't give me a name. But I'd seen the cigarette case in your kitchen. And I checked the gravestones in the churchyard, where you walk every day. There was only one English name among them."

"Francis Gardner."

"With the date he died written underneath. Ten years ago, here on this island. Only it wasn't really him, was it?"

Francis shook his head. "It was Grant McAllister. Though, in a manner of speaking, Francis also died that day. I haven't used the name since."

"Then who are you? And what were you to Grant?"

"I was a mathematician. I met him at a conference in London, a long time ago. We kept in touch afterward. He was in Edinburgh and I was in Cambridge. We started out as collaborators, but soon became more than that." Francis shrugged. "His marriage was a sham, and one day he moved out here to get away from it. That was just after the war. I gave it some thought and decided to follow him."

"Then you were more than just friends?"

"Yes. I loved him. And he loved me."

"And yet when he died you took his name, his identity, and no doubt his money?"

Francis turned a shrewd eye toward her. "What are you implying?"

"I'm asking the inevitable question. Did you murder him?"

"Murder him? No. Good God, no. It wasn't like that at all."

"Then what happened?"

• • •

Two men emerged from the line of trees, both dressed formally though the day was bright and warm. Before them, a grassy slope ran for about thirty yards to the edge of the cliff; beyond that was the cold, shining sea.

The younger man put his hand on the other's shoulder. "Worth the climb, don't you think?"

Grant nodded. "To the very edge then, since we've come this far."

He started to walk forward. Francis followed, with a hand clamped to his hat; the wind at this height was unpredictable. "Not too close, Grant. We need some room for the sheet." In his other hand he held a wicker basket, with a blanket balled up under his arm.

Grant briefly surveyed the breathing, monstrous sea and then turned back to his companion, who was busy clearing the area of stones, kicking them down the hill.

"Help me," said Francis, turning back to Grant. He held on to one end of the peach-colored blanket and threw the other into the air; the wind took hold of it, twisting it into a knot. It looked for a moment as if Francis had thrown a bucket of paint at Grant. The older man caught the other end, finding the corners and holding them out at arm's length. Together they spread it neatly over the grass and took off their shoes to weigh down the ends.

Then Grant sat down with his back to the sea. Francis was facing him. "Don't you want the view?"

Grant shook his head. "I have a view of the trees. And a glimpse of the town. It's the difference between us, Francis. I like to look at the things that are mine; you like to look at what's just out of reach."

"Do you include me in the things that are yours?" The wind was so loud that he had to shout, and the question sounded rhetorical. "You're in a literary mood this morning," he added.

Grant frowned. "It's cold up here."

Francis wedged the brim of his hat under a weighted corner of the blanket; it immediately began to twitch in the gale, up and down like the lid of a saucepan. He took off his jacket and gave it to Grant, the fragile fabric almost torn away from them as they passed it from one hand to another. Grant wriggled his arms into it. "Thank you."

Francis started to lay some of the food out on the blanket—a pot of honey and a loaf of bread. He tore the end from the loaf, then took a hard-boiled egg from the basket and placed it at Grant's feet, taking another for himself. Grant picked his up and tapped it sharply against the edge of his wristwatch, then started to peel the shell.

"Thank you," he said.

The two men ate in silence. While Grant was close enough to the cliff edge that he could simply throw his pieces of eggshell behind him and let the wind carry them out to sea, Francis was carefully dropping his into an empty wineglass. He was concentrating on removing a particularly sticky fragment from his fingertip when he heard a loud crack that came from somewhere behind him. The earth started to shake and the wineglass fell over; Francis tutted and set it right, as if that should be the end of the matter. But the shaking was followed by a horrific, magnified rasping sound that rose from the ground underneath him.

He looked up in disbelief and realized what was happening. The last two yards of the cliff top were falling away from him, falling in one piece like the hunk he'd broken from the end of the bread. And Grant was falling with it, his face showing only an instant of surprise as it dropped out of sight.

Francis blinked, struggling to comprehend what had just happened. The line of the cliff now ran directly under the square of the blanket, cutting it in half; the sheet hung down over the edge for a second—a defeated flag—until the wind lifted it up again and held it in the sky. The situation seemed to come crashing over Francis then, and he threw himself forward to the edge of the cliff. *He won't still be falling. He won't still be falling.* That was his single, absurd thought as he closed his eyes and leaned over. But the shock had muddied his sense of time, and when he opened his eyes there was Grant, still falling, spinning in circles through the air. A pair of shoes and the white speck of a boiled egg were falling beside him, with Francis's hat dawdling in the air above his head; Grant's face was a shrinking picture of terror. Did the two men make eye contact, or was that just a trick of perspective?

The falling rocks hit the water first, breaking the surface apart, so that Grant seemed to land a moment later on a cushion of soft white spray; it was a jarring incongruity as his body snapped in half.

. . .

"That's horrible," said Julia.

"Yes, it was devastating." Francis stared at the nearest tree, his eyes refusing to focus. "They'd heard the rockfall in town, so there was nothing suspicious about it. It was just an accident, a freak thing. I told the police exactly what had happened. But either they had trouble understanding my accent or I had trouble understanding theirs, because the next time I heard about the incident, it was Francis Gardner that had died tragically."

"And Grant McAllister that was still alive."

"I'd left my wallet in the jacket, you see, with my name and identification. And he was wearing it when he died. So they assumed that his body was mine. I was going to correct them, to begin with."

"But you thought better of it?"

"It all seemed to work out so neatly. We were living off Grant's money; I didn't have any of my own. His uncle would send it to him every month or so. All Grant had to do was write to him occasionally. Well, I could mimic his handwriting well enough."

"So you became Grant McAllister?"

"And continued taking the money. It's what Grant would have wanted, I'm sure of that."

"Then what about the book?"

Francis gave her a look of contrition. "When you wrote to me and said your colleague had found an old copy of *The White Murders* and wanted to publish it, the temptation was overwhelming. Grant's money doesn't go far these days. Besides, I'd been using his name for so long anyway, it seemed the obvious thing to do. And where's the harm in me having something to live off?"

Julia ignored this question. "But you'd never read the stories before?"

"No, that was the only problem. I knew he'd written some. But Grant didn't bring a copy of *The White Murders* with him when he moved out here. And he never seemed inclined to get hold of one. I think the fact that nobody had been willing to publish it was a source of pain to him. At one point he'd dreamed of literary fame and fortune."

"Then did you really think this would work?"

"Yes, I'm afraid I did." Francis nudged a stone with his shoe. "We lived together for years; we discussed just about all of Grant's work in mathematics. And that included his work on murder mysteries. So I know the mathematical ideas very well, and I thought I could bluff the rest. I never imagined you'd go to so much trouble."

"Yes, well, there's a lot you don't know about me." Julia picked up her bag and lifted the strap over her shoulder, brushing the dust from the bottom. "I just have one last question before I go."

Francis nodded. "What's that?"

"There's only one piece to this puzzle that I can't make sense of. The White Murder. Why did Grant fill his book with references to that crime? Is there really nothing you can tell me about it?"

Francis shrugged. "We never discussed it. But I knew Grant, and I know his sense of humor." He rubbed the back of his neck. "It was almost certainly a joke. He could be very macabre at times. It would have been just like him to put in all those references as a way of keeping himself amused. The more insensitive, the better; that's just how he was." Francis sighed. "I wouldn't go looking for any deeper meaning to it. A red herring, that's all."

"I understand." Julia smiled. "That's a relief, I suppose." She hovered at the edge of the clearing, hesitating before speaking again. "I think this is the last time we'll see each other, Francis. I did enjoy some of our conversations, but I wish I'd never met you."

And then she was gone.

16

THE FIRST ENDING

Thirty minutes later, Julia Hart was again climbing the dim staircase that led to her hotel room. She entered the shaded room with a hint of triumph. Her plan had worked; she had definitively outsmarted the man who was trying to deceive her. As if in celebration, she opened the shutters covering the window and let the brightness inside. A perfect square of clean white light appeared on the opposite wall.

Outside, the dreamy blue sea and the white cubes of the waterfront were becoming lively with human shapes. The hottest part of the afternoon had passed, and life was returning to the little town. Julia took two steps backward, away from the window, and sat down on the bed; the last few days had exhausted her. She lay back and kicked off her shoes and soon fell asleep, fully clothed, cradled in the arms of the sunlight.

She woke up twenty minutes later to find she had been crying; she could already feel the lines of salt forming on her skin. She took the nearest corner of the top sheet and laid it across her face—the triangle of white cotton pressed lightly against her eyes—and left it there until the sun had dried her tears.

Then she pushed herself up to a sitting position.

On a table beside the bed was her leather-bound copy of *The White Murders*. She picked it up and opened it on her thigh. The book had been given to her about six months earlier in another room with similar dimensions, with a bed and a window of about the same size. Though in that case the sky had been gray and the only thing to be seen outside was a pigeon perched on a streetlight. Julia's mother had been dying in that room, in the small house in Wales where Julia had spent her childhood. She'd sat by her mother's side, holding her hand.

"There's something you need to know." The older woman's breath rattled and sputtered; after a lifetime of smoking, her lungs were finally failing. "Please." She pointed at an unassuming book on a shelf beside the bed, and Julia stepped over to retrieve it. It was a slim volume called *The White Murders*. The book was bound in leather, but Julia recognized the thick pages and wide margins as being indicative of private publication. Julia was an author herself, with three romance novels to her name. She handed the book to her mother, who lifted the cover and slid her yellow forefinger over the name of the author, where it was printed on the title page. "Grant McAllister," she coughed. "That man is your father."

Tears had come to Julia's eyes then; she'd always been told that her father had died during the war, when she was a small child. "Is he still alive?"

The older woman closed her eyes. "I don't know. He might be."

"Then where does he live?"

"I'm sorry." Her mother shook her head. "He left us, when you were very small." She squeezed her daughter's hand. "He probably won't want to see you."

Julia considered this in silence, then answered so quietly that her mother couldn't possibly have heard. "I'm not sure I'll give him any choice."

The day after her mother's funeral, she'd worked out a plan. She knew enough about crime fiction to be able to fabricate a letter from a specialist publishing house, expressing an interest in Grant's old collection of stories. She'd given herself the title of editor and written under her middle name, Julia. The other details had come easily enough: Victor and Leonidas were the names of her two cats, and Blood Type Books was a simple pun. After a few weeks, Grant had written back, asking about money. She'd replied under Victor's name and had promised him whatever he wanted, if only he would agree to meet with her. Grant had suggested she come to the island. So she'd had the book typed up in manuscript form and set out on her trip: She would observe him for a few days while they worked on it together, then she would decide what to do next, whether to walk away or to confess everything.

And that was how she'd ended up here, lying on a bed in a dim hotel room after finding out her father had been dead for ten years. She turned to the first page of *The White Murders* and ran her finger over his name. Grant McAllister. And she realized, with a crushing sense of disappointment, that she was no closer to him now than she was when she'd first seen it. She would never get to meet him and would never know him at all, except through these stories. But at least she understood now why he'd left her and her mother and had come to live on this island: It wasn't to escape from an unwanted daughter, as she'd feared; it was to live openly with another man. That meager consolation would have to be enough.

A flock of seagulls landed on a nearby rooftop and startled her from her thoughts.

She closed the book and placed her palm on top of it. The dark-green leather was warm to the touch. Then she lay back and listened to the sound of the gulls.

It sounded like they were in terrible pain.

17

THE SECOND ENDING

Adrenaline had dragged Francis through that final conversation with Julia, and soon after she left him—sitting alone in the clearing, halfway up the hill—he walked back to the cottage by himself, drank a large glass of gin, and went straight to bed, exhausted. It was three o'clock in the afternoon. He slept for twelve hours and woke up early the following morning, when the island was at its coldest and darkest. His dreams had been of Grant, living out his life at the bottom of the sea; the man he'd loved, sitting underwater and staring mutely at the passing fish. The shredded skin around his wounds had looked like coral. Francis was glad to be awake.

He hauled himself out of bed and sat down on the porch of his house with a cup of coffee. He thought about what he would do for money, now that the book wasn't going to be published. He turned and looked at the small wooden hut, where he'd sat with Julia two nights before. It was just about visible in the moonlight, a quarter of a mile along the beach. It was full of things that he no longer used. Surely there was something in there that he could sell?

He closed his eyes and finished his coffee.

Two hours later, the sun was rising and Francis set out along the shore, whistling to himself. At that time of the morning it was impossible to believe that the day would ever be warm; it felt as if the summer had ended overnight. He decided to save some time and cut across the gentle curve of the beach, so he took off his shoes and held them in his hands as he walked out into the cold, shallow water. It felt like he was walking on ice.

A few minutes later he arrived at the patch of sand in front of the hut and let the shoes fall from his hands. Then he opened the two wooden doors as wide as they would go. There was no light inside, and the boat was before him in silhouette. If I get desperate, he thought, I can always sell the boat.

He squeezed past its cartoonish nose to a pile of old cardboard boxes that was hidden behind it. It was dark back there, even with the doors fully open, so he took down the antique lamp that was hanging from the ceiling and filled it from a small can of kerosene. He lit the wick and balanced it on the upturned hump of the boat, then knelt down and began to look through the boxes.

The first was full of books. That was no surprise to him—he'd looked in here only last month, searching for a copy of *The White Murders*—but he wondered if any of the volumes had any monetary value. He picked some out at random, but his eyesight made it difficult to work out the titles and he soon gave up in frustration.

The next box was full of musical instruments, most of them broken. A fiddle, a drum, and a lute without any strings. Grant had insisted he would mend them one day but had never found the time. The third contained fishing equipment, in good condition; he would return to that one later. The fourth was packed with various oddities. A telescope, a candlestick, and several packs of playing cards.

The fifth box brought him to a halt. He'd forgotten about this one, though he'd gone through it a few weeks earlier. It was a box of Grant's papers, together with a number of handwritten notes. Some of them must have been thirty years old. But there'd been nothing about *The White Murders*—no early drafts or structural notes—and nothing of any value, of course.

Then he remembered something.

Tentatively, he ran a fingertip down the side of the yellowing stack until he felt the hard edge of a sheet of card. He pulled it out and held it up in front of the light. It was a black-and-white photograph, cut from the pages of a magazine and glued to a white square of cardboard. A large photograph of a young woman. Francis didn't recognize her, but she was very beautiful and looked like she could have been an actor. In the bottom right corner was a tangle of black lines, written in thick, dark ink, that he'd previously thought to be illegible. But now he could just about see that they formed the name *Elizabeth White*. Then it wasn't a coincidence and Grant really had named the book after her? Francis turned the cardboard over and found that there was a note written on the back, in faint blue pen. If he hadn't known Grant's handwriting so well, he wouldn't have been able to read it at all.

Hampstead Heath. August 24, 1940. Her final signature.

One of the doors to the hut blew closed and its sudden shadow fell across the white square, hiding those words from view. Francis let the piece of cardboard fall to the floor and scrambled to his feet in recoil from it, stumbling backward against the boat. The whole vessel shook: The oil lamp slid from its place on top of the hull and fell directly into the box of papers, which immediately burst into flames. It was such a neat, self-contained calamity that Francis could only stand there at first, watching it burn. Then, in the fresh light of that miniature fire, he saw the note illuminated once again. The words were still there and the date hadn't changed.

The twenty-fourth of August, 1940. The day of the White Murder. If she had signed the photograph on that date, then he must have been with her just before she was killed. Taken together with everything else—the title of the book, the clues in the stories—it was too much to be a coincidence. "Grant, what on earth did you do?"

Francis knelt down again and picked up the photograph, folding it into his back pocket. A black circle of hot mold was spreading across the side of the boat where it was nearest to the flames; he saw it and started to panic. The bottom half of the cardboard box was yet to catch fire, so with his bare foot outstretched, he nudged it away from the boat and across the room, all the way to the half-opened door. Then he bent down, picked it up, and threw it toward the sea. When it bounced on the sand a moment later, the whole thing seemed to burst into a cloud of burning fragments; ashes and sparks rained down onto the beach.

Francis stumbled forward, his lungs full of black dust, and came to a stop in front of the empty pair of shoes that he'd left there earlier. They were still where he'd dropped them: in perfect formation, side by side on the sand. Francis felt that he could almost see Grant's ghost standing there, waiting to greet him.

"Grant," he said, reaching out to grasp the invisible hand, then falling forward onto his knees, "so you really did kill her?"

He took the photograph from his trousers pocket and examined it once again in the daylight. The glue had melted in the heat of the fire, and the printed picture was coming away from its cardboard base. There was a handwritten letter concealed between the two layers. Francis slipped it from its hiding place and started to read.

Dear Professor McAllister.

The writing was neat but so small that he had to squint.

My name is Elizabeth White. Francis held his breath. *We haven't met, but perhaps you've seen me onstage or you've seen one of my plays? I was lucky enough to attend the lecture that you gave on detective fiction in London last year, at the Royal Society of Literature. I found it to be a very inspiring talk. And I hope you will forgive the audacity, but I'm sending you the fruits of that inspiration, in case you'd like to read them. I've written seven murder mystery stories, based on your ideas: They cover a variety of characters and settings, but each one demonstrates a different permutation of detective fiction, to use your term. I'm hoping to publish them as a collection. The White Murders,* by Elizabeth White. *Forgive the egocentric title—I couldn't think of a better one. But I wondered if you might read them and give me your thoughts? It's my first attempt at writing this kind of thing. Perhaps we could meet and discuss them, if you'd be willing to let me buy you a drink? Be gentle, though; you're the first and only person I've shown them to. Gratefully yours, Elizabeth White.*

The last two words matched the signature on the photograph.

Francis crumpled the letter into a ball and threw it into the sea. He reached for the shoes, taking one in each hand, and cried out in despair. "Grant, how could you?" He put his head in his hands; the two shoes became a comical pair of horns. "You killed her, just to steal those stories?"

He imagined Grant, his vanity punctured by her success; he must have convinced her somehow to bring the original manuscript along to their meeting, then he'd killed her and taken it away with him. The inconsistencies in the stories, pointing to the details of the crime, must have been put in later; it would have amused him endlessly, Francis knew, to add those clues to the stories, knowing that no one would understand them except for himself. Had he kept her original title for the same unpalatable reason?

The tide was moving farther inland with every minute that passed. Francis looked out to sea and saw that a substantial wave was heading toward him. It broke a few yards before it reached the shore and splashed him all the way to the elbows. The water was freezing cold.

"How could you?"

The fire behind him had finished burning. But in his soaked white suit he looked like a snowman, already starting to melt.

Acknowledgments

Thanks to James Wills, my agent, and my two editors, James Melia and Joel Richardson, without whom the book wouldn't be what it is.

Thanks are due also to Rachel Richardson, Ciara McEllin, Maggie Pavesi, Amy Einhorn, Kerry Cullen, Kenn Russell, Patricia Eisemann, Caitlin O'Shaughnessy, Maggie Richards, Christopher Sergio, Tom Robson, Clare Bogen, Maxine Hitchcock, Grace Long, Jen Breslin, Jess Hart, Ellie Hughes, Nick Lowndes, Kit Shepherd, and Georgina Hulland Brown.